Sideline Confidential

BROOKE BENTLEY

GREENLEAF
BOOK GROUP PRESS

This book is a work of fiction. Names, characters, businesses, organizations, places, events, and incidents are either a product of the author's imagination or are used fictitiously. Any resemblance to actual persons, living or dead, events, or locales is entirely coincidental.

Published by Greenleaf Book Group Press
Austin, Texas
www.gbgpress.com

Distributed by Greenleaf Book Group

For ordering information or special discounts for bulk purchases, please contact Greenleaf Book Group at PO Box 91869, Austin, TX 78709, 512.891.6100.

Design and composition by Greenleaf Book Group and Kim Lance
Cover design by Greenleaf Book Group and Kim Lance

Publisher's Cataloging-in-Publication data is available.

Print ISBN: 979-8-88645-086-6

eBook ISBN: 979-8-88645-087-3

To offset the number of trees consumed in the printing of our books, Greenleaf donates a portion of the proceeds from each printing to the Arbor Day Foundation. Greenleaf Book Group has replaced over 50,000 trees since 2007.

Printed in the United States of America on acid-free paper

23 24 25 26 27 28 29 30   10 9 8 7 6 5 4 3 2 1

First Edition

To my home team—my husband, Jeff,
and my sons, Luke and Max.
Thank you for your unwavering love and support.
I am your biggest fan.

One

Welcome to the Big Leagues

Everything in Johnny Cook's corner office sparkled as if it had just been polished with Windex. There were cases holding autographed footballs and helmets, framed jerseys and memorabilia carefully placed on mahogany bookshelves. Even his bald head gleamed.

I crossed and recrossed my legs, trying to redirect the nerves raging inside me.

It was my first day of work. I had scored a job in the most powerful sports league in the world—professional football. To make it even sweeter, I was back in my hometown of Oklahoma City. I knew climbing the ranks in an industry coursing with testosterone would require toughness and grit. I had prepared myself for that. I just didn't expect my boss, the team's vice president of Media Relations, to march me into his office on day one.

"You have a lot of great memories here," I said. The sweat on my kneecaps was starting to bleed through my cream pants.

"These hanging up are my greatest moments. The All-Pro game, winning the championship, draft days. After three decades of blood, sweat, and tears in this league, you come away with some epic memories, lifelong friends, and a handful of enemies," Johnny said with a smirk.

"Have you always worked in the league?" I asked. My body uncoiled slightly as we eased into small talk.

"I'm a lifer. I started faxing stats here as an intern right out of college. I worked my way up the food chain, scrapping and clawing for the best job with the best team. As fate would have it, I ended up back in Oklahoma City, this time as a VP. The league is the only place for me."

"Wow, I can't imagine everything you've seen and done," I mused out loud.

"Blake, the stories could write themselves. Although, your ears are too innocent." Johnny winked.

I blushed at the wink, not knowing what to make of his offhand comment. Johnny had been difficult to read from the moment I met him in my interview with the team.

Three weeks ago he had barged into the conference room, his pristine white sneakers squeaking against the marble floor.

"I have ten minutes before practice starts. Blake, I'll cut to the chase. Your work impressed us. You're a solid writer and a natural broadcaster. An excellent fit to be our media coordinator."

He had spoken in short clips, bouncing between subjects.

"League teams like to own their media—radio shows, TV shows, podcasts, you name it. We own the media and sell the advertising. Cha-ching. But it all starts on the web. We need to build media platforms of content on our website. That's where you come in."

Johnny had paused and leaned halfway across the conference table, speaking closely and directly.

"You're a local girl. A huge plus. You've got the look to be the face of our team. Even bigger plus. But my question is: Why do you love football?"

I unclenched the sides of the chair. My knuckles had paled as I had braced myself for a barrage of questions. But this question I could answer with ease. It came straight from the heart, rolling off my tongue with fluency.

"I grew up on football. So much of my childhood revolved around going to games, watching games on TV, and reliving every moment Sunday night at dinner. My mom once said football is brutally physically and gracefully heroic. That always stuck with me. I love everything about this game."

Johnny had tapped a knuckle-sized, diamond-encrusted championship ring against the conference room table, his expression emotionless.

"Glad to know you're here for the right reasons. I don't tolerate any silliness. You're hired."

Now, a few weeks later, I was sitting across from this storied league executive as a colleague. Although, I felt just as anxious and clammy. I straightened my new pink silk blouse, discreetly fanning it below the armpits, and peered up at Johnny.

He was reclining back in his leather desk chair. "I've got great bullshit. You'll see. And I love to hear my own voice," Johnny said with a laugh.

"I'm sure people like hearing what you have to say," I said, smiling back.

"Blake, you're going to fit in here just fine."

Then he paused and looked down at the gold Rolex clasped around his thick wrist. When he looked up, the upturn of his lips had given way to a thin, straight line.

I had heard of pro football players flipping a switch. They were nice, affable men off the field. When they stepped on the gridiron, they became an alternate version of themselves—aggressive and primal. They would tackle another human with reckless abandon. Well, Johnny had just flipped his switch. I could see it in his narrow-set eyes, which were storming into a deep shade of gray.

"Blake, there is protocol we need to cover so things here run as smooth as possible," Johnny said. He folded his meaty forearms.

"I'm going to cut to the chase. No locker room. You aren't allowed in there."

I shook my head in confusion. *Wait, what?* The locker room was where most of the interviews took place. If my job was to interview players and write stories, how could I do that without going into the locker room? But before I could ask for clarification, Johnny delivered another swipe.

"You are going to ride your own bus. We don't want you sitting with the players and coaches on game days. So, we have chartered an extra bus. It's called the Blake Bus. Or I could call it the BB. In fact, I think BB is going to be my new nickname for you," Johnny said. His face thawed enough to crinkle in delight at his own joke. "Told you I've got great bullshit."

I blinked my eyes in confusion.

"Excuse me, Johnny. What's the Blake Bus?"

He squared his eyes to mine.

"The players and coaches don't know you. They aren't used to having you around. You aren't part of their routine. They thrive on routines. You, my dear, are a potential distraction. And we must eliminate distractions."

Questions popped and crackled inside me like someone poured a packet of Fizz Wiz in my brain. Who exactly didn't want me sitting with players and coaches? Johnny? The owners? And had Johnny just called me a distraction that must be eliminated?

I swallowed hard. My body trembled from the blows Johnny had dealt.

I looked up at a poster-sized photo of Johnny holding the league's iconic silver trophy. He had worked with teams who had won championships. He was a revered front office veteran. I had been with the team for just a few hours. Who was *I* to question *him*?

I took a sip of air and searched for my voice. "Does this happen often? The team needing an additional bus for new employees?" I asked, my lips wobbling over each word.

"Nope. This is the first time. You're the first girl to travel to all our games. It's new territory for us to have a girl on road trips."

There was so much more that I wanted to ask. But when Johnny swiveled his chair toward his computer, it was clear that he had nothing else to say. Those were the rules. Take them or leave them. And there was no way I was leaving this job.

I sat up in my chair and lifted my gaze to meet Johnny's profile. "I will do whatever it takes to exceed expectations here," I said with as much courage as I could muster.

The rules for engagement had been set. If I wanted to work in pro football, I had to prove that I wasn't some naive girl unable to navigate a team of supercharged egos and supersized men. I was a budding reporter with the skills and resolve to launch her career.

I inhaled deeply and stood up.

Johnny turned from his computer. "Blake, welcome to the big leagues."

In that moment, I had no idea how the job would unfold, but I did know I would never be the same because of it.

Two

Sweat Is Your Fat Crying

A couple of hours later, I thumbed through the team cheerleader calendar that had been in the welcome bag on my desk. Miss August splashed in the ocean as her white bikini bottom teasingly slid between luscious cheeks. Her highlighted hair fanned behind her as if an ocean breeze had delicately lifted it off her tan shoulders. Miss August radiated sexiness. I wondered what Johnny thought about her and the rest of the cheerleaders for that matter. Wouldn't playing on a field next to a Jennifer Lopez look-alike be more distracting than riding a bus with a young woman in a Gap button-down?

As I filled in the travel schedule for the two remaining preseason games, I couldn't shake the Blake Bus from my thoughts. On Friday, the team departed for New Jersey. It would be my first road trip. I imagined myself sitting alone on a luxury charter bus with my USC satchel sitting on my lap, the players and coaches standing on the curb and gawking. *Why's the new girl riding her own bus? Johnny doesn't trust her around us. Too distracting.*

The humiliation made me shudder. I needed to remind myself why this job meant so much to me. Why it was my dream job.

I unbuckled my satchel and pulled out a photo that my mom found in an old scrapbook. It was a picture of my dad and me holding hands in front of Oklahoma City's palatial riverfront stadium before the team kicked off the season in its new home on national television.

I'd been only five years old. I'd worn my hair in pigtails with navy blue bows and a #1 gold and navy jersey. So much of my early childhood remained a jumble of images tucked into corners of my mind. Not that night. I could still hear the country music pulsating from speakers in the parking lot. I could smell the hot dogs sizzling on tailgating grills. I could close my eyes and vividly picture the sea of over 70,000 fans standing in their seats before kickoff. And I could feel the electric current that coursed through the stadium when the kicker sailed the ball into the air to start the game. Energy had buzzed from my head to my toes, and I'd shaken my blue pom-poms wildly.

That night was one of my favorite childhood memories. It was also the first time I saw a woman reporter working the sidelines of a football game. She paced regally past the players in her tailored blazer, microphone in hand. When she took her place in front of the camera, I could tell her words mattered. She knew things that only a person immersed in the game could reveal. She was magnificent in my eyes. My dad said that I pointed at the reporter and declared, "That's what I want to be when I grow up."

The following year, I convinced my parents to enter a drawing for discounted season tickets. The team's new owner had launched a "True Blue" family-friendly package to engage young fans and ensure the stadium would sell out during a rebuilding year. When the team notified my dad that we had been selected, there was no way he could decline. And from that moment on I felt like fate had inextricably linked me to the team.

The young squad that season managed only a handful of wins, but that didn't matter to me. I loved the pageantry of the games. The cannons that lined the field shaking the rafters as they exploded with thick smoke. The players emerging from the clouds like a magical apparition while the announcer bellowed their names. I leaped from my seat for the fingertip catches and buried my head in my hands with every turnover or sack. At the end of the season, I set my mind to work in football. I was determined to be the next great sideline reporter.

To break into the league right out of graduate school seemed like a gift from the football gods. Especially because I had no connections or strings I could pull. My resume just happened to be on the top of the pile. The team was in a crunch after initially hiring a veteran print reporter who struggled with the on-camera work. When he decided to go back to his former paper, the team fast-tracked their search and I was the first person they called.

. . .

"It's a great morning in Oklahoma City. How can I help you?" Sheila asked.

Through the frosted glass of her desk, I caught a glimpse of the gold cowboy boots she had paired with a denim prairie dress. Team colors. This wasn't Sheila's first rodeo.

"No, I can't help you get an autograph. Believe you me, I wish I could!" Sheila clicked her earpiece with a long red fingernail.

"Here you go, darlin'," she said and handed me a security badge with a photo I had taken earlier that day. "Now you're free to move about the building. This here badge unlocks the doors in the stadium and opens the parking lots too."

"Thanks, Sheila," I said.

"When I saw your name, I expected a man. But you are pretty as can be with those long trim legs," Sheila said. "You must have some good genes. And I don't mean Jordache."

"That is very kind of you to say. I guess I come from good stock," I said, conjuring up my best hometown twang.

"Well, if you need anything, just holler."

"Will do."

I turned down the hallway and came face-to-face with a young man with floppy brown hair and a dimpled chin.

"Excuse me," I said.

He looked down at the badge I was holding. "Are you Blake? Hi, I'm Ryan."

"Yes! Nice to meet you," I said with a burst of enthusiasm. I had been eagerly waiting for a tour of the stadium with Ryan, Johnny's intern.

"I was looking for you. Johnny said to show you around and grab lunch before the afternoon practice begins."

"That sounds a lot more exciting than the HR meetings I've been sitting in all morning."

"The first day is boring. It will be a whole different story tomorrow. Get ready for fifteen-hour days and running around like a crazy person."

Light brown freckles trailed across Ryan's sunburned nose and cheeks. There was something inherently boyish about him. It was like Ryan spent his time tossing the football in his backyard instead of grinding out long days in a stadium.

"What kind of work do they have you doing?" I asked.

"Whatever Johnny tells me to do," Ryan said dutifully. "I run stats, transcribe quotes, pick up dry cleaning. It isn't glamorous, but it's worth it when you're standing ten yards away from the players at practice."

"I bet. Not a bad gig to land right out of school."

"No doubt. I went to Oklahoma State. My OSU buddies living here are jealous that they are toiling away in offices while I'm working on the sidelines of a pro team."

"I'm ready to get to the field myself. This seems like a typical business office, just transported to the second floor of the stadium," I said, motioning to the cubicles surrounding us.

"Yeah, that's because we're on the business operations side. Business ops are the suits—the lawyers, sales team, HR. On the other side of the reception desk, that's football ops. That's where the magic happens."

We walked a few yards past the reception desk. Ryan pointed to a large suite. The double doors had been closed when I arrived early that morning.

"That's the owner's suite," Ryan said in a hushed voice. "He's got like millions of dollars of art in there."

I believed it. Overstuffed patterned furniture sat under a crystal chandelier. Two assistants occupied antique desks, and oil paintings adorned the wood-paneled walls behind them. The room looked more like a grand salon in a Southern mansion than an office in a stadium.

"Wow. It's fancy," I said.

I followed Ryan around a corner to Johnny's office. The door was cracked. Johnny was talking on the phone with his Tod's loafers propped on his desk. Directly across from his office a copier was spitting out press releases.

"That's where I sit." Ryan pointed to the copier.

I had walked by Ryan's makeshift workspace on my way to meet Johnny and noticed the binders and press clippings strewn across the small desk. There was barely room for a bottle of water and Ryan had zero privacy. But his location was central. He sat feet away from Johnny, the general manager, and the head coach.

My cubicle, on the other hand, was located past the sales bullpen in a receded corner of the second floor. I initially had figured it was the only cubicle available. Now with the conversation about the Blake Bus gnawing at my subconscious, I couldn't help but wonder if Johnny had purposely distanced me from the coaches and football personnel.

"I wonder why my cube is so far away," I said, subtly probing Ryan for insights.

"Maybe because it gets rowdy down here," Ryan said with a shrug. "The coaches play their music loud and the language is R-rated."

"Sounds like a locker room," I said.

"You've got the picture." Ryan smiled.

"Do any women work in football ops?" I asked.

"All the assistants are women. They pretty much work nine to five. After they leave, that's when things turn up." Ryan motioned for me to follow him to a staircase.

"Got it," I said. "I'm just trying to get a better sense of how I fit into things around here."

I still did not fully understand the team's org chart, but it was becoming clear that women didn't populate the higher levels, at least not on the football side.

"I'm sure you'll settle in quickly. And I know you'll love our next stop on the tour—the team cafeteria," Ryan said with a grin.

"You must have heard my belly growling. Please tell me they have a salad bar," I said.

I had been too nervous to eat my usual bagel breakfast, and the black coffee I drank during the health insurance PowerPoint was eating away at my stomach lining. "Team cafeteria" was music to my ears.

"They've got everything. Carving station, pasta station, sandwich bar, dessert bar. And want to know what makes the food here so good?

It's free! It's an all-you-can-eat free buffet." Excitement frothed from Ryan's mouth.

"Free" was also music to my ears. When I signed my employment contract a few weeks ago, everything about the job felt like a dream come true—except the salary. Unfortunately, working in a billion-dollar industry like pro football didn't pay the big bucks unless you were in a big-time front office position or a player or coach. Since I was still paying off car notes and student loans, I had moved into my parents' house to save money.

"I am definitely all about free these days," I said as we reached the bottom level of the stadium.

"Then you have to check out another great perk," Ryan said and led me down the cinder-block concourse.

Bass thudded from a glass door that had been propped open with a free weight. I peeked inside. There were bench press bars loaded with 100-pound plates and squat racks balancing weights the size of truck tires.

"Is this the players' gym?" I asked.

"Yep. You should see the o-linemen. They can squat like 750," Ryan said.

On a wall, signs read: SHUT UP AND TRAIN. INTENSITY BUILDS IMMENSITY. SWEAT IS YOUR FAT CRYING.

"Do we get to use it?" I asked. It looked like a few normal-sized men were jogging on the treadmills.

"Yep, it's like having a free gym membership."

"That's awesome. Working out clears my head. I think I'm addicted to the endorphins from all my years of playing volleyball."

Ryan's eyes widened. "Did you play in college?"

"Yep. I walked on the volleyball team at USC. I'm under six feet. I wasn't tall enough to play outside hitter. My specialty was defense."

"The players are going to think that's really hot. A SoCal volleyball player," Ryan said. As soon as the words left his mouth, his cheeks flushed a deep crimson. "I'm sorry. That was inappropriate."

"Maybe a little," I said. But Ryan's slipup gave me the opening to say what had been nagging me all morning. "Well, now that we've broken the ice, there's something I want to ask you. Did Johnny mention anything to the media group about specific locker room rules for me or me riding my own bus?"

Ryan chewed on his bottom lip. "Yeah, we had a department meeting about it this morning."

"What did he say?" I asked. My soft voice betrayed my heart, which was hammering my rib cage. I was trying not to take Johnny's rules personally, but it was hard given he had coined my mode of transportation the "Blake Bus." The thought of him nicknaming me BB and explaining the locker room ban to my coworkers made my insides twist and knot. Being singled out at work never felt good. Being singled out on the first day and relegated to your own bus was mortifying.

Ryan bit down harder on his lip. He was visibly uncomfortable.

"Johnny said this is the first time he's had a girl on his media team. He's edgy about it. He wants to make sure he can trust your intentions before he lets you in with the players and coaches."

Ryan kept his gaze downward.

My chest heaved. Johnny really did not trust me. But why? Did he think that I would flirt with players while they undressed at their lockers? That I wanted to make googly eyes with them on the bus rides to the games? That wasn't why I was here. This was my big break into sideline reporting. My chance to ignite a career covering pro football teams. I wasn't going to jeopardize that.

I straightened my shoulders and lifted my chin. "Well, Johnny is soon going to see that I'm not a girl. I'm a woman. A woman who can excel at her job. A woman he can trust implicitly."

Three

A Taste of Home

"There she is! Our media guru, team expert extraordinaire!"

Dad held open the back door of our house. He wore a navy T-shirt with the team's logo, khaki shorts, and a black apron that said "The Grillfather."

"Blakey, come in here and tell us about your day. I've been too excited to think about anything else!" Mom shouted from the kitchen sink, where she was peeling carrots.

I had been reluctant to move home. I loved my parents. They had always been kind and supportive, cheering at all my games and helping me late at night with my homework. When I went away for school, we talked on the phone at least once a week. Still, moving into their house in my midtwenties felt confining, like I couldn't fully embrace this exciting new chapter of life.

I tried to make the financial math work with my student loans and car payments, but renting an apartment would put me in the red. Living in my childhood room and sleeping in my old four-poster bed was the most prudent option. And getting home-cooked meals certainly sweetened the deal.

"I can't believe you guys are making a big dinner. You don't have to do that," I said as I perched myself on a barstool.

"Don't be silly. We are soaking up every second with you before you get busy with the season. Tonight, we're toasting to your dream job!"

Mom hoisted an imaginary wine glass in the air.

"I wish I had exciting news for you, but there's not much to report. Aside from touring the stadium, I spent most of the day dealing with HR and meeting with my boss."

I dipped a pita chip into a bowl of hummus that Mom set on the kitchen counter.

"Dealing with Human Resources is a part of any job, even if you work in pro football," Dad said as he patted his famous rub on three generous cuts of filets.

"Yeah, but there were a few things I didn't expect that sort of shook me."

I had driven home feeling conflicted about telling my parents the details of Johnny's rules. They wanted to celebrate my job. Their giddiness over the last couple of weeks had reached unquantifiable proportions. They had boasted to family, friends, our mailman Landon, Rita at the hair salon, really anyone who would listen that their oldest daughter "had landed her dream job as a pro football reporter!" Revealing Johnny's "Blake" policies made the job seem a lot less dreamy, and that made me feel like I was disappointing them in some way and pulling their bragging rights out from underneath them.

I was also embarrassed about the distressing reality that my boss didn't trust me around the players or coaches. But I couldn't withhold all of this from my parents. In fact, I needed their guidance. They had both dealt with bureaucratic human resource departments—my mom as a career counselor at the local community college and my dad at the law firm where he had worked for the last twenty years.

"My boss Johnny called me into his office and laid out some strict rules for me. I can't go in the locker room and I have to ride my own bus to games," I said with a grimace.

Mom tilted her head quizzically. "Why do you need your own bus?"

"Johnny is worried I might distract the players and coaches on game days. He wants me to prove I can be trusted to act professionally around them," I said.

"Well, that's because they don't know you. They don't know the integrity you have," Mom said in a measured tone. "They'll see. Very soon."

"That isn't all of it. Before I left for the day, the head of HR had me meet with her to sign an anti-fraternization agreement. It says that I won't date or pursue romantic or sexual relationships with players or coaches. If I do, I'm subject to termination."

"As an attorney, I understand where they're coming from on this one," Dad interjected. "The team has to be very protective of the players and coaches. They are the team's biggest assets."

"I guess. But I couldn't help but take it personally, that there was something about me in particular that concerns them," I said.

"No, I would assume this is procedural and subject to change after they get to know you," Dad said matter-of-factly.

"You're probably right. For all I know, there've been issues before— maybe employees chasing after players. I don't know. It just caught me by surprise," I said, downplaying my concerns. There was something about Johnny that made me uneasy. I had seen his personality turn instantly from affable to steely cold, and I suspected his stout frame housed a volatile temper. I could see it in his wily eyes.

"Blake, you're going to win over the team in no time. Just think, women journalists have been covering football for years. Lesley Visser started working in pro football locker rooms in the eighties. The league Network reporter who covers the team is a woman. They must be comfortable with her because she's interviewing players inside the locker room every time I turn on the TV," Dad said.

"But, Dad, those women don't work for the team. It's different because I'm a team employee."

"Work hard and earn the team's respect. Show them they have nothing to worry about. That team is going to love you. Now, make way. It's time for the Grillfather to get sizzling."

"Why don't you open a bottle of wine and bring in a couple glasses while I clean up?" Mom said while placing a roasting dish of vegetables in the oven.

A bottle of Mom's favorite chardonnay, one she only drank on special occasions, glistened in the chiller. I poured two glasses.

"You and Dad are spoiling me tonight. Fancy wine, steaks, a tray of apps. My palate isn't used to this. Between college and grad school, I've spent the last six years eating mac and cheese and drinking cheap beer."

"The glamorous life of a student," Mom said, winking. "Really, Blake, we couldn't be prouder of all you've accomplished over that time. You not only kept up your grades during the volleyball season, but you also managed to earn a partial scholarship to journalism school. Your dad and I worried that you'd never find a broadcasting job and we resigned ourselves to losing you to California. But here you are, back in Oklahoma City, on the path to fulfilling your dreams. Our hearts are bursting."

"I really hope this job is everything I'm envisioning it to be," I said.

For some reason, pleasing my parents had always mattered a little too much to me. Maybe it was in my DNA; being an overachiever was inherent to my construct as a person. Or maybe it was because I wanted to prove to my parents that I could carve out a career in a cutthroat and fickle industry, which I knew unsettled them. Either way, I was hellbent on making this job work, partly for them and mainly for me.

"Yes, there will be an adjustment period for you and the team," Mom said. "But I've never seen you back down from a challenge. You're tough. Plus, you're a good judge of character. You're going to do great."

Mom tucked her caramel bob behind both ears and smiled.

I watched my dad remove the steaks from the grill. My absolute favorite meal, which I reminded myself I was eating for free. In fact, I hadn't paid for a single meal that day. Saving on food would certainly help my bottom line and allow me to incrementally increase my loan payments. I swirled my glass of chardonnay with satisfaction.

"Fine meat coming through," Dad said, marching to the butcher-block island. "You two looked like you were in deep conversation. I better not have missed anything important."

"I was just about to show Mom one of my job perks."

I removed a book of tickets from the front pocket of my satchel.

"Two lower-level seats to every home game, plus a parking pass. Not bad, huh?"

Dad's eyebrows arched high.

"You've got season tickets! In the lower level. With a parking pass. That's got to be worth thousands of dollars."

"Consider it my rent for the season."

"Let me check my calendar to see if I'm available," Dad said, scrunching his face in faux concentration. "Yep. I'm free. I can go. To every game."

Mom and I simultaneously rolled our eyes.

"I figured as much."

I took a long sip of wine and savored the taste of home.

Four

The Geek Out

The next morning I pulled into a secured area behind the stadium and scanned my employee badge. The gate rolled open, revealing two parking lots separated by a chain-link fence and a security booth. The lot on the left looked like a Mercedes-Benz showroom with luxury cars glistening in the sunlight. The lot on the right resembled the used car dealership where I bought my Jetta.

The officer standing outside the booth motioned for me to roll down my window. "Welcome, young lady. Just so you know, employees park here," he said and pointed to the used car lot. "Players and coaches are on the other side."

"Thank you, sir," I said and turned into a parking spot next to an old Ford truck with an OSU bumper sticker.

With a spring in my step and a travel mug of coffee in my hand, I bounced down the stadium concourse and up to the second level.

It was 7:00 a.m. and the football ops hallway was bustling. Coaches were pecking at their keyboards and yelling at each other from their desks. The smell of dark roasted coffee permeated the air.

"Did you say fifty-five has a hamstring?" the cornerbacks coach barked with a thick, raspy voice.

"Yeah, it's strained. That slappy is out for at least a week," the linebackers coach barked back.

"Watch what you say. A pretty young lady is walking by." The corner-backs coach nodded in my direction.

Ryan had advised me to follow army protocol when approached by a coach. Only speak when spoken to and keep your answers short. "Yes, sir" or "No, sir."

I wasn't sure what to say since the coach wasn't talking directly to me, so I smiled politely and bounced merrily through the maze of offices back to my cubicle in the corner.

Sitting on my desk like a Christmas present, shiny and new, was my team-issued phone. I tore open the plastic wrapping and extricated my first ever iPhone.

I hadn't been able to afford one in college and had resigned myself to cheap droids and green text boxes. I held the gold and white device, complete with a full data package, in my hands and squealed with delight. There was something about it that made me feel important, like I had pressing work to do and urgent calls to make. And all of it was paid for by the team. I squealed again.

"Ahem," I heard and jerked up in surprise.

In the opening of my cube partition stood a lanky man with spiked black hair.

"Am I interrupting something?"

"Sorry. I didn't think anyone would hear me back here. I just got this phone and I'm geeking out over it."

I stood up and extended my hand.

"Hi, Garrett. I'm Blake. We met during my interviews."

He nodded, leaving my hand awkwardly suspended between us.

"Yes, I'm Garrett, and I try to avoid handshakes. They spread too many germs."

I retracted my hand and shoved it into my pocket.

"I need to brief you on today's duties and the details of your job. I wanted to meet with you yesterday, but I was presenting in business development meetings which ran longer than expected."

"I totally understand. I was stuck in HR meetings that consumed most of my day," I said with a smile that went unnoticed. Garrett was halfway out of my cube, searching for an empty chair at a neighboring station.

"As I'm sure you know, I'm the team's digital media manager," Garrett said as he pushed a chair into my cube.

"I manage the content that goes on the website, from stories and videos to ads and promotions. That means I have one of the few jobs that reports to both business ops and football ops."

"Ryan was telling me about the organizational structure," I said.

"It's hard to put the media group into parameters. We work with football ops to create content about the team and we work with business ops to make sure that content sells. I, personally, do a lot for both sides. Of course, Johnny wields even more influence. He's the only VP with standing meetings with the head coach, the GM, and ownership. He's relied upon by many."

"I can see that," I said. "I'm also learning that he possesses the unique ability to be terrifying and charming in the same moment."

"Johnny's biggest gift is that he gets people to do what he wants," Garrett stated emphatically.

I couldn't tell if he revered or resented Johnny for it.

"So, Garrett, how will we be working together on a daily basis?"

"Actually, you'll be working for me," Garrett said as he peered down at me through his black, rectangular glasses. "Each day, I will get Johnny's approval on story and video topics. Once approved, you will write and produce the content and post it to the website. Johnny will get the final say on your final product. If he doesn't like the content, we take it down or edit it to his liking."

He tapped a legal pad next to my keyboard.

"You should be taking notes."

"Of course," I stammered, embarrassed I hadn't taken the initiative earlier.

"Today, we'll keep things simple. You'll write a story about the battle at backup quarterback. I've requested interviews with Seth and Marcus, the players vying to be number two. We'll edit their sound bites together for an accompanying video."

Garrett proceeded to give me detailed technical information about the website posting and editing process, as well as a laundry list of important resources.

"This is a lot to digest. If you have questions, send me an email. Also, Ryan can help."

"What exactly does Ryan do for the website?" I asked.

"Ryan is a busy man. Aside from being at Johnny's beck and call, he records interviews with players and coaches and transcribes all the audio. He updates the site with the most current stats and depth chart."

Garrett folded his pale arms across his chest.

"Also, Ryan can conduct interviews on your behalf that must be done in the locker room."

My body stiffened. "Johnny mentioned that I wouldn't be able to go in there. I figured I would interview the players elsewhere."

"For the most part, yes," he told me. "But there will be times when the only way to talk to a particular player is in the locker room. Really, the locker room rule benefits you and the team."

I wasn't sure how I came out ahead, but I didn't see the point in challenging Garrett.

"I'm sure we will make it work."

"Good. I just forwarded you the team's daily schedule," Garrett said, holding up his phone. "Practice starts in thirty minutes. I'll be skipping most of it. Too much to do building the cheerleader web pages. But I'll come down in the final period to make sure you're set up for interviews. Plan to post your story and video by 5:00 p.m."

Garrett stood up. His flat-front khakis hovered above his anklebone by at least an inch.

"I'll be pestering you with questions way before then," I said with a laugh.

Garrett shrugged his shoulders and dragged his chair back out of my cube. I thought that was appropriate because working for him looked to be a total drag.

Five

Cobra Kai and Monster Calves

While I waited outside the locker room for Ryan to change into his team-issued practice clothes, I texted friends my new cell number. I felt a surge of pride sharing the news about my job. A few friends messaged back immediately that they had seen an announcement about it on the team's site and some had even shared the post on social media.

A grin stretched across my face as I imagined the news circulating not only in my own social media circles but in the vast network of Oklahoma City football fans.

OKC was a city, but it felt more like a big town. People here treasured their cowboy roots and football fandom. I hoped that having one of their own reporting on the team would rally our fans and give them someone else to cheer for when they visited the team's site.

"What are you smiling about?" Ryan said as he pushed open the locker room doors. He was wearing a Dri-FIT T-shirt and shorts, both stamped with the team logo.

"Some friends are texting me about my job. It's fun hearing from people I haven't seen since high school," I said.

"Pretty soon fans all over the city are going to know who you are. Your face will be on every video on the site. It's so badass."

"Not going to lie. That makes me feel like kind of a big deal," I said and winked playfully. "Unfortunately, I'm not a big enough deal to get team apparel to wear to practice." I tugged at the collar of my linen dress.

"Did you talk to Johnny?" Ryan asked.

I nodded. "He said he'd look into it."

Johnny had emailed me about his strict dress code. Our media group wore business attire in the stadium and team apparel at practice. The equipment staff had purchased team gear for each media employee prior to the season—shirts, shorts, shoes, sweatshirts, rain jackets, ski jackets for cold-weather games. Between the orders for the players and coaches, there was plenty of extra apparel in storage. It's just that none of it fit me unless I wanted to wear a T-shirt that hung to my knees, so I had asked Johnny about placing a special order on my behalf.

"I met with Garrett this morning," I said, choosing my words carefully as I pivoted subjects. "He's a tough nut to crack."

"He's a little different," Ryan said. "But he runs the website like a well-oiled machine. His job performance is judged on page views, and he knows how to get them. Our site is top five in the league."

"He's obviously good at his job. I just couldn't tell if he liked me."

"I'm not sure he likes any humans. He only has eyes for metrics," Ryan said with a chuckle.

"Does that mean if my stories or videos don't get a lot of views, I will hear about it?"

"You betcha," Ryan said. "Did he assign you a story for today?"

"The battle at backup quarterback. Garrett said the players give interviews on the field during training camp, so I can get my sound bites there."

"Get ready for the gang bangs—that's what Johnny calls the media frenzy around the players. Reporters push and shove their way closer to the players and shout over each other's questions. But you shouldn't have much of a problem with Seth or Marcus. Backups don't get as much attention."

Gang bangs. Not the most socially appropriate terminology. It was becoming clear that Johnny said what he pleased and didn't care what anyone else thought.

"Why don't the players and coaches do their interviews at a podium so there's no media scrum? Isn't that what they do during the season?" I asked out of curiosity.

"Johnny said he's always done it this way during camp. He likes seeing reporters scurry around the field to interview players. It shows him which reporters want it more than others."

"I'm not complaining," I said. "The arrangement helps me because it takes the locker room out of the equation. I can knock out all my interviews on the field."

"Johnny talked about all of this in a meeting a couple of weeks ago. He said media protocol changes for the regular season but I'm not sure of all the details."

"Well, I'm sensing that not being allowed into the locker room is going to affect my job more than I initially thought. Garrett mentioned an open locker room period. He said that's when most of the interviews take place."

"That sounds right," Ryan said.

"Since I can't go in the locker room, you'll be helping me with those interviews," I said.

Ryan ran his hands through his floppy brown hair. The humidity was causing his frat boy waves to swell and puff into a mushroom-like shape atop his head. "I really hope they figure something else out. I have major stage fright and don't want to be anywhere close to a video camera."

"We'll cross that bridge when we get there," I said as we climbed up the final steps of a small hill to a concrete plateau. Below us sprawled three football fields and an indoor practice complex. The state-of-the-art facilities, along with the stadium, stretched beside the Oklahoma River. From our vista, I could see the city's skyline to the west with Devon Tower seemingly piercing the clouds above us.

It all felt surreal. This was the place where I had grown up and found comfort in the familiarity of my surroundings—holding hands with my mom at the zoo, taking school field trips to the botanical gardens, going out to dinner in Bricktown. But from that perch at team headquarters, OKC sizzled with newness and excitement.

I inhaled it in and followed Ryan down the stairs to a large folding table by the entrance to the fields. A woman with brown curly hair spewing out of a team visor sat with two young men wearing *Training Camp Intern* T-shirts. They picked up clipboards and wristbands when we approached.

"She doesn't need to check in," Ryan said to the woman. "This is Blake. She's the new media coordinator."

"Nice to meet you, sweetie. I'm Tammie. I work in scouting, but each year I perform my saintly duties and help Johnny with media check-in during training camp."

Tammie pinched her navy blue shirt and fanned it away from her large bosom.

"It's hotter than Hades out here. I'm one step away from melting."

"You could have fooled me," Ryan said. "You look great."

"Aren't you a dear!" Tammie batted her eyelashes as clumps of black mascara smeared against her eyelids. "I will take all the compliments I can get. Sheridan Lane from the league Network is here, and I always feel like a bag lady when I'm next to her."

My eyes widened.

"Sheridan Lane is one of my favorite reporters," I said, unable to contain my excitement.

"She covers our division for the Network, so she spends a lot of time in Oklahoma City," Ryan said.

"That I did know," I said. I leaned toward Ryan and elbowed him teasingly. "By the way, your compliment might have given Tammie a hot flash."

"Tammie's been an assistant in the league since she graduated from high school. Back in her prime, Hall of Fame quarterbacks were begging for her number. Even now, coaches take her out to smoke cigarettes," Ryan said.

"Damn, how do you know so much about this team?"

"It pays to keep your eyes and ears open around here. It also pays to sit in earshot of all the coaches and GM. The stories I hear could fill a book."

• • •

The fields bristled with activity. The coaches were dividing the players into position groups, with each group practicing on an assigned section of the field.

The offensive linemen stomped past us like a herd of elephants on their way to the end zone for blocking drills, their thick legs quaking the ground below us. My eyes immediately landed on one player's bulging calves, which rivaled bowling balls. I scribbled "Monster Calves" next to #74 on my roster. I had never seen a human as big as Monster Calves in my life.

Ryan chewed on his lower lip as we approached a throng of reporters who were congregated on a rubber track between two fields. Their heads swiveled back and forth as they searched for certain players and scribbled on their notepads.

"I have to admit something," he said, stopping me before we got any closer to the media. "I get really nervous around all the media. I think it's because I've been reading or watching them for so long that I've built them up in my head. I completely clam up around them." Ryan wiped his sweaty palms on his Dri-FIT shorts. He really was nervous.

Before I could say something comforting, like I was a little nervous too, a round man with a balding, sun-spotted head approached us. A pair of cutoff sweatpants clung to his swollen legs, which looked like a couple of bratwursts ready to burst. It was hard to find him intimidating in the slightest.

"Hi, young lady. You must be Blake, Johnny's newest addition."

I immediately recognized his raspy Southern drawl and throaty laugh.

"You're Hal from the morning show!" I blurted out.

"The one and only."

"I've been listening to you since I was a little girl. I would make my mom tune in to your show when she was driving carpool."

Hal smiled, revealing a row of Chiclet-sized, coffee-stained teeth.

"Thatta girl. I'm glad to see OKC got you back. We wouldn't want to lose a good one to California."

I blinked, surprised Hal knew anything about me.

"I loved USC," I told him. "It's hard to top a school where you can go to the beach and watch your football team beat Notre Dame in the same day. But I always knew I wanted to end up here."

"You went to journalism school there, right? Smart cookie."

"I learned a lot, but I'm quickly seeing this business boils down to on-the-job training."

"This business is about who you know," he said. "And you gotta know Sheridan Lane. She's a pro's pro. She'd be a good mentor for you."

Hal pointed to an impeccably dressed woman taking notes in front of the quarterbacks. Her aqua silk tank accentuated her athletic figure. Her light brown hair curled softly at her shoulders, every strand in place—an act defiant to the August heat and humidity.

"C'mon, I'll introduce you."

Hal lumbered toward her. Ryan and I looked at each other with wide eyes and followed behind him.

"How is it that you've been here five minutes and are buds with Hal and meeting Sheridan Lane?" Ryan whispered.

"I have no idea," I said with a shrug.

Hal nudged a reporter out of the way and assumed a spot next to Sheridan.

"What did we do to deserve Sheridan Lane at practice today?" Hal said, flashing his Chiclet smile.

"Hal, just the man I was looking for. I need to pick your brain later for a story I'm doing about Andy Miller."

"I'm happy to help if it means I can get you on our morning show this week. We're broadcasting from camp."

"Deal. I can do it between my Network hits tomorrow morning."

"Sheridan, there's someone I want you to meet."

Hal motioned for me to step forward.

"This is Blake Kirk. She's new to the media team here. A local girl who just graduated with a master's in journalism. I thought you could give her some friendly advice this season."

"Good to meet you, Blake," Sheridan said, firmly shaking my hand. "This industry can be a lot of fun, but it isn't for the faint of heart. Let me know if I can help you in any way."

"I would be honored to get your advice!" I said, brimming with eagerness.

"I'm here because a few pioneering women advised me when I was a cub reporter. I guess it's time for me to do the same for the next generation," Sheridan said and glanced at my notepad. "Are you working on a story today?"

"Yes, my first assignment is on the battle at backup quarterback."

"That's an important story, especially when you have an injury-prone starter at QB," Sheridan said. "I'm working on answering the million-dollar question: Can starting quarterback Andy Miller live up to his contract?"

At the start of training camp, Andy signed a four-year contract extension worth more than $160 million. It was a whopping deal that put Andy's salary on par with top-tier quarterbacks. It also was a lightning rod for controversy. Some media praised Andy's ability to manage the offense. The majority questioned his ability to stay healthy and complete deep passes.

"If you ask me, he's the team's best option. There was nothing in free agency, unless you want to gamble on veterans well past their prime," Hal said. "Don't forget that Miller led this team to the playoffs the last two years."

"Still, it's a rich deal for a player who has missed games in three of the last four seasons and is coming off shoulder surgery," Sheridan said.

"It was a minor surgery," Hal contested.

He wiped his forehead with a red handkerchief.

"Only Miller can settle this debate when the season gets underway," Sheridan said.

"The o-line and d-line are going one-on-one. Don't want to miss that," Hal said, tying the handkerchief around his meaty neck.

Hal made his way down the field and Ryan scampered behind him.

I stood next to Sheridan and followed her gaze. Where she looked, I looked. And her eyes were glued to the team's star wide receiver Devonte Harris.

"Devonte can make any quarterback look good," Sheridan said.

Devonte pushed himself up from the grass and flipped the football to an offensive assistant. From ten yards away, I could see the veins popping in his biceps. The proximity of his perfectly chiseled V-shaped body made me gasp. His broad shoulders were accentuated by abs so defined I could make out the deep indentations through his jersey.

"Devonte's got a lot to play for this season. He's entering the fourth year of his rookie deal. If he sets records, you know the team is going to lock him up with a monster contract," Sheridan said, her eyes fixed on the receiver as he jogged back to the line of scrimmage.

"He said he wants to spend his career in Oklahoma City. He told Hal that last week on air," I told her.

I had listened to the interview on the way to the dentist and sat in the parking lot with the car running until the end of the segment.

"Devonte will spend his career here for the right price. He and his people are applying pressure on the team through various channels. That includes the media."

I lapped up Sheridan's insights like a thirsty puppy. The game of football that I knew was being played before me in pads and helmets. But Sheridan drew inside knowledge from the shadows of the field where agents lingered, backroom deals were made, and the politics behind the sport played out. I didn't have access to that world. Not yet at least.

"So, are you interviewing Miller for your story?" I asked, trying to prolong the conversation.

"I will be sitting down with him this afternoon. Miller is an unlikely franchise quarterback. He isn't flashy and he's injury prone. But this organization clearly believes in him. I want to ask him why the team should invest that much money in a quarterback who has delivered so little."

I smoothed back the sweaty strands of hair that were pasted to my forehead and mustered the courage to offer my own insights.

"Miller put up career numbers two years ago and led the league in completion percentage. If he can stay healthy and the defense can pick up where it left off, this team should be hard to beat."

Sheridan raised a perfectly arched eyebrow.

"That's a big *if*," she said. "And while you do make a good point about the defense carrying this team, we all know this is a quarterback-driven league. If you don't have a star QB, you can forget getting the trophy."

"What do you think of the backup quarterbacks?" I asked.

"I suspect Seth will receive significant playing time, and Marcus is an intriguing prospect."

When the team selected Marcus Dixon in the fourth round of April's draft, fans across the city cheered. Most draft picks beyond the second round don't get much attention. But Marcus had stolen the hearts of many Oklahomans. He grew up in a small *Friday Night Lights* town where he took his team to the state title game. He went on to the University of Oklahoma and made dazzling plays as a running quarterback, darting out of trouble and slipping past defenders. League scouts cautioned that Marcus was a system quarterback and his scrambling style wouldn't translate to the pro ranks. But OKC's general manager saw potential and said he gave the team a different look under center.

"Do you think Marcus will play this season?" I asked.

"Doubtful. He's got a strong arm but some mechanical issues. If the coaches here can work with him while he's on the practice squad, he'll have a fast learning curve because he's an incredible athlete."

"What about Seth?" I continued.

"Seth is a very capable career backup in my eyes. He's got a much bigger arm than Andy. Seth's issue is turnovers."

An air horn blasted, signaling the end of practice. The players jogged to the center of the field and dropped to one knee in front of Coach Bush.

"I really enjoyed meeting you. Thank you for taking the time to talk to me," I said, smiling at Sheridan.

"It's a pleasure meeting a smart young woman who wants to talk about the game. You asked important questions. You should come out on a story with me. See how we do things at the Network."

"That would be amazing!"

"I'll talk to Johnny. We'll set something up."

As if he heard his name, Johnny began walking toward us, waving antsy reporters back with his clipboard.

"Speak of the devil," Sheridan smirked.

"No media steps foot on this field until the huddle breaks," Johnny said.

I looked around for the team's photographer, Sam Boswell, who preferred the nickname Boss. When a man with light brown stubble covering his narrow chin and legs the size of toothpicks handed me a microphone, it took me by surprise. With his long hair pulled back in a low ponytail, Boss looked artsy and cool. His appearance starkly contrasted with the display of jumbo-sized muscles on the field.

"You must be Blake. I'm Boss. How about a quick audio check?" he said.

I turned on the wireless mic and he nestled an earbud in his ear. "All good." He gave a thumbs-up.

"So, do I just go up to Seth and Marcus and ask questions?" I asked, suddenly feeling anxious about my interviews.

"Pretty much. They won't get big crowds. We'll tell Marcus to wait around. The rookies usually do what they're told. We'll interview Seth first," Boss said, scanning the field.

"What about Coach?"

"Coach speaks last. He likes to run laps around the far practice fields. Get his workout in. He'll talk after the players get back to the stadium."

As a whistle blew, the players pushed off the ground with their helmets in hand and broke their huddle. The media promptly burst off the track, racing to catch the players they needed for their interviews.

Marcus was easy to spot because he was surrounded by offensive linemen handing him their helmets. He was dutifully carrying out the pro football tradition of rookies lugging veterans' helmets to the locker room, and he was doing it with the kindest smile.

"Hi, Marcus, I'm Blake. I need to grab you for an interview. Can you wait a couple of minutes?"

"No problem," he said, stacking the helmets on the ground next to him. Sweat streamed down his round, soft face.

"Thanks. I'm going to find Seth. I'll be back."

"You got it," Marcus said cheerfully.

Seth was on the field about twenty yards away. He was bending at the waist in a hamstring stretch and talking to Monster Calves, who was splayed across the grass.

As we approached them, my throat seized. It hit me. I was about to conduct my first interview with a pro player. It felt like someone had shoved Monster Calves's sock in my mouth. I stared at his calves, which looked like half-deflated basketballs flattened against the grass. Forcing a swallow, I looked up. A pair of glistening hazel eyes gazed down at me. Seth's sweaty auburn hair was tousled in a bedhead style.

"I'm . . . I'm Blake," I stammered.

"I know who you are," Seth said and grinned.

"Do you mind if I interview you for a few minutes?" I asked, ignoring how he could possibly know me.

There was a cockiness about Seth that was both attractive and intimidating. He was like Johnny from *The Karate Kid*—you didn't want to like him; you were rooting for Danny. But Johnny was just so darned cute. Seth was really darned cute.

"You want to interview this guy? Don't waste your time," Monster Calves said, sitting up and tugging at a black knee brace. It reluctantly folded below his kneecap.

"Don't be jealous just because no one wants to talk to o-linemen," Seth said.

"Whatever. I'm hitching a ride on a cart," Monster Calves said, rolling onto his knees as Seth pulled him up.

"In case you can't tell, we're good friends. Known him since college," Seth said.

"I've been protecting his ass for far too long," Monster Calves said. He gave Seth a fist bump and then whistled at a trainer who was loading Gatorade coolers on the bed of a golf cart.

Their ribbing quelled my nerves, and my jaw began to slacken.

"He has the biggest legs I've ever seen," I blurted out.

"He's solid as a rock in every way. But you're not here to talk about our starting left tackle."

"No. Just a few questions for you," I said, trying to ignore Seth's dimpled chin.

"Let's do it," Seth said and smiled wider, revealing his perfectly straight gleaming-white teeth.

I glanced down at my notes and quickly reviewed the questions I had scripted. I needed to immerse myself in the interview before I noticed another handsome feature on Seth.

"You're coming off a season where you finished the year as the starter because of Andy Miller's injury. How has that impacted your mentality in training camp?" I asked, relieved to have shifted into reporter mode.

"It really hasn't. I am the number two guy, but I always prepare like I'm going to start and play every snap. That's my mentality no matter the situation."

I nodded as Seth spoke and steadied my gaze on the collar of his jersey. Looking into his eyes would certainly derail my focus.

"How would you assess your play so far in training camp?"

"I like to be aggressive. That's always been my style of play. It probably cost me early in camp. I was overthrowing guys and had too many interceptions. But now I'm finding my rhythm. Today was by far my best of camp."

I could feel Seth's smile, warm and bright, beaming down at me. My pulse raced. Pheromones ignited my skeletal system.

"That was fun. How about we do it again tomorrow?" Seth said, cocking his head to one side.

I couldn't tell if Seth was flirting with me, but I needed to defuse the giddiness I was feeling.

"I'm sure Johnny has other plans for me," I said, trying to sound businesslike.

"Don't let Johnny boss you around," Seth said teasingly and jogged away.

I exhaled loudly. What was going on with me? I had just crushed on a player in my first interview, and that was not OK. I looked up at the cloudless sky to clear my head.

"Come on, Blake. Time to interview Marcus," Boss said as he walked toward the rookie quarterback.

Marcus was standing patiently in the same spot where we left him with a stack of four helmets at his feet.

"Thank you for hanging around," I told him.

"It's OK, ma'am. My meetings don't start for another thirty minutes."

"Marcus, you can call me Blake."

"Where I grew up, you show a lady proper respect. So, I'd prefer ma'am."

"OK. Ma'am it is." I smiled and planted my sandals firmly in the grass field. After my interview with Seth, I needed to regain my equilibrium and feel grounded into the earth.

I took a sip of air and motioned for Boss to begin shooting.

"Marcus, what are you working on during training camp?"

"Everything. The coaches are focusing on my throwing motion. I need to be more consistent with that, more accurate. I'm working on everything they tell me. I can hardly sleep at night. Practice film keeps playing in my mind."

Interviewing Marcus was effortless. It was like conversing with an old friend.

When we finished, Boss dropped his camera at his feet and shook out his neck. "You're a pro. We're going to work great together," he said.

I soaked up his compliment. It was exactly what I needed to hear after my interview with Seth, which had unsettled me. Maybe I was imagining the sparks crackling between us. Regardless, I needed to turn my thoughts away from the pro quarterback and concentrate on being a pro reporter.

· · ·

I walked with Ryan and Boss back to the stadium.

"We need to shoot intros to the videos before we post them on the web," Boss told me. "We can do that after the late practice. That will give you time to freshen up."

The long curls I worked so hard to achieve that morning had transformed into limp clumps of sweat-matted hair. I could only imagine the melted mess my makeup had become.

"I could use a few hours in the AC," I said. "By the way, did anyone see Garrett? I thought he was coming out here."

"That dude always avoids practice," Boss said. "The only reason he knows what's going on is because he reads the interview transcripts we post on the site."

"We should stop by his office and check in," I suggested.

We approached the cafeteria, where players with bags of ice wrapped around their knees and shoulders were filing out with Styrofoam boxes of food.

"Catch ya later," Boss said. He slipped into the cafeteria, passing a cornerback holding a tray loaded with grilled chicken and bottles of Gatorade.

"How did your interviews go?" Ryan asked as we walked upstairs.

"Actually, really well. The guys gave me good info."

"I still haven't interviewed a player one-on-one. I just hold a recorder up with the rest of the media and let them ask the questions. And that's just fine with me," Ryan said.

"Don't get me wrong. I was super nervous before I interviewed Seth. But the adrenaline rush is part of the fun," I said.

"Speak for yourself," Ryan said and knocked lightly on Garrett's closed door.

"Come in," Garrett grumbled. His office looked like a tiny beige box. Two photos were taped to his computer, one of a young woman in a cap and gown, who looked like his sister, and the other of his parents. A framed Brett Favre jersey leaned against the wall next to boxes of old media guides and file folders.

"Are you from Green Bay?" I asked.

"Howard, Wisconsin, to be exact," Garrett said. He typed on his computer, barely looking up at me as he spoke. "I've been in this office two years and still haven't hung that jersey. Too busy."

"You seem busy right now. We just wanted to check in."

"Keep it quick. I need to finish the cheerleader pages," he said, his eyes still glued to his computer screen. "Did you get all the interviews done?"

"Yes, I have everything I need for my story. Boss and I will shoot the video intros this afternoon. I wanted to confirm that the interviews with the players were going to be edited into one video."

"Yes, Boss will edit them together," he said. "Now, get started with your stories. You have a lot to get done."

Ryan and I looked at each other and both shrugged.

"Was it just me or did Garrett seem annoyed with us?" I asked Ryan as we walked down the hall.

"That's how he operates. Always busy. But if you don't check in with him, he can get pissy."

"There sure are a lot of egos around here," I said.

"The biggest ones aren't even on the field," Ryan said.

· · ·

Grains of rice from the cafeteria's stir-fry special stuck to my keyboard, a by-product of working through lunch. I wedged the granules out with a paper clip and swept the remainder with my hand into the to-go box. Time to proofread my story.

Oklahoma City has a problem. And it's a great problem to have. Their backup quarterbacks are gunning for playing time.

Veteran Seth Barker and rookie Marcus Dixon may be entrenched in supporting roles behind Andy Miller, but the quarterbacks don't approach practice that way.

"I am the number two guy, but I always prepare like I'm going to start and play every snap," Barker said.

I leaned back and admired my leading paragraphs. Sheridan would be proud. Unfortunately, it took me a couple of hours to write, twice the time Garrett had allotted.

I dialed his number and cringed.

"Is your story done?" he asked abruptly.

"Yes, I just finished the first draft. Do you want me to email it to you?"

"Nope. Put it in the web publisher. You should head to the practice now. Coach usually finishes early in the afternoons."

"OK," I said, wishing I left myself more time to improve my hair and makeup.

"What about the transcriptions?" he asked.

I cringed.

"I didn't finish them. I just did the quotes I needed for my story."

"You need to manage your time better," Garrett told me curtly. "Post the transcripts ASAP when you get back."

"No problem."

I quickly swiped on a coat of lip gloss and bolted from my cube.

• • •

"Stand-up, take six."

I nodded at Boss.

"Welcome to our training camp report. I'm Blake Kirk here at team camp headquarters in Oklahoma City. Today we caught up with the backup quarterbacks to talk about their roles on the team. Here's what they had to say."

"That one should work," Boss said, removing his camera from the tripod before I could protest.

"Are you sure? I think my voice cracked midway through. My first video has to be flawless."

Boss and I stood on a practice field adjacent to the indoor training center. The afternoon session was over, but players still were trickling out of the facility.

Several coaches and media members stopped to watch me shoot my intro, which caused me to trip over my words. I had pretended a mosquito was swarming my head when Coach Bush paused behind Boss. There was no way I would be able to remember my lines with the head coach evaluating my talent. At least, not during my first shoot. Luckily, the team's offensive coordinator ushered Coach away to talk about a third-and-long play in practice.

"Your voice sounded fine to me. You looked good. That's the most important thing," Boss said, folding the tripod, marking an end to our discussion.

"I thought my words would be the focus," I said.

"The trolls who go to our website care about how you look. Trust me. That's why it didn't work out with the print guy before you. Smart dude but no one could stand the sight of him. The team didn't want to make that mistake twice, so they scooted you in here real fast."

"I haven't put much thought into the appearance part of the job. I really want to prove that I know my stuff," I said.

"Don't get me wrong. You need both to succeed. It's just that if you don't look good, no one will listen to you. It's a harsh broadcasting reality," Boss said.

I nodded and made a mental note to google makeup tips for heat and humidity.

When I got back to my cube, I cracked open a Diet Coke and refreshed the team website. Front and center was a photo of Seth and Marcus at practice under the headline "The Dynamic Duo Vying for Number 2," by Blake Kirk.

I clicked on the story. It already had double-digit page views. I watched the video. The stand-up wasn't flawless—my voice was pitchy. But Boss was right; I looked good, and I was learning that mattered. A lot.

Six

Bootylicious Goldilocks

Three days into the job and I had started to fall into a routine. Wake up early to run. Fill a giant travel mug with dark roast coffee and vanilla creamer. Leave the house by 7:00 a.m.

I had learned from my rookie mistakes and better strategized for the sweltering heat. I was wearing a sleeveless cotton sundress and flat sandals. A wool cardigan was neatly folded in my satchel to insulate me from the subarctic temperatures on the second floor.

I skipped up the stadium stairs and past the cornerbacks coach, who was pecking at his computer with one hand and holding an oversized mug that said "Coffee Makes Me Poop" with the other. He thrust the poop mug in my direction and began to whistle the chorus to Seals and Crofts's "Summer Breeze."

"The Summer Breeze just blew in, and she's big-time now. Got her own video on the website."

My knees buckled slightly. The coaches had watched my video! "Hi, Coach, my name is Blake Kirk. I wanted to formally introduce myself."

"I know exactly who you are. Us coaches have been locked away in this stadium since training camp started. Then you come through here like a fresh breeze on a summer day."

"I'll take that as a good thing." I leaned against his doorframe.

"It's a very good thing. By the way, sweetie, you can call me Scooter. Need anything, my door is always open."

"Thanks, Coach."

"That's Scooter to you," he said and winked.

. . .

Ryan squatted on his heels like a baseball catcher, loading paper into the copier trays.

"Are you ready to walk to practice?" I asked.

"One sec," he said as he popped to his feet and tucked his Dri-FIT shirt into his shorts.

"Aren't you lucky getting to wear athletic clothes on the second floor like one of the coaches," I teased.

"Johnny called just after I had changed and asked me to make him a quick copy," Ryan said.

"Isn't he inside his office? He can't make the copy himself?" I whispered.

"He doesn't know how to work the copier," Ryan said and slid the papers under Johnny's closed door.

"I asked Johnny about practice clothes," I said as we walked toward the staircase. "He said that the team can't order any player apparel in my size, so he gave me clothes that the cheerleaders wear."

"How cool," Ryan said, sounding genuinely impressed.

"It's not my style. The T-shirts are skintight and bedazzled with rhinestones and sequins. I'd feel ridiculous wearing that to practice," I said.

"But it could up your page views," Ryan offered.

"I refuse to impersonate a cheerleader to get clicks," I said, defiance rising in my voice.

Ryan looked down at his running shoes. "I'm sorry, Blake. I didn't mean to offend you. I was just trying to say that . . . I mean . . . you would . . ." Ryan chewed on his words.

I knew what he was trying to articulate. Ryan thought he was paying me a compliment by saying I would look good in the cheerleading apparel. He had no idea that Johnny's suggestion felt more like an insult.

"I get what you were trying to say, Ryan. But I'm not sure you under-stand where I'm coming from on this. Wearing a mega-tight shirt makes me look like I'm trying to be a sexy cheerleader and not a serious journal-ist. It discredits my work. Even more confusing is that this was Johnny's idea. On Monday, he told me that I need to prove I'm here for the 'right reasons' and not because I want to date a player. Today, he gives me a bunch of provocative clothes I'm allowed to wear to practice. It's a lot of mixed messages."

"I didn't think about it that way," Ryan said.

"I suspect that Johnny subscribes to the mindset that women work-ing for pro teams should have pom-poms—not microphones. When I told him that I would stick with my sundresses, he was shocked and annoyed."

"To be honest, I thought you'd be excited to dress like a cheerleader. It didn't even cross my mind that you could be offended."

"I'm trying not to let it get to me. Johnny is still figuring out where I fit in an organization that has been run by men, for men. It's all uncharted territory," I said and pushed open the stadium doors.

"You're going to carve out a place for yourself in no time," Ryan said reassuringly.

"I sure hope so," I said and waved at Tammie at the media check-in desk.

The players had begun practice and there was a horde of media sur-rounding the receivers.

"I wonder what all the excitement is about," Ryan said.

"Let's ask Hal," I said and motioned for Ryan to follow me to where Hal was standing to the side of the fray. The collar of his faded Bubba's BBQ shirt hung heavy with sweat.

"Morning, Hal. What's going on?" I asked.

"Apparently, Devonte got a new tattoo—a woman's face," Hal said, sounding unimpressed.

The tattoo covered Devonte's entire right forearm. It was the profile of a woman with long flowing hair and pursed full lips.

"Who do you think it is?" I asked.

"I suspect a girlfriend who lives in Jersey. You know he's from there. Probably wants to show it to her at Saturday's game," Hal said. "Seems like a whole lot of something over nothing. But us media folks gotta have something to talk about."

When the horn sounded after the final period, Johnny and a staff of training camp interns funneled the media to the back of the field.

"A couple of announcements while Coach is talking to the players," Johnny said and placed two fingers in his mouth, whistling loudly to silence the media. "We leave for New Jersey on Friday. Players have meetings in the morning. There's no media availability on Friday. Next week, we will begin interviewing players during open locker room. There will be no interviews on the field after practice. Did you hear that? Let's start getting ready for the regular season."

Johnny ceremoniously clapped his hand against the clipboard, signaling the media's release.

The herd plowed toward Devonte, Boss and I following in step.

"Have to ask you about the new ink. Who's the lucky lady?" a local blogger said, pointing to Devonte's arm.

"Someone special to me. I'll leave it at that," Devonte said, looking down at his cleats.

Johnny, who was standing in his dutiful position behind Devonte, jumped to his toes and thrust his head over Devonte's shoulder.

"We are here to talk football. Anyone got football questions?"

"Devonte, what does it mean for you to go back and play in front of your hometown?" Hal asked.

"It means the world. I didn't grow up with much. But my family, we overcame a lot. To have my friends and family in the stands on Saturday means everything. They helped me get this far."

It was the perfect quote for my story.

• • •

After hours of transcribing quotes, my stomach was growling and my vision was blurring. I scurried downstairs to the team cafeteria. The lights were dim and empty chafing dishes lined the hot food section, waiting for the next meal. At the far end of the room, the frozen yogurt machine purred invitingly. I pulled down the chocolate lever and the lights popped on bright, causing me to drop my plastic bowl and land a dollop of yogurt between my feet.

"Sorry, didn't mean to scare you," a luscious woman said. "I'll get some napkins for that chocolate turd on the ground."

She strutted to a napkin dispenser, her long golden curls swaying over her shoulders. The stitching down the seam of her tight white pants labored with every move of her voluptuous, opposing butt cheeks.

"Here you go."

Her pink acrylic fingernails grazed my palm as she handed me a wad of napkins.

"You must be the new girl. I'm Emily."

"Hi, I'm Blake. Nice to meet you. I would shake your hand but mine's a little sticky at the moment."

I wiped the yogurt dripping off my fingers.

"I'd help you clean up," she told me, "but I'm going to bust right through these pants if I bend over."

Emily moved her hands to her waist and stuck out her rear to emphasize the point.

"It's OK. I've got it. I don't want a player coming in here and slipping. Although an injury at the yogurt machine would make for a sensational headline," I said with a laugh.

There was something about Emily that made me feel like I'd seen her before. And it was not because she looked like someone straight out of *The Real Housewives of Oklahoma City*.

"Gotta book it for a meeting. Glad I'm not the only one here with a sweet tooth," Emily said, licking a chocolate chip off the tip of her spoon and sashaying out the door.

I was so hungry that I ate most of my frozen yogurt on the walk back upstairs. When I got to my cubicle, the phone rang. Ryan.

"Hey, I found the perfect photo of Devonte for your story. I went ahead and tagged it for you," he said.

"You're the best."

I stirred the remnants of crushed Oreo toppings and lowered my voice.

"So, I just met a bootylicious Goldilocks in the cafeteria. What's her story?"

"You must mean Emily," Ryan whispered into the phone.

"Should I know her from somewhere?"

"Devonte's tattoo," Ryan said and hung up.

Seven

I Think I Just Saw Her Birth Canal

I heaved my overstuffed, frayed rolling bag up a couple of steps. The worn suitcase had dutifully accompanied me back and forth from Oklahoma City to Los Angeles for the previous six years. Now, it was getting a taste of the big leagues. A chartered plane ride with a pro football team.

But neither the bag nor I appeared fully equipped for this trip.

The night before, I had emptied my closet in search of the perfect outfits for a one-night stay in New York. Well, New Jersey, to be exact, since New York's team played its games on the other side of the Hudson River and we were staying close to the stadium.

Still, New York adjacent felt a lot more sophisticated than OKC. And after watching Emily strut around the cafeteria in her tight white pants, all my clothes looked frumpy in comparison. Emily wouldn't have been caught dead in a flowy faux wrap dress.

I finally settled on black slacks and a black silk blouse for the plane ride and jammed everything piled on the floor into my bag. Even after I coerced the zipper shut, washed my face, and collapsed into bed, my mind kept circling back to Emily. Did HR make her sign a nonfraternization agreement? Did the team know about her relationship with Devonte?

I balanced my bag on the fourth step and shook my cramping hand.

"A pretty girl like you shouldn't have to carry her luggage," Seth said, standing at the bottom of the stairs, holding a plate piled with egg whites and bacon. He bounced up the steps and handed me his plate.

"You take this. I'll get the bag."

"You don't have to do that," I said. I could feel my pulse quicken. There was something about Seth that stirred up my insides.

"I most certainly do," he said.

He picked up the bag as if he was lifting my purse and carried it nonchalantly to the landing.

"You do realize we're only going for one night?"

"I know. But I couldn't decide on what to wear. I need options. Not all of us are lucky enough to wear a uniform."

"You'll look great no matter what you wear."

My cheeks blushed. I didn't know what to say, so I stood there motionless and let them warm to a deep shade of pink.

"I can take that," Seth said, motioning to his plate. Our fingers grazed as I handed it to him, and I felt the energy flicker between us.

"Thank you," I said and looked up to meet his gaze. His hazel eyes crinkled at the corners.

"Pleasure was mine. See you on the plane," he said and bounced back down to the concourse.

I allowed the second-floor door to slam behind me and caught my breath. Seth had been sliding into my thoughts since my interview with him earlier that week. I tried not to indulge myself in daydreams about his dimpled smile, but there was only so much self-control a girl could have.

I wheeled my bag past Ryan's cube and did a double take. It looked as if someone blasted a leaf blower over it. Notes, stat sheets, and Post-its covered his desk. Dr Pepper cans and candy wrappers littered the floor.

"This place is a pigpen."

Johnny's voice startled me.

"I think Ryan worked late last night," I stammered in Ryan's defense.

"I work past midnight all the time and don't treat my office like a frat house," Johnny said, kicking a soda can under Ryan's chair. "Blake, follow me. There's someone I want you to meet."

I wheeled my bag behind him. Johnny stopped abruptly. "Why did you bring your bag up here?"

"Was I supposed to leave it somewhere?"

"Yeah, the locker room," Johnny said, then tilted his head upward as he had an epiphany. "But you can't go in the locker room. Hmm. Next trip, have Ryan drop your bag in the locker room so you don't have to roll that thing all around the stadium."

Satisfied with his solution, Johnny resumed marching down the hall, stopping in front of a plaque that read, "Lenny Jones Player Operations Coordinator."

"It's Johnny," he said and knocked, opening the door before getting an answer.

Lenny clicked on his mouse and then stood up from behind his computer.

"Come in."

Lenny and I hadn't formally met, although for several days he greeted me in the hallways with a warm smile. From what I'd read, Lenny had starred as a defensive back for a small college in Ohio. He bounced around practice squads with a few pro teams before taking an internship with a front office. With his lean, muscular physique, he often was mistaken for a player. Only when he took off his aviator sunglasses were wrinkles revealed around the corners of his eyes. Lenny was a behind-the-scenes guy and part of the team's safety net, the last line of defense to make sure nothing slipped through the cracks.

"Lenny, meet Blake Kirk," Johnny said. "Blake, meet Lenny. He handles all the logistics when it comes to the players and team travel."

"Nice to meet you." Lenny nodded.

Before I could reply, Johnny interrupted.

"Blake, I trust you read the travel itinerary Lenny emailed. I want him to walk you through the details before we leave. The team travels like a well-oiled machine."

"Great," I said and began to pick at my fingernails, my default nervous habit.

Lenny sat down and leaned forward on his muscular forearms.

"We will begin departure from the stadium around noon. Equipment managers and staff—that includes you—will ride on the bus together to the plane. The players and coaches will be on the other three buses.

"You'll have an assigned seat on the plane. Your hotel room will be on the same floor as the rest of your department. No one except players and coaches are allowed on the players' floors. We'll have security stationed just outside the elevators of the players' floors to enforce that. We'll set up a ballroom as our team cafeteria. That cafeteria is only for players and coaches.

"Before the game, that's when your bus will be used. The buses will go in shifts to the stadium. The players, coaches, and most of the staff will ride on earlier buses from the hotel to the stadium. Do *not* get on one of those buses, even if other people from your department are doing so. Just use bus number four before games.

"I know this is a lot of information being thrown at you. You'll pick it up quickly. The most important thing is that on Saturday you ride bus number four, the Blake Bus, as Johnny calls it."

By the time Lenny finished talking, flecks of chipped fingernail polish speckled my black pants. I wasn't sure if the entire team knew about the Blake Bus, but clearly the front office was well aware.

"Blake, we appreciate your work and are excited to have you aboard. Great story on Devonte, by the way," Lenny said.

"Thanks," I said, grateful to be changing topics.

"Lenny, you're the man," Johnny said, fist-bumping him from across the desk. "Blake, now you know the drill. Don't forget we have a department dinner tonight. My treat."

. . .

The police escort motored through highway traffic, leading the four team buses to the airport without so much as a pump of the brakes. The buses parked on the tarmac and the team's equipment managers hopped out to unload massive duffel bags and trunks.

Ryan grabbed our suitcases from the belly of the bus, and I followed him up the plane's staircase. Three attractive flight attendants stood in the galley, cheerfully greeting us as we boarded.

"Hi, sweetie," twanged a petite blonde, patting Ryan on the arm. "I have extra hot fudge just for your sundae."

"Alyssa, the only thing sweeter than you is that sundae," Ryan said, flirting.

I coughed back laughter.

Ryan glanced back at me, having forgotten I was in line behind him. His face turned beet red.

"Alyssa, this is Blake," he stammered. "Blake's part of the media group. Alyssa is the senior attendant."

Alyssa took my hand, clutching it warmly between her palms. She had full pink lips, bright green eyes, and a thick coat of tan foundation lacquering her face. At first glance, it was hard to guess her age. But the dark sunspots marking the tops of her hands suggested she was at least fifty.

"Pleasure to meet you, honey." She winked. "If you want anything special, let me know. I've got it all—warm cookies, M&M's, Twizzlers. I even have a special stash of something stiffer, if you know what I mean."

Each seat on the plane was accounted for with a name tag. I spotted my name on an aisle seat, next to Ryan.

"You sure got to know Alyssa quickly," I teased.

"I needed a dessert hookup," he told me, blushing.

"That may not be the only hookup she's looking for."

"Ha ha," Ryan said, scooting into the middle seat. He grabbed a paper bag from underneath him and ripped it open like a kid on Christmas morning. "I'm starving. These plane snacks are the best."

Ryan unwrapped the foil off a sub sandwich oozing with cheese and marinara sauce. Red sauce dripped down his hands and he licked it off before it reached the cuff of his jacket.

"A meatball sub for a snack?"

I rummaged through the contents of my paper bag and handed Ryan a wad of napkins.

"It's the perfect snack for the guys in the trenches," he said, cheese dangling from the corner of his mouth. "They'll pound this down in three bites."

Hal's belly brushed against me as he sidestepped into the seat behind me. "Thataway, Ryan. Show that sub who's boss."

"Ryan, you need a bib," I said, handing him more napkins.

"I heard they're serving chicken parm for lunch. But I'm always a sucker for the sub sandwiches. It's nice to have options," Hal said, plopping into his seat.

"Have you always traveled with the team?" I said, twisting my neck toward the aisle to face Hal.

"Ever since the station bought the rights to be the team's official home on the radio. The station negotiated for the talent to ride on the team plane to games. So, I get to fly private and lap up a three-course meal while talking to some of my favorite people."

"Do you ever go back and talk to the players?"

"They're off-limits. But sometimes the coaches invite me into first class for a little chat, off the record of course," Hal said, popping open a bag of chips from the snack bag.

Monster Calves was the first player to board the plane. He grunted and groaned as he wedged himself down the aisle, proclaiming, "Creamed spinach last night was a bad idea. It's going to look the same coming out as it did going in."

"Did the quarterbacks take you out?" Hal asked.

"Yep, to Cattleman's. Steak always tastes better when someone else is paying."

The rest of the offensive line followed Monster Calves to the back of the plane, all in billowing suits made with enough fabric to slipcover all the couches in my parents' house.

Next came the running backs and wide receivers in a procession of custom suits, oversized watches, and designer luggage. Most players wore headphones and bobbed their heads to music as they walked past. A running back wore gold-rimmed sunglasses with diamonds encrusted on the sides. A fullback sported a pink silk pocket square and matching pink Hermès tie.

But no one sparkled or shined more than Devonte. His large diamond earrings refracted rainbows on the walls of the plane. He wore a pale blue fitted suit with thin white pinstripes. Large silver-knotted cufflinks adorned the folded cuffs of his bespoke white shirt. He dragged a Louis Vuitton suitcase and carried a matching backpack.

I looked down at my gossip magazine. The show unfolding in front of me was better than anything on the magazine's pages.

"When you're done reading that, will you pass it back?"

I looked up and found Seth grinning down at me, looking handsome in a charcoal suit with a light blue shirt.

"I assume you're kidding," I said.

"None of these guys would be caught dead buying those magazines, but we all read them in the training room. They're addicting. We call them crack mags."

I handed him the magazine. "Consider it my gift to the team."

"I promise to repay you," Seth said and mischievously raised an eyebrow.

I looked down as he walked away, suddenly self-conscious of our banter. Had Seth and I been flirting again? Did anyone hear us? Suddenly, a vision of my signature on the nonfraternization agreement popped into my head, and I clenched the armrests.

"Can you make room?" Garrett said, peering down at me. His plain black suit and skinny black tie appeared austere in contrast to the players' parade of colorful, custom clothes.

"Of course," I said and stood up.

"I was in first class talking to Johnny until the coaches arrived," Garrett announced, proudly. "They're all here now. We should take off soon."

. . .

I scooped the last of the fried calamari appetizer onto my plate and leaned back in my red velvet chair to take in the scene. We were at Graziano's, which Johnny had proclaimed was "the best Italian joint in Jersey." Red wine and pasta sauce sloshed onto starched white tablecloths. People talked loudly over Dean Martin playing in the background. And Johnny presided over our long table in the back of the room like a godfather in an old mobster movie.

"This year is going to be big," Johnny said from the head of the table. "We have talent on the team. Devonte is going to be the next Jerry Rice. Mark my words."

Johnny wore a bright blue button-down with a paisley print on the cuffs, which he had rolled up twice before diving into a heaping plate of veal piccata.

"Tomorrow is our third preseason game. It's getting real." He raised a glass of iced tea. "Let's toast to the grind."

There were six of us at dinner. It was Johnny, Ryan, Garrett, me, and two longtime PR coordinators—one who handled all of Coach Bush's press and the other who handled the general manager's press. They followed Johnny to and from the various teams and had worked for him for nearly a decade. Both were in their midforties, married, and battling receding hairlines. Johnny trusted them implicitly. They were his right and left hands. Carson and Carleton. And I was having the hardest time remembering who was who. To me, they were interchangeable and identical, like a pair of corporate Bobbsey Twins.

Johnny usually saved places on either side of him for Carson and Carleton. That night, he reserved one of those seats for me, and one of the Bobbsey Twins had glared at me when Johnny had told him to find another seat.

"Johnny, are we the only native Oklahomans at this table?" I asked him.

"OKC is my roots. I was born there. I've worked most of my life there. In fact, I started out as an intern like Ryan. I slept in a sleeping bag under my desk at night, always available to the coaches. At midnight, you could find me making copies or making coffee," Johnny said. "The league was different back then. Coaches smoked cigarettes on the team plane. The players cracked open beers. It was another era."

"It's hard to believe that any team would subject players to a bunch of cigarette smoke," I said, shaking my head.

"We didn't know any better," Johnny said. "But not all change is good. I miss some of the old ways. I'm old school, Blake."

I wasn't sure where Johnny was going with this. It was clear that he resisted change, and that likely included hiring a female for my position. I also got the impression that he liked me and believed in my potential, but he didn't know what to do with me.

"Why did you leave Oklahoma City for Dallas?" I asked.

Johnny banged his championship ring against the table.

"Dallas had an opening for a coordinator job and OKC wasn't going to promote me. I wrote and called the Dallas front office every day for three weeks until they hired me. I spent nine years with Dallas. Their PR staff is first class and ironclad. That's where I really learned how to do my job. My boss there told me, 'The media may blitz you, but you have to keep ownership upright. Always protect your owner.'"

With two glasses of wine in me, Johnny didn't seem so intimidating. We almost felt like friends. Almost.

Johnny took a long sip of iced tea.

"After Dallas, I took a VP job in Los Angeles and eventually got hired away by OKC."

He tore off a piece of bread and soaked it in the pool of lemon butter sauce on his plate.

"Blake, I may seem tough, but you're about to see it takes skin thicker than a rhino to survive in this league. I've seen entire coaching staffs fired at Christmas. The media has called me 'Johnny the Jackass.' But I've lasted thirty-five years in the league because I know how to take one on the chin and survive."

Johnny swallowed down the bread with the last of his iced tea and untucked the napkin from his designer jeans.

"All right, party people, I'm heading out," he said, standing up and clapping his meaty hands. "I've settled the bill. Most of you have company cards. Enjoy some department bonding and buy Blake something nice to drink. Not that crap in a paper bag."

"Who are you meeting now?" one of the Bobbsey Twins asked.

"Drinks with a major league GM. You know me, always working," Johnny said, giving him a fist bump.

"Will we see you at the club?" the other Twin asked.

"No, we have a back room at a steak house. You'll have free rein of The Bling, and that includes you, Blake. This is your chance to get to know your coworkers, show them what you're made of." Johnny winked and pointed in my direction.

I smiled enthusiastically, but I had no idea why going to a bar was such a big deal. Was there some sort of department initiation, like a tequila shot contest? I really hoped not. Alcohol shots made me queasy.

"And, Blake, you better have your dancing shoes on." Johnny gave me a double wink and waved to the rest of the group.

"What was that all about?" I asked the Bobbsey Twin sitting next to me.

"You mean Johnny big-timing us? That's his MO. He's always double-booking, never missing a chance to meet up with big shots. He drinks iced tea with us so he can sip cognac with the power players," he said.

"What's this place he's talking about? The Bling?" I asked.

"You'll see, Blake. You heard Johnny. You're coming with us," the other twin interjected.

All of us except Garrett piled into a minivan taxi.

"Where did Garrett go?" I asked.

"Who cares? He's no fun. First stop, the liquor store," a twin said.

"Why do we need to buy drinks? We're going to a bar, right?" I asked.

The car fell silent.

"'Cause you going to Bada Bling!" The driver broke the awkwardness with a jubilant Jamaican accent.

. . .

The taxi pulled next to a building that looked like an old double-wide trailer with a neon sign reading "Nude" illuminating the parking lot.

My stomach fell. A strip club. This was way more unnerving than a shot contest.

"I don't know about this. I should take the cab back," I said nervously.

"Don't worry. Stick with me. We'll have fun," Ryan said, assuring me with a pat on the knee.

"I've never been to a strip club before. I had no idea people brought their own drinks," I told Ryan, motioning to the 40 he clutched in a brown paper bag.

"Bada Bling is actually one of the most famous strip clubs in the nation. All the pro athletes come here. Come in for just a few minutes. If you don't like it, I'll go back with you."

"Fine," I conceded, grabbing a 40.

A neon-lit runway illuminated the cavernous main room. Thick cigarette smoke hung in the air, making the scene happening before me appear even more surreal. There were businessmen with their shirts unbuttoned to their navels, cigars hanging from their mouths, ogling as naked women shimmied between their legs. A bachelor party drunkenly tossed dollar bills in the air as a woman gyrated her bare bottom in the bachelor's face. Carleton and Carson took prime seats at the end of the runway and cheered as a tall brunette dipped to a full squat before them and opened her legs wide.

I lingered by the door, thankful Ryan hadn't left me. That's when I sensed something moving above me. I looked up and saw a naked woman balanced on a trapeze, her legs stretching into the middle splits as she swung from the ceiling. Her full genitalia on acrobatic display.

"I think I just saw her birth canal," I said, the words tumbling out of my mouth.

Ryan looked uncomfortable. I couldn't tell if he wanted to shield me from what I was witnessing or join the Bobbsey Twins.

I was about to tell him to sit down when a tan platinum blonde approached us. Her breasts were so inflated they barely bounced as she walked. She wore nothing but fuchsia high heels and her perfume smelled like vanilla birthday cake.

"Want a lap dance?" she asked Ryan.

"I'm not sure. I'm here for work," he stammered. "This is my boss. Well, she's sorta my boss. I'm an intern and she's not."

"She can get one too," the dancer said.

"Hi, I'm Blake," I said, beginning to extend my hand. She stared at me blankly, leaving my hand to dangle in midair. I retracted it slowly and self-consciously crossed my arms.

In my white jeans and sleeveless blouse, I had never felt or looked more out of place in my life. Why would Johnny think I had any interest in getting lap dances with my colleagues? How would this experience strengthen our workplace bonds? A night of revelry and tipsy conversations—that I got. But Johnny had duped me into going to a strip club, and that felt really icky.

"It's totally fine if you want to give him a lap dance," I said. "Really, Ryan. I'm going to leave."

"Are you sure?" Ryan said, picking at the torn edges of the paper bag around his 40.

"Yes, you stay and hang with the guys. Department bonding," I said and forced a smile. "I'll see you tomorrow."

There was a line of Escalades waiting outside The Bling. I hopped in one and watched the neon lights recede behind me.

I pressed my head against the window, unable to shake the vision of the naked middle splits. It swung back and forth through my thoughts. The irony. My boss had encouraged me to whoop it up at a strip club with my coworkers but wouldn't allow me to enter the team's locker room.

Eight

Prime Slime

It was just after dawn. The sun smoldered through the smoggy haze that blanketed an untamed marsh near our hotel. The murky morning captured the exact state of my brain.

I was struggling to make sense of "department bonding" that included the Bobbsey Twins motorboating a pair of low-hanging breasts. Why had Johnny been so intent on me going to a strip club with my coworkers? Was the initiation ingrained in his "old school" mentality?

I began to run the Mill Creek Trail around the marsh. I needed to stride the night out of my consciousness and sweat out the toxicity that had come with it.

Johnny warned me I needed thick skin to handle this job. Could it be that I was blowing this all out of proportion? My driver on the ride back to the hotel had said that famous athletes regularly visited The Bling. Going to strip clubs could be a routine extracurricular in pro sports, something I just needed to get used to.

I stopped and gazed at the New York City skyline in the distance. As much as I tried to justify my trip to The Bling, it didn't sit right with me. In fact, it made me feel downright icky. But I couldn't let Johnny see that. I needed to show him that I could handle anything he threw at me—even a front seat to the naked middle splits.

. . .

My beige heels pinched my pinkie toes as I crossed the checkered marble floor of the hotel lobby. I had never been much of a high-heel person. I already was tall and usually preferred dressing comfortably to wearing the latest trends. I had bought these heels for my cousin's wedding and never worn them since. But seeing Emily strut around in her stilettos had inspired me to trade in my low wedges for something sexier. Now, I was cursing that I had stuffed my feet into the Louboutin knockoffs.

I rounded the cascading floral arrangements centering the lobby and saw a bushel of black, spiky hair buried into a laptop. A nylon computer bag with the team logo rested beside a pair of clunky lace-up shoes.

I sank into a leather chair across from Garrett.

"Hi there. How's your day been?" I asked.

Garrett continued to type without acknowledging me.

"I need to send a couple of emails before I get on the bus," he finally said.

"I'll let you work."

I stood up and straightened my navy wrap dress.

"You were smart to duck out last night," I told him. "I'd never been to a strip club before. It's not my scene."

Garrett looked up, his brow pinched.

"You ended up going?"

"Johnny really pushed me on it. He said it would be good department bonding."

"Oh," Garrett said. "Strip clubs aren't my thing either. I'm not a big drinker. And I don't like being tired on game days."

"I don't blame you," I said. "I got up early for a run and then went back to sleep for a few hours. I have a little more time since my bus doesn't leave until 4:30. Are you going on the first bus?"

"Yeah. I like to get to the stadium at least three hours before kickoff. That way I can get the website primed for everything we post during the game. There's also a lot of gear to set up. You'll see."

"Is Ryan riding with you?" I asked.

I was hoping Ryan would stay behind to ride the Blake Bus. I was anxious for the companionship and to hear about the rest of his night.

"He's supposed to meet me down here any minute," Garrett said, looking expectantly at the elevators. "I want us to load into the bus before the players do."

On cue, the elevator bell rang and the gold doors slid open to reveal Ryan—or what Ryan would look like if the washing machine flung him out mid-cycle, rumpled and soaked. Wrinkles traversed down his blue dress shirt and the corner of a collar bent upward toward his chin. His normally fluffy hair hung over his head like a wet mop, dripping water down his shirt.

He slumped toward us. Garrett sighed disapprovingly.

"Jesus, Ryan. You look like shit. Did you decide to towel off with a wadded-up shirt and then wear it?"

"It's been a rough day," Ryan mumbled. When he looked up, I gasped. His lips were dry and cracking, as if he hadn't swallowed water for days. His face was a putrid pale yellow.

"Maybe Ryan should ride the last bus with me so that he has more time to get ready," I suggested to Garrett.

Ryan's puffy eyelids lifted, sensing a glimmer of hope.

"Yeah, it would be nice for Blake to have one of us ride with her before her first game."

Garrett shook his head.

"That's not going to work. I want you there early to help with site maintenance."

"Could I ride the third bus? I could use a little more time," Ryan said, trying to smooth down his rumpled shirt collar.

"Fine. But don't make these pregame benders a habit," Garrett said, shoving his laptop into his bag.

"I'm going to board the bus before the players and coaches come down. Ryan, I suggest you return to your room before anyone sees you like this."

Ryan nodded and Garrett walked out of the lobby to the bus idling outside.

"Geez, you really tied one on last night."

"Yeah, we got carried away," Ryan said and rubbed his bloodshot eyes. "Listen, Blake, I'm sorry if you were uncomfortable there. I felt bad bringing you. But I didn't know what to say. I really want these guys to like me and offer me a full-time job."

I smiled sympathetically.

"It's OK. I was uncomfortable, but that wasn't your fault."

I stood up and draped my work satchel over my shoulder.

"Want to grab a bite? I was going to have a late lunch before my bus leaves."

"No, thanks. I had breakfast with the team earlier and don't have much of an appetite."

"You mean the buffet in the ballroom?" I asked pointedly.

Ryan gnawed at a flake of skin on his lower lip.

"We ran into Johnny in the lobby when we got back from The Bling this morning. He told us to meet him for breakfast so he could hear about the night."

"Lenny told me the ballroom meals are only for players and coaches," I said.

"And Johnny. Johnny can go anywhere, and we were with him," Ryan stammered.

"It just seems like Johnny has a different set of rules for me," I said.

"If you'd been with us, I'm sure Johnny would have asked you to breakfast too."

The pitch in Ryan's voice rose. It was clear he didn't believe that to be true. Neither did I.

· · ·

At 4:30 p.m. sharp, the Blake Bus pulled away from the hotel lobby. To my surprise, it was about a quarter full of scouts and front office executives.

I looked out the window at the two policemen on motorcycles leading the bus. Traffic moved aside as we cruised to the stadium. The bus continued inside the complex and parked on a loading dock next to the team's three other buses. The policemen, who were idling on their bikes, waved at the bus driver and rode off. At least Johnny had deemed the Blake Bus worthy of a police escort. It felt like a positive sign, which I badly needed on this trip.

I followed three young scouts who were heading to the press box elevator. The scouts were talking about a new analytics software system they were using when the tallest one with a closely shaved buzz cut glanced back at me.

"I hear you had a big night at The Bling," Buzz Cut said.

My face burned red. How did he know?

"Well, sort of. I was there less than ten minutes. But The Bling did leave a big impression."

The scouts stopped in front of an elevator. Their collective age couldn't have been more than seventy-five. The shortest one adjusted a pair of Oakleys nestled atop his thick, red hair and extended a freckled hand.

"Hi, I'm Joseph, but everyone calls me RJ. It's short for Red Joe," he said, and we exchanged a friendly handshake.

"Nice to meet you, RJ. I'm Blake."

"I know. I've watched your videos. Good stuff," he said.

"Thanks. I forget that people know me from the web. I wish I knew everyone on the team. There are so many people on staff, and I'm still putting faces to names. You guys are scouts, right?"

"We're the pro scouting interns. The three of us evaluate the back-of-the-roster guys. It's intense right now with roster cuts coming up."

"I bet. It's amazing how much goes into putting a pro team together. I really had no appreciation for it until I started this job."

"Yeah, you won't see most of the scouts because they're on the road 300 days of the year. The college scouts basically live out of suitcases until the national championship game. Their job is to make sure we draft future superstars."

"Wow, you scouts are under a lot of pressure."

"Not all of us can be Blake Kirk, flashing 100-watt smiles and hitting up strip clubs," RJ teased. "But seriously, you were getting mad props at breakfast this morning. You earned major street cred by going to The Bling."

I flinched. Why were people talking about me going to a strip club? How could that make me popular on the team?

"Who exactly was giving me mad props?" I asked, feeling uneasy about the direction of this conversation.

"Johnny couldn't stop bragging about it. He was going up to all the assistant coaches and trainers, saying, 'Did you hear my girl Blake was at The Bling last night?' Johnny must have high-fived half the dining room. He was really proud of you."

"Oh." It was all I could manage to say. My stomach knotted thinking about Johnny parading around the ballroom and reveling in stories about me with naked women at a strip club. And "my girl." I was not Johnny's girl. It was all too slimy for words.

But I didn't want RJ and the scouts to see I was upset. I needed to play it cool with them. Johnny was testing me. He wanted to see if I had the fortitude to play by his rules. I could not show weakness. Not this early in the game.

Nine

Oh Lord

Inside the press box, Sheridan Lane was standing at the soda fountain talking to a man who looked like Cam Newton's body double, complete with a defined jawline and twinkling brown eyes. He was one of those men who was universally agreed-upon handsome. No one would object. Sheridan waved at me to join them.

"Blake, there's someone I want you to meet."

Sheridan placed a neatly manicured hand on the man's broad shoulder.

"This is Jeremiah Wood. He's our new fantasy football expert. He's launching a midday show on the Network. Jeremiah, this is Blake. She's OKC's new reporter."

"Nice to meet you," we said in unison and shook hands. Jeremiah's brown eyes sparkled when he smiled. He was instantly likable.

"Jeremiah is high on Devonte," Sheridan told me. "He's doing a big piece on Devonte for a fantasy draft special. You two should collaborate. Blake, you can interview Jeremiah, produce a fantasy piece for the team's website."

Sheridan's dewy lips curled in satisfaction.

"You're what I like to call triple threats—proficient in print, TV, and digital. You two are the future of this business."

As I opened my mouth to respond, a sharp elbow dug into my back.

"Can you scoot over, Blake? I'm trying to get a Diet Coke."

Garrett shoved a plastic cup under the soda fountain.

"We need you to help us when you're done chatting."

"I'm coming right now," I said and turned to Sheridan and Jeremiah, who were looking at each other with raised eyebrows. "Excuse me, I better get to work. Jeremiah, it was so nice to meet you."

I scurried behind Garrett as he walked down the tiered press box. Our media department was sitting in the second row, behind the large glass window overlooking the field. Carleton and Carson, both in navy suits with white shirts and gold ties, stood at the entrance to our row, talking to their PR counterparts from New York. With their team pins perfectly straight on their pressed lapels, the Twins didn't look like they partied until the wee hours of the morning.

I waved politely so as not to interrupt their conversation and scooted behind them. Garrett nipped at my heels.

"You're second to last, next to Ryan," he barked. "It's a hierarchy. Ryan is at the tail end. Then you. Then me. Johnny sits at the head of the row."

"Got it," I said and began to unpack my bag.

"An hour before game time—that's crunch time in the press box. You arriving late really puts us in a bind," Garrett said, hovering behind me.

I stared at my laptop as I connected to the stadium's wireless signal and suppressed the urge to glare back at him.

"Garrett, you do realize the reason I'm later than you is because Johnny has me riding a later bus?" I asked measuredly.

"You stopping to gossip with Sheridan and Jeremiah didn't help matters."

Resentment simmered inside me. But as much as I wanted to snap back, I forced myself to swallow any fighting words. Garrett was trying to assert his authority. Remind me that I ranked below him in the pecking order. While he could be aggravating and borderline rude, I had bigger issues to manage. Namely, Johnny.

I looked up at Garrett.

"You're right. I should have been more aware of the time. What can I start working on?"

Garrett nodded in approval. "I've divided up tasks between you and Ryan."

Ryan, whose face was progressively drooping closer to his computer, jerked up upon hearing his name.

"Blake, you will handle the photo slideshow, manage social media, and keep a running list of game notes.

"Ryan will write a live game story that I'll supervise. I'll do the game story during the regular season, but I want to give Ryan a chance to work on his skills during a preseason game when things are more lax."

More lax. I suppressed an eye roll.

"Blake, the camera bag is next to Ryan's computer. You should get going. The team is warming up," Garrett said and pointed to the navy and gold jerseys spread across the field.

"Won't it be easier if I ask the team photographer for his photo cards?" I asked.

"He takes thousands of photos. Those cards take forever to load. You won't have the pregame slideshow up until halftime."

With that, I slung the camera strap around my neck and darted back to the press box elevator.

• • •

Lights from atop the stadium bathed the players, as if exalting their superhuman physiques. With their pads on, they appeared larger than life. Otherworldly. Fans filled the stands, but their noise hummed lowly in the background. The drums crashed in Phil Collins's "In the Air Tonight," drowning them out, the music encasing the field in a protective layer as the players prepared for battle.

Just inside midfield, Coach Bush stood with his arms folded and legs planted wide. He was dressed in his signature coaching attire: a long-sleeved navy polo, khaki pants, unscathed white running shoes, and a helmet of perfectly coiffed chestnut hair. His eyes narrowed as Andy dropped back and threw a pass.

Seth waited his turn and pumped his head rhythmically.

I raised the camera to my eye to capture the shot and Seth looked directly into the lens and mouthed, "Oh Lord."

I let go of the camera. The strap pulled against the back of my neck and the camera bounced off my chest. Flustered and embarrassed by Seth's stare, I angled myself to Andy. I clicked away as Andy took snaps from an offensive quality control coach. I didn't care that I was taking crap shots or that my high heels were sinking into the grass. I hid behind the camera until the red drained from my face.

"Secure the catch!" a coach yelled. I unearthed my heels from the field and shuffled toward the wide receivers. The players moved so fast that most of them outran the camera frame. I scrolled through the digital viewer. Not one good shot. Devonte's famous gold gloves looked like fuzzy clown hands.

A few feet away, the team's photographer wielded a camera with an extended lens the size of a traffic cone. There was no doubt he was capturing Devonte at the apex of his catch in perfect lighting and crisp focus. When he broke to glance at a digital preview, I made my move.

"Did you get some good ones?"

"Devonte turning back, directly facing the camera, ball squarely between his two golden gloves. And evening lighting, to boot. That's perfection."

He was right. It could be blown up into a poster and tacked in kids' bedrooms across Oklahoma City.

"What do you do with all these images?"

"I give Johnny's crew the photo cards after the game. They use them for promotional materials, posters in the stadium, marketing, the website. They'll send images to news outlets. You name it."

"Would you mind if I used one of your pregame cards for an online slideshow?"

"As long as I get photo cred, the more people who see these shots, the better. I never understood why Garrett sent people down here when the team's already paying a professional."

He nodded at the camera hanging from my neck.

"That's a nice camera—if you're going to take pictures of the Grand Canyon. If you want to capture guys who run a 4.4 in the 40, you need a lens like this."

He pointed at the monster lens attached to his Cannon.

"You're telling me."

The photographer ejected the card from his camera. It was hard to tell his age. His face was young and smooth, but there was a shock of gray hair spewing over his visor.

"Here you go."

He handed me the card, his hands tan and hardened at the fingertips.

"Come down and find me at the end of each quarter. I'll give you as many photo cards as you need."

"Thank you. My name is Blake, by the way."

"Blake, I'm Monte."

When I got back to my seat in the press box, Ryan was tinkering with the opening paragraph of his game story. "Get some good pics?" he asked.

"I sure did."

I shoved Monte's card into my photo reader.

. . .

At precisely two minutes before kickoff, the team captains gathered at midfield for the coin toss. The press box was eerily quiet.

"Oklahoma City called heads. It's heads. They choose to receive," the official said.

It was go time. Print writers affixed themselves to their laptops, TV reporters scribbled notes, and radio reporters used landlines at their desks to dial into their stations.

Garrett leaned over me to jab Ryan.

"Make sure you include the coin toss in the story."

Ryan's fingers quivered as he updated his work.

I leaned into Ryan. "You do realize your story is live on the web for the entire world to read, including the team owner."

"Not funny, Blake. Earlier, I misspelled the name of one of New York's captains. Garrett saw it and lost his mind."

As the pregame clock expired, Johnny bumped fists with the Bobbsey Twins and wished them good luck.

"Blake, it's my pregame tradition. The good-luck fist bump," he said and leaned toward me.

I had been so consumed with my pregame duties that I had shelved my exasperation with Johnny. Sensing his face inches from mine reminded me how perturbed I still was with him, but I was determined not to show it.

"Good luck," I said, and we bumped fists.

The kicker placed the ball on the tee. One of the Bobbsey Twins looked through binoculars and called out the jersey numbers on the field.

Garrett nudged me with a bony elbow.

"You should be writing down the starters for the game notes."

I scribbled down the numbers just before the kicker blasted the ball out of the end zone. First and ten.

Andy clapped his hands to break the offensive huddle. Devonte set his feet at the line of scrimmage and pointed to the official to indicate he was an eligible receiver. Andy floated a ten-yard pass to the sideline. I cringed. An interception, I thought. But Devonte outjumped the cornerback, grabbed the ball out of his hands, and broke away for a twenty-yard gain.

"That was Devonte Harris with a twenty-nine-yard catch. Oklahoma City with a first down at the forty-yard line," the PA announcer said.

Devonte continued to abuse single coverage and the offense marched down the field for a touchdown.

"Here's the headline for your sidebar story," I told Ryan. "Devonte Delivers Against New York."

"I'm going to use that," Ryan said, grabbing the pen tucked behind his ear.

With five minutes left in the quarter, I saved my game notes and headed to the press box elevator.

Monte's shock of gray hair made him easy to find on the sidelines. I walked behind the metal benches where the linebackers and defensive linemen sat, their position coaches crouched in front of them, showing the players pictures of formations from the last series. Coach Bush paced in front of the players crowding the sideline. He spoke into his headset and looked at a large, laminated, multicolor sheet of plays that resembled a Denny's menu.

I walked up behind Monte, who balanced on one knee. "Did you get the touchdown?" I asked.

"You bet," Monte said. "Devonte at the apex of his jump."

"Awesome. See you before the half."

I walked back behind the team's bench and caught Johnny staring at me. He put his hand up for me to stop and walked toward me.

"One of the coaches keeps saying you've got the best legs," he whispered. "Just thought you should know."

The sliminess of Johnny's warm-breathed message lingered on my ear. Gross. His message. The delivery. The speck of spit he'd left on my cheek. It was all gross.

Did he think I would be genuinely flattered? Or was he once again trying to see how much of his "old school" boys' club mentality I could take?

I wasn't sure. What I did know was that Johnny was right about one thing—I would need to layer on rhino skin to survive him.

· · ·

By the fourth quarter, open blisters stung my pinkie toes. I kicked off my heels and dabbed the perspiration at my hairline with a press box napkin. Between dashing down to the field and furiously updating the social media accounts and slideshow, I felt as if I was operating in fast-forward.

"I'm supposed to write about the quarterback play and I need to figure out a story line," I said to Ryan.

"I think Seth was perfect in the red zone," Ryan said and pulled out the latest stat sheet.

"Aha," I said and typed the title and byline.

Barker Sees Red.

Seth Barker is perfect from the red zone, throwing two touchdowns and leading his team to its second preseason win.

I smiled in satisfaction.

"Way to think ahead, Blake," Garrett said.

My head recoiled in surprise. A rare compliment from Garrett.

"The game moves fast, but it's nothing compared to postgame. And we need to be prepared," Garrett said, looking down at his spiral notebook. "Blake, you will go to Coach's postgame presser. Record it on this."

Garrett handed me a pocket-sized digital recorder.

"After the presser, meet me outside the locker room and I'll grab Seth for you to interview."

My stooped shoulders jerked upright.

"Seth? I'm interviewing Seth?"

Seth, with the tousled, auburn hair and light brown freckles dancing above his cheekbones? Seth, who flirted with me on the team plane and thought I was taking adoring pictures of him before the game?

"Is that a problem?" he asked.

"Not at all," I told him, my voice cracking.

Garrett turned to Ryan. "You will stay up here and finish the game story. When you're done, meet Boss in the locker room. You can stick the microphone into media scrums around each player."

I nodded along with Ryan, but my eyes were locked on the field. Seth was resting on the bench, wearing a blue cap and scrolling through game photos on an iPad. Johnny walked behind him, placed a hand on his shoulder pad, and leaned in close. They laughed, Seth cocking his head back so far I could see his open mouth.

I looked at the game clock. Five and a half minutes left.

"Blake, you should head down. They close the press box elevators soon for the coaches who are in the boxes," Garrett said.

I painfully wedged my feet into my heels and joined the media drove heading to the elevator. Sheridan strutted along with her leather-bound notepad and cameraman.

"Ready for your first postgame interviews?" she asked.

"I hope so. Any advice?"

"Coaches loathe dumb questions. Every coach is different and requires a unique approach. But all the coaches are smart. Ask intelligent questions and ask them the right way," Sheridan said. It was hard to imagine her ever asking a dumb question.

I followed Sheridan and her photog down the elevators to a workroom on the concourse. A backdrop with the team's logo was draped from a metal stand behind a wooden podium. Sheridan took a seat in the front row and chatted with the ESPN reporters and local beat reporters sitting around her.

A few minutes later, Johnny ceremoniously threw open the door and introduced Coach with the grandeur of a royal entrance. "Ladies and gentlemen, I present Head Coach Bruce Bush."

Coach Bush sauntered to the podium, his bowed legs pushing against the seams of his khaki pants. He unfolded a stat sheet and hunched over the microphone.

"Good evening. Overall, it was a good night for all our quarterbacks. But this league is about consistency. It's about doing things right all the time. Right now, they're doing things right only some of the time. We need to fix that. Any questions?"

"Seth with two impressive touchdown passes. What struck you about his play?" Sheridan asked.

"Seth was at his best in the red zone. That back shoulder fade he threw is one of the toughest throws in football. We are lucky to have him as our number two."

I scribbled down the time codes of Coach's quote. It was perfect for my story.

After seven minutes of back and forth between the media and Coach, Johnny cleared his throat loudly.

"That's a wrap, people."

Johnny promptly ushered Coach out of the room and brought in Andy.

I should have logged Andy's press conference, but I was too distracted by my interview with Seth. I imagined looking into his hazel eyes and forgetting what to say, standing there tongue-tied like a middle schooler with a burgeoning crush on the most popular boy in school. I shook the thought from my head. I needed to focus on my questions. I needed to be a journalist.

Intro: Hi, my name is Blake Kirk and I've got your postgame report. I'm with Seth Barker, who threw two touchdowns in a win against New York.

I was so engrossed in drafting my questions that Devonte's deep voice caught me by surprise. He was the picture of cool, standing behind the podium in his signature diamond necklace and a black Gucci polo.

"I saw that everyone gelled together and worked together. We were moving the ball and blocking pretty well on offense," Devonte was saying, keeping his gaze low.

Everything about Devonte was flashy—his clothes, girlfriend, play on the field. The only thing subdued about him was his demeanor in front of the media. There was a shyness about him that made him seem like a gentle giant.

Instinctively, my hand shot up. I knew what would open him up. I could ask Devonte if he felt like he was playing a home game with so many fans in the stands. I leaned forward in my seat, anxious to ask my first press conference question.

I tried to catch Johnny's attention, but he avoided looking back at me and pointed to a local TV anchor. Then, like a maniacal robot, Johnny's head spun toward me. His penetrating glare smacked me back in my chair. He lowered his chin and mouthed, "*No.*"

I flinched like a child who was spanked for no reason. What had made Johnny so mad? He said I couldn't ask Coach questions. He hadn't said anything about the same rule applying to players.

After another question, Johnny shouted from behind the podium, "Press conference is over. Time for open locker room."

The media stampeded out of the workroom. I sat, still clinging to my seat.

On her way out, Sheridan crouched next to me.

"I saw that stunt Johnny pulled. Don't let it get you down."

· · ·

For more than thirty minutes, I fidgeted in front of the locker room, checking my phone, rehearsing my interview, applying lip gloss, and then blotting the sheen. I watched the door fly open, providing brief glimpses of players buttoning dress shirts or addressing circles of reporters who held out microphones with hyperextended arms. When the door slammed, I went back to fidgeting.

I heard the familiar sound of dress shoes clapping against the concrete floor. I thought it was another TV anchor going in and out between live shots, so I looked down at my phone and pretended to be busy.

"You going in?" Jeremiah asked, smiling kindly.

"I'm waiting on someone," I said, trying to sound casual.

Jeremiah flung open the door.

"Come in for a few minutes. Maybe we can talk to Devonte offline."

I stood, paralyzed, debating whether to tell Jeremiah that the team had forbidden me from entering the locker room.

Before I could speak, Johnny appeared at the door with Seth at his side and Boss trailing behind.

"Let's roll, BB," Johnny said, shoving Jeremiah inside the locker room and closing the door behind him.

"Never leave our locker room door open. Too risky. Someone outside the media could hear or see something they shouldn't. I can't risk some fan or stadium worker posting a naked picture of a player on TikTok."

Seth shook his head.

"You're so damned paranoid."

"This league is built on paranoia," Johnny said, quickening his pace.

My feet throbbed as I strained to keep up. From behind, Seth's broad shoulders bulged through his light gray suit jacket. His muscular thighs pushed against his fitted slacks.

"Johnny, where are we going?" he asked.

"Here," Johnny said and turned sharply into the media workroom where the press conferences took place. "You can stand in front of our drape. I want our logo in the background."

"We'll have to move the podium," Boss said, setting down the camera and microphone on a chair. "Blake, can you help me with this?"

Seth waved off Boss.

"I've got it, dude. You can't expect a lady in heels to help move furniture." Seth looked at me and winked. My body warmed in response.

As Seth carried the podium to the wall, Johnny tapped me on the shoulder.

"Now is your time for questions. Not in press conferences. You have to earn my trust before you can ask questions in pressers. Got it?"

"Got it," I replied mindlessly. I was too consumed by Seth—his knowing glances and devilish smiles—to process what Johnny had just told me.

"Good. Let's get rolling. We've got seven minutes until we need to be on the bus."

Seth moved next to me, our bodies inches apart. I could feel his heat on my skin. My hand trembled so hard that the microphone knocked against my lower lip. Seth was igniting my insides and it terrified me to think that all three men in that room could sense it.

I gripped the microphone harder, my knuckles turning white. Seth was gazing down at me, but I didn't look up; my raging hormones couldn't handle meeting his eyes.

"In three, two, one," Boss said, pointing in my direction.

Shit. Shit. Shit. What is my first line? My name. I need to say my name.

"Hi, my name is Blake Kirk and I've got your report."

Ugh, I forgot "postgame." Keep going.

"I'm with quarterback Seth Barker, who had an impressive night in a win over New York. Seth, thanks for being here."

I looked up at his chin, avoiding his hazel eyes at all costs. I had mangled my script, but there was nothing I could do about that now.

"Blake, good to be here."

"A strong night for you. Two touchdown throws. What did you take away from your performance?"

"Everyone was on the same page," Seth said. "Guys were getting open and making the plays. It was just one of those nights where everything clicked."

I robotically recited questions, and Seth's words floated over my head. I was too busy trying to remember the next question from my script to pay much attention to his answers.

Finally, Johnny waved his finger to wrap up the interview.

"Thanks, Seth, and congrats on a great night," I said with too much excitement.

"Thank you, Blake. I hope to be back on your postgame report."

I exhaled in relief. I had finished the interview without committing a major gaffe, professing my crush, or fainting. I would take victories anywhere I could get them, but what was happening to me?

Ten

Duly Noted

Drake's "Nice for What" thumped in the back of the plane. The players packed the aisles, their ties unknotted and dress shirts flapping open at the navel. Alyssa shimmied through the makeshift club, hand-delivering Crown and Cokes and accepting booty bumps from the players along the way.

The smell of whiskey wafted to row 10, where I sat with Ryan and Garrett. Ryan and I had split duties. He was writing every word of every question and every word of every answer uttered in the locker room. I did the same for the press conferences and my interview with Seth. When we finished, we would pull quotes for our respective stories and merge the transcriptions together to post on the site.

"This is a first. My eyes are closing and crossing at the same time," I murmured to Ryan.

"Flag down Alyssa for a pick-me-up. We have a long night ahead." Ryan yawned. "We won't get to the stadium until three in the morning."

I dinged the call button. Alyssa's gold anklets jingled as she walked toward me.

"Flying is so much more fun after a win," she said, smacking her cotton candy–pink lips. "What can I get you, honey?"

"A bag of Twizzlers for me and a Snickers for him." I nodded at Ryan.

"Sure thang."

Alyssa gripped the seat armrest with her fuchsia talons and bent toward me.

"And, honey, if you need to use the potty, I suggest you go up front. It's pretty wild back there."

I hoped to avoid the restroom altogether and eliminate the challenge of navigating between 200-pound men barricading the aisles. But holding it wasn't an option after two Diet Cokes and a bottle of water.

"Are you sure the coaches won't mind me going into first class?"

"They'll understand. You're a lady, after all."

I unbuckled my seat belt and followed Alyssa to the first-class curtain. She stepped into the galley and gave me an encouraging nod. I nervously pulled open the blue cloth.

The coaches were reclining, watching cut-ups of the game on iPads. Johnny and the GM sat in the front row, huddled over an armrest and deep in conversation. The special teams coordinator saw me out of the corner of his eye and nudged the tight ends coach. Within seconds, the entire first-class cabin was staring at me.

Johnny shot up.

"Blake?"

"Sorry to interrupt. Alyssa suggested that I use this restroom."

Coach Bush chuckled. He sat across the aisle from Johnny with bare feet propped up on the wall in front of him.

"Girl, I don't blame you. You couldn't pay me to dip my big toe in that mess back there. Much better that you come up here," he said. The rest of the coaches laughed and went back to their iPads. Johnny smiled and leaned back in his seat, seemingly satisfied with Coach Bush's show of approval.

I was tempted to joke back to Coach and recite one of my dad's bathroom jokes about avoiding hazardous work conditions, but I didn't want to push it. I was happy I had come this far.

• • •

The offices in the stadium were completely dark. Ryan flipped on the switches next to a staircase and we wheeled our bags to our cubicles in silence.

With the team off on Sunday, most of the coaches and players went directly to their cars when we arrived back in Oklahoma City. A few members of the equipment staff were putting things away in the locker room, but other than that, the stadium sat eerily empty.

I logged into my desktop and navigated the portal to find my interview with Seth. I hit play and cringed. I spoke too fast and smiled too big, but Seth didn't seem to notice or care. He answered each question thoughtfully, providing a measured pace to our exchange.

I sank my head into my hands. What was I doing crushing on a player? I needed to get control of myself and act like a professional. For the sake of my job.

I rolled my bag down the deserted hallway. A lamp flickered at Ryan's cubicle. The side of his face was planted on the desk, his bushy hair tangled in his mouse cord. Drool slid down his mouth as he snored softly.

"Ryan, wake up," I said, patting his shoulder.

He rubbed his eyes sheepishly.

"Guess I shouldn't have stayed out so late last night."

"What do you have left?"

"Just my story on Devonte."

"You need to get home and get some rest."

Ryan picked at the crust in the corners of his mouth.

"Yeah, it's painful to think we have to be back here in ten hours for Coach Bush's press conference."

"Ugh, thanks for reminding me."

· · ·

The smell of coffee percolated into my room. Dad's spoon banged against his mug. It was the family cattle call he resorted to when he really wanted to get us out of bed.

I knew my parents were anxious to hear every detail from the road trip. They were probably unfolding the sports page on the breakfast room table and tapping their fingers in anticipation of a complete digest of the game. I tossed the covers aside and threw on a USC hoodie.

"Blakey! Sit down, sit down. I just pulled the muffins out of the oven. We can't wait to hear about the game!" Mom said, throwing her arms around me like she hadn't seen me in months.

"Yesterday was the longest day of my life. I got up at 7:00 for a run and didn't get home until 4:00 a.m."

"Oh, sweetie. You must be exhausted. I hope you can rest today."

"Actually, I have to go into work this afternoon for Coach's press conference."

"My goodness. You don't get a day off?"

Dad peered over his bifocals.

"There are no days off during the football season. Coaches sleep in their offices. Players watch tape before dawn. Blake's fine. She's young and energetic."

Mom plated her famous carrot muffins with fruit.

"I was hoping she could go to church with us and take a nap this afternoon. She needs to take care of herself."

"I'm fine. In dire need of coffee, but fine," I said, picking up the front page of the paper. "For the first time, I don't feel like I need to read the sports section. I lived it."

"We want to hear about every detail," Mom said, pouring me a glass of orange juice.

"Thank you, Mom. You're making it very hard for me to leave and find my own place."

"That's the plan. Now, start from the beginning."

My parents leaned over their plates. I fed them juicy tidbits—tidbits that didn't involve the strip club or Johnny. The complexities of my job were too meaty for them to digest.

· · ·

Heat steamed from the concrete in the team lot. I recognized Johnny's black Escalade, Coach Bush's F-350 XLT truck, Garrett's Mini Cooper, Ryan's Ford truck with the passenger mirror reattached with duct tape, and a few luxury vehicles I assumed belonged to the assistant coaches.

It was hard to believe I was in this lot just hours earlier. I closed my eyes for a few seconds and let the blistering sun burn away the final vestiges of the New Jersey haze.

The low hum of country music floated through the hallways around the coaches' offices. Ryan sat at his cubicle, reviewing his story online.

I patted his fluffy, unbrushed hair. "Did you get any sleep?"

"A couple of hours. We shouldn't be here long. Garrett told me that all we have to do is transcribe the press conference and post a video of it."

"Ryan, don't you dare use the t-word. Transcriptions are becoming the bane of my existence."

"You better gear up for a season full of them," he said. "Did you know that Johnny sends the transcriptions out to all our media contacts so they have the quotes at their disposal for stories?"

"That surprises me. I would think he would want them to attend the pressers."

"No, he wants to make it as easy as possible for media to cover the team. Of course, if there's a question he doesn't like, he'll tell us to remove it from the transcripts."

"Well, that does *not* surprise me," I replied.

I rounded the partition to my cubicle. The framed photo of Dad and me in front of the stadium wasn't in its usual spot on the right side of my monitor. Someone had moved it to the left of my keyboard, leaving fingerprint smudges on the silver frame. On my chair sat a folded, handwritten note.

You looked good in your white pants. Keep up the good work.

—JC

A wave of queasiness washed over me. *WTF?* It was creepy enough to think about Johnny snooping around my cube and touching my things, but the note—that was next level. It surpassed creepy and landed closer to disgusting, disturbing, and demeaning.

I stared at his chicken-scratch writing as nausea crested in my gut. What could I do? March into HR? The team would much rather replace me than Johnny. He was a venerated veteran executive. I was only one week into the job. The team brass was not going to have my back. And confronting Johnny seemed futile. He would probably fire me on the spot.

I had to put on my big-girl, rhino-skin panties and tough this out. It felt like the only option if I wanted to set foot in the locker room and, more importantly, keep my job. Still, I just wondered how much of Johnny's "old school" boys' club ways I could take before I reached a breaking point.

I began to crumple the note in my palm, but something deep inside me told me otherwise. I smoothed it against my desk and slid it between the pages of an old directory in my file cabinet. I had a hunch I would need this note later.

Eleven

Buckle Up

"Buckle your chinstraps," Johnny said, slapping his hand against his desk so hard coffee sloshed out of his mug. "Week one of the regular season. From here on out, no fuckups. No excuses. Too much on the line."

Everyone nodded silently. One of the Bobbsey Twins momentarily closed his eyes as if he was overcome by the Gospel of Johnny.

It was Monday morning, and our department was convening in Johnny's office for our weekly 8:00 a.m. meeting. Johnny had been holding these meetings since training camp, setting the agenda for the week, reviewing talking points for players and coaches, confirming media schedules, storytelling about hanging out with Hall of Famers. But that day, there was no reminiscing about hanging out with Warren Moon at a party where the waitresses wore coconut-shell bikini tops. Johnny's tone was completely different. He was all business.

Over the last couple of weeks, I hit my stride with the team. I shared a friendly rapport with the coaching staff and players. We slapped together sandwiches at the deli bar and greeted each other in the hallways. They gave me a "Hey, Blake. Nice story" or "Liked that video." I replied with a jovial "Thanks! Just doing my best."

I truly got the sense the team enjoyed having me around and accepted me as one of their own. And to my relief, I had hardly heard from Johnny since the note incident. He and the Bobbsey Twins were cramming to finish a slew of publications and press releases before the start of the regular season.

"Let's get down to business," Johnny said, turning his tufted leather chair toward his computer. "Coach will have his usual presser today at three. Tuesday is the players' day off. We always do community appearances on Tuesdays. This week is all about first responders since the game is on the anniversary of 9/11. We are hosting a large group of first responders for lunch in the club level. Seth will speak because his dad was a fireman. It's the perfect tie-in."

Johnny scrolled down his computer screen.

"Practice Wednesday, Thursday, and Friday. We'll take Devonte, Andy, and Coach to the podium. Open locker room after that. Saturday, the players will have a walk-through and I'll meet with the broadcast team. Sunday, it's game time."

Johnny cracked the knuckles on his index fingers.

"Any questions?"

I had a million.

What were community appearances? Did I go to the walk-through on Saturday? And most importantly, could I finally enter the locker room now that I'd earned my stripes?

But I didn't say a word. Johnny's invitation for questions was more rhetorical than genuine. Plus, no one said a word in this meeting, much less shifted their weight.

The Bobbsey Twins occupied their usual seats, the two tan club chairs facing Johnny's desk. Garrett was perched on a desk chair, which he rolled in from Ryan's cube. Ryan and I stood against the wall, flanking a blown-up photo of Johnny and Devonte from the All-Pro game. Johnny was puffing his chest proudly in a black silk Hawaiian shirt with a bright parrot print, both arms clasped behind his back. Devonte, who wore his red and white All-Pro jersey and a wreath of leis around his neck, stared at the camera. There was no discernible expression on his face. He stood straight and stoic, several inches from Johnny, looking like a cardboard cutout, a prop in Johnny's vacation photo.

"Isn't that a great photo?" Johnny said, leaning back in his chair and folding his arms. "Nothing like the luau in Hawaii. Pig roast. Hula dancers."

Johnny raised his eyebrows toward the Bobbsey Twins a couple of times, as if to say, "You know what I mean?"

"Hawaii is always on my mind. We have to get more players there. That's a big goal for us this season. Devonte was our only All-Pro player last year. Just one of our players went to Hawaii. Unacceptable."

Johnny shook his head.

"Let's enhance the All-Pro campaigns on the website this year," Garrett interjected. "We can do mock pitches, like they're running a political campaign. Give the players slogans. Get not just OKC fans but all league fans to vote for our players."

Johnny took a swig of coffee.

"Garrett, I like where your head is."

Garrett smiled so wide I thought his face might crack open.

"It's on our department to build these players up. Frame their stats. Get them in front of cameras. Write stories about them on our site. Beef up their campaigns. This year, I want at least three players going to Hawaii," Johnny said, wagging his finger at each of us as we scribbled furiously in our notepads.

Johnny plunked his mug on his desk, the dark roast coffee cresting to the rim.

"I'm sure it goes without saying what our top priority is. What we must accomplish day in and day out."

Johnny cocked his head and stared at Ryan. For several seconds, Ryan's head was falling forward and jerking back as he fought to stay awake. He had spent the weekend in Stillwater with his fraternity brothers. The effects of the bender were written all over his pale face.

Johnny's eyes narrowed as Ryan's head bobbed.

"Ryan, go on, tell the group. Give them a refresher."

Ryan jerked so fast he almost fell forward and face-planted into the Bobbsey Twins. He blinked hard, as if to reorient his eyes, and looked down at his blank legal pad.

"Um, um, we want to win the championship," he stammered.

The room collectively braced for Johnny's response.

"No shit, Sherlock. But this department has no control over that unless you can put on pads and sack a quarterback," Johnny snapped. "Every day we make sure everyone here looks good. Ownership, Coach, general manager, and players. If they don't look good, we look real bad. Our top priority is to make the top people look good. You've got that? Now, go drink a cup of sludge and get your ass in gear."

Ryan nodded feebly.

"OK, I've got a call with the Network. Sheridan wants to sit down with Devonte this week. You guys can leave."

Johnny waved us out.

I held the door open as Ryan slumped back to his cube.

"You OK, partner?"

"Just embarrassed, that's all. It felt so good to be back on campus. Not to rush for a deadline or stand in front of a copier for hours. Being back in the frat house was so fun, I didn't want the party to stop. But a Sunday fun day with beer and cornhole wasn't the best idea."

I lowered my voice to a whisper. "There are plenty of people who party here. Have you heard the Bobbsey Twins talk about going to Harrah's in New Orleans? They gambled until 7:00 in the morning before a preseason game. But once you step into this stadium, or any other stadium in the league, it's go time, and you better be ready for it."

Ryan looked up at me with eyes so wounded that it was hard not to feel sorry for him.

"The worst part is disappointing Johnny. I really need to impress him if I want a full-time position here. I don't want him to think I'm some frat dude, always looking to party."

"You have an entire season to prove yourself," I told him. "This is just week one. Plus, being a frat guy is probably a step up from being a woman, at least in Johnny's eyes."

Ryan shrugged.

"Being a girl has a lot of upside. I'm pretty much invisible to the players and coaches. They walk by and don't say a word. For you, they smile, say your name. Players happily give you interviews outside the locker room after practice. They'd never do that for me."

Ryan was right. As a woman, I stood out among a team of men. The players and coaches noticed me, gave me extra attention. But I was also under a microscope. My every move—like accessing the locker room or going to a strip club—was scrutinized.

"I do have some advantages," I said. "I just don't know yet if they outweigh the disadvantages."

Twelve

Best Seat in the House

"You are the true heroes. What we do on the field is easy compared to the danger you face. I know from experience. My dad was a firefighter." Seth paused and swallowed back his emotions. "For twenty-two years, my dad reported for his shift at the Cedar Hammock Fire Department in Florida. I would ask him if he was scared to go to work. He would say, 'No, son. I'm honored.'"

Applause thundered across the room. Policemen and firefighters wearing starched dress uniforms stood from their tables, clapping and nodding at each other in solidarity. Seth beamed from the podium and pointed to the crowd, as if to redirect the appreciation back to them.

With the season opener falling on the anniversary of the 9/11 tragedy, Johnny worked with the Community Affairs Department to structure an event that paid tribute to these local heroes. To that point, the event was flawless. The first responders posed for photos with cheerleaders, received miniature footballs signed by Seth and Coach Bush, and dined on a four-course meal. More important to Johnny, cameras from the television stations' sports and news departments were there, ensuring double coverage on their broadcasts.

I savored the final bite of flourless chocolate cake and wiped the evidence from the corners of my mouth.

"This is a nice break from covering practice," I said to Boss. "It's also nice dressing up."

I adjusted the collar of the blue and white shirt dress I bought with the Nordstrom gift card my parents had given me for my twenty-fifth birthday a few months earlier. While form fitting, the dress hit just above the knees, making it conservative enough for work.

"Whatever you say. I'm here for the food," Boss said between bites of cake.

"How on earth do you eat so much and stay so skinny?"

"I run around with a thirty-pound camera. That's how."

"Did you get enough footage during the luncheon for our videos? We are producing a video for the website and a separate one for the jumbotron during the game."

"We should be covered, but I guess it wouldn't hurt to get some shots of Seth talking to the first responders," Boss said, reluctantly dropping his fork on a chocolate-streaked dessert plate. He pulled his camera from under his chair and dutifully marched toward Seth, who was shaking hands with a table of firefighters.

Hearing Seth talk about his father tugged at my heart. Now, watching his kindness and warmth opened my eyes to a softer, more vulnerable side of him.

I felt a tap on my shoulder. It was Johnny.

"I'm gathering the media at the side of the stage. You guys can interview one of the cops here. Ask him about today's event. Then Seth will talk. Got that, BB?"

A small pack of photographers, all of them without reporters, assembled near the stage. I motioned Boss to join us.

"Since we don't have reporters with us, we'll let you ask most of the questions," a photographer said, handing me his microphone. "Do you mind holding this for me?"

"That's fine," I said as my nerves began to prickle. Leading the media scrum in asking questions was usually reserved for seasoned reporters.

As Johnny walked toward the media with a stout police officer, I met them in stride.

"Is it OK for me to ask questions?" I whispered.

"Definitely."

Johnny then situated the officer in front of the cameras.

"Here is Sergeant Manny Perez. Blake, you get us started."

I inhaled deeply.

"Sergeant, what did today's luncheon mean to the first responders?"

Sergeant Perez embraced his moment in front of the cameras, talking about how humbled the first responders were to be honored by the team, the importance of the community acknowledging their work, and even touching on Seth's speech.

"I'm good," a photographer said when Perez finished.

"Me too," I added.

Johnny then ushered Seth toward the media. He smiled widely. "Just so you know, I'm only answering her questions."

The photographers chuckled and hoisted their cameras on their shoulders. My cheeks blushed. I gripped three microphones and bashfully looked up at Seth.

"Why was this event so important to you?"

Seth smiled back and began to talk. The scent of woody musk wafted toward me. My body warmed instinctively.

This time when he talked, I let my gaze meet his. Our eyes latched and it felt as if we were having our own conversation. Everything else faded away—the rest of the media, the cameras, everything.

When the interview ended, a photographer shouted, "Hey, can you ask him a football question? Like about his role this Sunday?"

Johnny pushed back a camera and stood next to Seth.

"Today is about the first responders. If you want to ask a football question, come to practice tomorrow. We are done for today."

The photographers groaned and dismounted their cameras. Johnny squeezed me on the shoulder and whispered in my ear, "Great job today, BB. Way to make us look good."

• • •

Hal lifted the collar of his faded, orange OKC Rodeo T-shirt and sopped up the sweat cascading from his forehead.

"I came so fast from the station that I forgot my handkerchief. I'm sweating like a pig in a bacon factory."

Hal released his shirt and the collar fell low against his chest, stretched and drenched.

"I didn't want to miss a second of practice. The first Wednesday of week one is the official first day of the season. At least, in my book. This is when things get real."

Hal and I stood on the practice field sidelines along with a handful of media members, watching the team install the game plan on both sides of the ball. A whistle blew and an assistant coach shouted, "First down!"

The starters rushed to the line of scrimmage. Coach Bush stood behind the offense, his bowed legs planted wide as he alternated studying his play sheet and the team. Coach's eyes squinted as he watched Devonte sprint fifteen yards and then brake downfield to haul in a catch.

"Bush doesn't look happy," I told Hal. "I thought Devonte made a great catch."

"Devonte ran the perfect curl route and made a hell of a catch," Hal said. "Problem is the quarterback. He threw it behind him. Andy has made more throws to the water boy on the sidelines than he has his receivers today. It's been pretty ugly."

I jotted down, *Devonte curl route/Andy inaccurate* in my notes.

"Hal, this may sound like a dumb question, but what's a curl route?"

"Girl, I'm glad you asked," he told me. "Most people who come out here don't give a flip about the x's and o's. They just want to scoop you on stories. We need to sit down and go through all routes. For now, all you have to know is flat and slant because those are the safe, short routes Andy likes to throw."

"You sound really down on Andy. I'm surprised. You've been defending him on the radio."

Hal looked around. Most of the reporters were on the other end of the field, talking to Johnny about player availability for the week. Hal leaned close and a bead of sweat dripped from his brow onto my arm.

"Blake, I work for the radio station *and* the team. When the station signed the deal to be the team's official broadcast partner, I effectively became a team employee. If I say something on the morning show or during the game that the top brass doesn't like, someone calls the station. Usually Johnny, occasionally the owner. This team controls its message. So, I criticize cautiously."

Hal stepped back and looked around again.

"Just about every journalist in town knows about how the team pressures my station. It's no big secret. But I try to use my words carefully around here."

"I won't say a word," I told him. I was not surprised Johnny vigilantly monitored the radio station's broadcasts. As Johnny said, the primary objective of his job was to make the team look good. I was just surprised Hal had confided in me about it.

"I know I can trust you. I also know that you are going to go far in this league, and one day you'll say it all started with an old radio guy who taught me a curl route," Hal chuckled.

"Hal, you've really taught me so much already," I said, before an air horn blared, signaling the end of practice.

"We better mosey down to the other end," Hal said.

Johnny stuck his thumb and index finger in his mouth and whistled at the media.

"All right, people. It's the regular season. Most of you know the drill, but here's a refresher. No footage after practice. No interviews with players and coaches as they walk off the field."

Johnny glanced back at the players. They were breaking the team huddle with "Win on three."

"We will bring Coach and two players to the podium around 2:00 p.m., and open locker room is after that. No questions to players or coaches about plays or drills you see during practice. If you talk about plays you saw, if you put it on social media, you will be banished from our facility."

Johnny flipped to the second sheet clipped on his clipboard.

"Coach has been kind enough to offer lunch to the media who want to stay. The media workroom is open. Any questions?" Johnny said and then reached for his phone, which was vibrating in the holster attached to the waist of his shorts. "Gotta take this." He unsnapped the phone and walked toward the stadium.

"I swear he has people call him just so he can avoid questions from us," Sheridan said, tucking her notebook into her purse.

Johnny walked to the bridge connecting the practice fields to the stadium. He placed his phone back into the holster and fist-bumped the Bobbsey Twins, who took their place behind him.

"Like a duck with his ducklings," Hal said, laughing.

"I'm waiting for the day when one of Johnny's ducklings quits following and bites him in the ass," Sheridan laughed back. "It's bound to happen."

· · ·

I kicked off my sandals underneath my desk. It was just past 8:45 p.m. and all of the business staff was gone. The only people left on the second floor were the coaches, scouts, Garrett, Ryan, and me. Even Johnny left for the day.

I refreshed the team website to peruse the story and video I posted: "Preparing for the Rush: How the Offense Is Game-Planning for the Season Opener." Over thirty hits and a comment in less than a minute.

I closed my eyes and thought about what Sheridan said after practice. *I'm waiting for the day when one of Johnny's ducklings quits following and bites him in the ass.* Who in my department had the guts to defy Johnny, let alone go after him? Certainly not the Bobbsey Twins. I snickered, picturing them scurrying behind Johnny, all in matching navy Dri-FIT polo shirts and khaki shorts.

My growling stomach interrupted my thoughts. I had about an hour of work left to do and needed an energy boost. I walked out of the maze of cubicles and headed to the break room for a Diet Coke. The smell of buttery fajita meat and skillet onions filled the hallway. I passed Garrett's office and glanced to see if he still was working.

"Good story, Blake," Garrett said from his desk. "It's racking up hits already."

His flattery stopped me in my tracks. Garrett didn't dole out compliments unless he was highly impressed. There was no casual encouragement.

Garrett made you earn praise with results, and several weeks into my job the results were materializing. My writing had become tighter, more concise and poignant, and I was selecting story lines that resonated with fans.

"Thanks, Garrett," I said, leaning against the doorframe of his office. "It came together really well because I got some strong quotes from Devonte."

"Keep up the good work. Traffic on the site is up. It always increases at the start of the season, but your stories and videos have given us an added boost."

"Wow, that's exciting! I feel like I'm starting to find my rhythm," I said through a huge smile.

"You've come a long way. But don't get comfortable. That will breed complacency."

"Oh, I'm not getting comfortable. I'm just getting going," I said. "Hey, I'm smelling some delicious fajitas. Want to walk to the break room with me to see what's cooking?"

Garrett shook his head.

"Hate to burst your bubble, but that food is only for coaches. They cater dinner upstairs during the week because they're here so late, working on the game plan."

"That's a bummer," I said, unable to hide the disappointment in my voice. "I guess I'll just get a soda."

I slid open the door to the soda fridge and stared longingly at the buffet of Mexican food curling around the perimeter of the break room. A large basket of chips glimmered at the end like a pot of gold. The tight ends coach was piling beef onto tortillas. His bare, calloused feet scratched against the nub carpet as he moved to the refried beans.

"Well, girl, are you going to fix yourself a plate?" Coach Bush said, walking past me to the front of the buffet line and picking up two plates. "Some of the best Mexican food in town. Only thing that would make this meal better is a beer."

"Are you sure? I heard this food is for you coaches," I said.

"Girl, if I eat all this meat, I'm going to have more problems than a math book. Come on, ladies first."

I let the refrigerator door slide closed and took one of the plastic plates he was holding.

"You see, when the suits on the other side of the office leave, us coaches can finally get comfortable. I play my country music. We order greasy food."

I scooped guacamole onto my plate and piled chips on top.

"That makes working late sound like fun. I don't know how you coaches do it with the hours you keep."

"I didn't choose coaching. Coaching chose me. My old man coached high school ball in Lubbock. I used to wonder how he could obsess over some other kids—spend every waking minute thinking about them between the months of August and December. So, I started helping out at practice and games, handing out water bottles, things like that. I saw what coaching really meant to him. The lessons of perseverance and humility he taught those young men. That's when I knew I would follow in his footsteps."

Coach Bush grinned wistfully. It was the first time we had exchanged more than workplace pleasantries, and the personal nature of our conversation disarmed me. Coach Bush hadn't talked at me like a head coach. He had spoken to me like an authentic human being. It dawned on me that I probably knew more about Coach Bush's personal life than I did Johnny's.

"Your dad must be really proud of you now. Not many people can say their son is a pro football head coach."

"Pa passed away from cancer right after I got this job." Coach Bush looked up. I couldn't tell if he was blinking back tears. "He said he wanted to watch the games from heaven. Best seat in the house."

"I'm sorry, Coach," I said.

"Aw, Blake, you got me all teary eyed over here," he said and shook his head.

"Well, it was nice talking. And thank you for the dinner. There is nothing better than fajitas and queso," I said, trying to lighten the subject matter.

"Anytime, Blake. You're doing a real standout job. I was glad to see the team hired you. I have daughters myself. One is about to go to college. I want these opportunities for them too," he said.

"I will make sure to do right by them," I said and turned down the hallway with a heaping plate and a full heart.

Thirteen

Let's Be Honest, You Show Better than Garrett

"Blakey, your eggs are getting cold!" Mom shouted from the bottom of the stairs.

I studied myself in the blotchy full-length mirror that had been adhered to the back of my bedroom door for at least two decades. I was wearing a new white shift dress that I bought with my last paycheck. The dress hit me about four inches above the knee, a little shorter than I normally wore to work, so I was opting for flat shoes. Comfortable flats that wouldn't give me blisters or sink into the field when I chased Monte around for the photo cards.

I spritzed my hair with a final layer of hair spray and shoved my makeup bag into my satchel. My parents sat at the breakfast table, reading the paper. Mom was wearing the rhinestone shirt I gave her as a gift from the cheerleading collection. It would have been a midriff on me, but it fit my petite mom perfectly.

"Looking good," I said, spearing a strawberry. "Are you excited for the game?"

"Excited is an understatement. Your dad was up before 6:00," Mom said.

"I wanted to make sure my new shirt was clean. You can't buy these in the stores. I looked online," Dad said, swelling with pride in a team polo shirt that Johnny had found in a box in his office and given to me. "It's going to be lucky. I can tell."

"If the team wins every time you wear that shirt to a game, Johnny will fly you on the team plane to away games," I teased.

Dad's eyes flickered as if there could be a shred of truth in what I told him.

"Now you're talking!"

I took a bite of eggs and poured coffee into a thermos.

"I better run."

"But you barely ate, sweetie." Mom frowned with concern.

"There's plenty of food in the press box. I'll look for you when I'm on the sidelines."

"Section 108!" Dad yelled as I walked out the door.

I pulled into the stadium lot and parked across from the CBS broadcast crew. The network's extended, generator-powered semitruck and satellite took up the back third of the lot.

Across the street, tailgaters filled lots surrounding the practice field. The sounds of country music and hip-hop mixed with the radio's pregame broadcast. Industrial meat smokers churned out a haze of brisket that floated above the crowd.

Fans spent the entire week preparing for this game. They shopped for beef, brats, and beer. They pitched tents, set up televisions, made signs. They listened to Hal in the mornings and surfed sports sites for the latest stats and injury news. They even read my stories and watched my videos. I watched a fan toss a beanbag onto a cornhole board and envisioned him sitting at a computer, scrolling through my "Keys to the Game" piece.

In that moment, I felt like I mattered. I did not have the name recognition of Sheridan or Hal, but a sense of importance welled within me.

"Good morning, Miss Blake," said Officer Pete, a security officer with brown, spiky hair that was bleached at the tips. The team jokingly called him Officer Frosted Tips.

Officer Frosted Tips and I had become friendly in the team gym. We were working out and I had asked about a tattoo of a badge on his forearm. He explained he had gotten the tattoo after he retired from the police force as a tribute to the twenty years he spent serving and protecting the fine people of Oklahoma City. I asked when he joined the team. He said he received a call from the front office three years earlier, asking him to join the team's security detail. It was an offer he couldn't refuse. Traveling with the team, working games, helping players when they were in a bind—how could he say no to that? Being a huge football fan only made the job that much sweeter.

"Hi, Officer. How did you get stuck out here?" I asked.

"I'm waiting for the CBS crew. Gotta help escort them inside. Another guy is supposed to be manning this post. He's inside, taking a leak. Got a bladder smaller than a black-eyed pea."

Officer Frosted Tips dipped his head closer to mine and I could smell his wintergreen chewing gum.

"Go in there and kick some major internet butt. I will be checking the site tonight."

"Thank you, Officer," I said as he opened the stadium door for me.

I walked through the tunnel toward the morning light illuminating the field.

It was my first regular season game and I wanted to stand on the pristine, green grass and appreciate all the emotions bubbling inside me. I looked up at the nosebleed section, where it all started, and closed my eyes. I envisioned my view twenty years earlier from high in the rafters, an endless stream of fans cascading below me. The field had stretched distantly beneath me like a magical, unreachable destination.

But now here I was, walking the freshly painted sidelines and making my dreams come true. My swelling heart tugged at my insides, making them dance in delight.

Then, I felt a hand gently squeeze my shoulder.

"Hard to believe this is real," Ryan said. "I had to take a knee and soak it all in."

"Since I was five years old, I have imagined what it would be like to step on this field on game day. It's almost surreal that I've journeyed from the last row in the stadium to the sidelines. It makes everything we endure—the long hours, the huge egos—all worth it," I said.

"Amen," Ryan said and turned toward the players jogging on the field before us. Most wore headphones and stared intently straight ahead. They were locked in, flipping their switches to warrior mode.

A few yards down the sideline, Sheridan stood in front of a cameraman and an ultrabright lighting kit. Her royal blue blazer shone in the artificial light.

"Coming to you in one minute, Sheridan. The Network will count you down," her cameraman said.

Sheridan nodded and pushed an IFB earpiece deep in her ear. I moved closer to their makeshift set so I could hear her pregame report.

Sheridan held the microphone to her red lips and nodded.

"About two hours until kickoff here in Oklahoma City. As you can see behind me, the players are getting loose, stretching. Warm-ups here aren't to be missed. This is when receiver Devonte Harris practices his acrobatic one-handed catches in the back of the end zone."

The camera panned to Devonte on the field as Sheridan continued.

"Devonte told me earlier this week that practicing those one-handed grabs helps him establish his timing and gets him hyped before the game. He's looking hyped now, don't you think, guys?" Sheridan laughed into the microphone and made small talk with the broadcasters in the studio before signing off.

"All clear. They're coming back to us in twenty minutes," her cameraman shouted.

I waved at Sheridan.

"See you upstairs," she said, waving back.

"You totally have a girl crush on her," Ryan said.

"How could I not? She's the best in the business. I really want to learn from her."

"I have no doubt that one day you'll be standing right where she is," Ryan said with a grin.

"You just made my day," I said as we headed to the press box elevator.

The press box was about half full and fairly quiet. Ryan and I walked to our department's assigned row in the middle of the first section of seating near the entrance. The Bobbsey Twins had plugged in their computers, but Garrett was the only person sitting in our row. He was near the end, wearing his favorite black suit with a skinny, gold tie.

"So nice of you to make it," he said, without looking up from his laptop.

"Believe it or not, we were here early. We just got caught up in the excitement on the field," I said.

"I know. I saw you ogling Sheridan Lane," Garrett said, turning from his computer, his thin lips pursed. "In case you didn't notice, you're sitting down there with Johnny and the guys."

I looked at the name tags taped to each desk area. Mine was affixed to the space usually reserved for Garrett, and Garrett was assigned to the very last spot where Ryan usually sat.

"There must have been a mix-up. Want to switch around seats?" I said, sensing the bitterness emanating from Garrett.

"Nope. Johnny wants it this way. Said it is better that you're closer to him for content purposes. Don't know what that means. But you should sit down and start working. Get the pregame photo slideshow started. I want a lot more photos and social media for this game."

I silently unfolded my laptop. There was nothing to say to Garrett to soften his edge. His pride was far too wounded. The only way to appease him was to work hard and produce stellar content.

Once I built the slideshow page, I went back to the field to locate Monte. The sidelines were packed with VIP fans, including local NBA players, CEOs of major oil companies, and the team's owner, Garland Morgan, and his family.

Mr. Morgan was decked out in his trademark white linen suit, which he had worn for every season opener since he bought the franchise. He was tall and lean, towering over his petite wife, who was known for her pouf of gray bouffant hair and double strand of pearls. Mr. Morgan joked that his wife was born wearing those pearls. He, however, wasn't born into a privileged life. He was a self-made billionaire who went from farming chickens in Mississippi to building the nation's largest privately owned oil company. It was a rags-to-riches story that made him one of the most beloved philanthropists in the city.

Behind the owner stood his son, Whittaker, and Whittaker's much younger third wife. Whittaker matched his father in a white linen suit, and his wife wore a tight, white sheath dress with a blue silk scarf around her neck. There were rumors that Whittaker had been begging his dad for years to run the team alongside him and that Mr. Morgan was finally relenting and beginning to groom his son to be the franchise's next owner.

There were also rumors that Whittaker wasn't the most capable heir. He had blown through most of his trust and never held a steady job. He liked to accompany his father to practices and team meetings, and the players had dubbed him "Sir Dim Whit" for his lack of intellect and presumed inheritance of the team.

I hadn't formally met Mr. Morgan or Whittaker. I'd only seen them stand beside security details at practices or games. But their family dynamics fascinated me, especially Whittaker's marriage to a gorgeous, leggy brunette who was just a year older than me.

I made a mental note to include photos of her in social media posts. Johnny had reminded me several times that she expected to see photos of herself and Whittaker in our feeds.

As the final notes of the national anthem pumped through the stadium, Johnny slid behind me for his pregame fist bump.

"BB, how do you like your new seat?" he asked and reached out his meaty knuckles.

All of Johnny's actions were calculated. I needed to know what his motives were on this.

"I'm happy, but why did you move me?" I asked.

Johnny squatted down to eye level.

"Let's be honest; you show better than Garrett. I'd like you up front with me where people can see you. It's good for our department."

Johnny winked.

I let Johnny's words settle between us. He had just likened Garrett and me to a dog and pony show, which was incredibly disrespectful to both of us. If anyone was a dog in this scenario, it was Johnny. But I couldn't tell him that and cause a scene in the press box. Not if I wanted access to the locker room, which seemed within my grasp. Things had been going so well with the team. Johnny certainly would reverse his policy soon.

I envisioned standing next to Sheridan at Devonte's locker with a microphone in hand. There was nothing I wanted more. So, I bit my tongue and gave Johnny a forced smile.

. . .

At the end of the second quarter, Devonte gave the team its first touchdown of the game. Andy hit him with a quick slant pass; Devonte slipped through a tackle and reached the end zone for a 34-yard score.

"Finally, a touchdown. We needed that," I said to Ryan.

Ryan refreshed the official stat tracker site.

"Devonte's got almost a hundred receiving yards in the first half, but it doesn't feel that way because our drives keep stalling," he said.

"Andy fumbling was costly. We're lucky to be up 10–7 with the way he's playing," I said.

Ryan sat up in his chair and pointed his nose in the air like a Labrador sniffing out a steak dinner. "I think they're serving buffalo wings. There's nothing I love more than buffalo wings dipped in blue cheese dressing. Did you know that I won a wing-eating contest in college? There's a plaque in my frat to prove it."

"And you're proud of this accomplishment?" I teased.

"You bet!" Ryan popped up from his chair. "I'm getting in line. You want some?"

Next to me, the Bobbsey Twins were tucking napkins into their shirt collars and waistbands, preparing to tackle a pile of wings dripping in spicy sauce.

I imagined my face stained with buffalo sauce as I shot stand-ups on the field after the game.

"I'll pass and leave the wing eating to the pros."

"You're such a girl," Carleton taunted me, licking his greasy fingers.

I rolled my eyes as he thumbed through the stat sheets, staining them with orange fingerprints.

The third quarter opened with Devonte shaking a cornerback on a crossing route and scoring a 72-yard touchdown. He leaped into the stands with the ball, and fans cheered wildly, slapping high fives and dancing in the aisles.

"Devonte will be the big story," Garrett yelled from the far end of the row.

With Garrett not constantly breathing down my neck with his coffee breath, I'd almost forgotten he was there.

"Blake, you'll cover him. And get his touchdown photo posted ASAP."

"You got it," I said.

"Ryan, you'll go to the locker room for quotes and do something on the defense," Garrett said.

With just more than five minutes left and the team leading 23–17, I packed my laptop.

"Garrett, I'm heading down to the auditorium," I said.

"Don't forget to shoot the intros for the videos," Garrett said as he updated the live game story.

I took a step toward him. "You know what video would really get hits—a one-on-one interview with Devonte."

Garrett turned from his screen. "That's up to Johnny. You have to ask him."

Johnny was already on the field, getting ready to debrief Coach Bush and escort him to his obligatory media appearances after the game. I wouldn't be able to talk to Johnny until after the pressers, but I knew he would be in a good mood after a win. Plus, I had played along with his *best in show* comment. That had to count for something.

· · ·

I took a seat behind Sheridan in the auditorium and waved at Boss, who was setting up his camera in the back of the room.

"Hi there. I'm sure you're doing a story on Devonte, just like the rest of us," Sheridan said. Her makeup was just as fresh as it looked on the sidelines six hours earlier.

"The game was pretty uneventful except for his performance out there," I replied.

"Well, unlike us, you get the inside track, something more meaningful than the company line at the podium."

"Actually, I'm still working my way toward going in the locker room and doing interviews with the players."

Sheridan's forehead crinkled.

"What do you mean? Isn't that what you were hired to do?"

I shrugged.

"We'll talk later," she said as Johnny thrust open the door to reveal Coach Bush standing behind him. Coach sauntered to the stage and gripped each side of the podium.

"Before we get started, I want to say it was a heck of a day for Devonte. On the way in here, I had Johnny show me the stats. Unbelievable—228 receiving yards and two touchdowns. That young man was impressive in every aspect of the game, and boy are we lucky he plays on our team. Any questions?"

A local beat writer asked, "What makes Devonte so hard to cover?"

Coach Bush chuckled. "Everything. He's fast, tall, strong. He can outjump and outrun cornerbacks. He's got hands the size of a catcher's mitt. He can catch anything in a five-foot radius. And he wants it more than the other guy. Don't let Devonte's quiet nature fool you. That boy is driven. He wants to be the best."

The questions poured in about Devonte, until Sheridan raised her hand.

"Coach, Andy's fumble in the second quarter. What did you see on that play? Was it a bad snap?"

"You know, Sheridan, I didn't see the play happen, so I'll need to look at it on tape."

"One more," Sheridan said before another reporter could jump in. "Andy threw an interception late in the game, but the defender dropped it. Despite a few big throws to Devonte, not a very crisp game for your quarterback. What were your impressions of his play?"

"Yeah, not a great throw by Andy on that one that almost got picked off. I think it was a timing read. That's something that he and I have to get corrected. But you have to remember that this is his first regular-season game since December, back when he hurt his shoulder. He's still working some things out."

After a few more questions, Johnny escorted Coach Bush out of the auditorium and paraded in Devonte as if he were a Derby-winning horse. Johnny yanked the microphone from the podium and announced, "Ladies and gentlemen, All-Pro receiver Devonte Harris."

In his soft, low voice, Devonte patiently and humbly answered questions. Most of what he said was generic. He was able to take advantage of some single coverage. The entire team contributed to his performance, especially the o-line. But Devonte's final response quieted the room and raised eyebrows. An ESPN reporter asked him about the rhythm he had established with Andy.

Devonte lowered his head, his diamond necklace grazing the podium.

"I don't know about our rhythm. I just catch the balls he throws me."

Reporters looked at each other quizzically and clamored for follow-up questions, but Johnny cut them off at the knees.

"All right, last question. Last question. Blake, go ahead."

I gulped. I wasn't raising my hand. I hadn't prepared any questions for Devonte. Johnny explicitly asked me not to ask questions in press conferences. Of course, the logical question, the question burning the tongues of the media, was if Devonte and Andy needed to work their chemistry. But Johnny's narrowed eyes and steely gaze indicated I shouldn't touch that topic. He had called on me to deflect attention and lob a softball to Devonte.

So, I did.

"Devonte, where does this game rank for you among your best?" My voice quivered as I imagined reporters rolling their eyes at my powder-puff question.

"Man, this has to be at the top. To go down in the record books and get us a win to start the season. Man, it feels good. I'm going to enjoy this one."

"OK. That's it, folks. Andy is up next."

Johnny led Devonte off the stage to the exit, letting the door slam behind them.

Within seconds, my phone vibrated. A text from Johnny. *Way to be a team player.*

I texted him back, *Can I interview Devonte one-on-one?*

Johnny replied, *Not today. Next time.*

My face fell in disappointment.

. . .

I was finishing my story on Devonte in my cubicle when I heard the clattering of bangle bracelets. Emily strutted toward me. She wore her favorite tight white pants and a gold halter top. A white suit jacket hung out of her Louis Vuitton tote bag.

"Hey, I thought I heard typing back here," she said, leaning against the cubicle wall, which I was not confident could support her ample bottom. "You should take a break and get some barbeque. The guys are in the players' lot whooping it up."

"I wish I could, but I still have a lot of work to do." A plate of brisket sounded heavenly. I had barely eaten all day. But I still had to finish my stories and I wasn't sure how Johnny would feel about me hanging out with the players in such a casual way.

"That's lame. It's not like they can fire you for going," Emily said like she was reading my mind.

"Actually, they probably can and would."

Emily jutted out her hip. "Did they make you sign some bullshit agreement?"

"Yep."

"What a scam. This team picks and chooses who they want to sign that garbage. There are two sexpot scouting assistants who work under Tammie. They're always partying with the players and coaches. They're probably eating barbeque with them right now. No one seems to care what they do."

I looked at Emily quizzically and racked my brain for anyone who looked like "sexpots" in the stadium.

"I met Tammie at training camp," I said. "She's the lady who's been here forever. But I didn't meet anyone else."

"That's because those chicks work in closets on the other side of the building doing data entry for the scouts. They're so far removed from business ops that HR probably forgot they even work here."

Emily twirled a long, blonde curl.

"Occasionally, I'll see them in the cafeteria wearing crosses, looking all sweet and innocent. After games, they hit the club with their boobies hanging out of their dresses."

I smiled at Emily's candor. "Just when I thought I knew most of the team."

"Girl, there's so much you don't know." Emily handed me a business card with her cell phone number. "I'm going to gnaw on some ribs. If you change your mind, text me."

Then she turned on her stiletto heels, leaving my cubicle with the smell of cotton candy musk.

Fourteen

You Can Find Me in the Lounge

The sidelines were pretty much empty at practice that Friday, just a couple of beat reporters and the team media. Even Hal decided to forgo the heat to get ready for the next day's trip to Florida

"There's literally no one here," I said to the Bobbsey Twins. We were standing in a small patch of shade near the shed at midfield.

"Yeah, lots of media skip Fridays. Most of the players have already talked, so writers have their quotes. Plus, this is basically a walk-through practice anyways," Carson said and crossed his arms. Thick, white sunscreen matted the pale skin from his wrist to his elbows.

"Well, I get to write the coolest story today," Ryan blurted out.

"Is that so?" Carleton asked, one of his strawberry-blond eyebrows arching in curiosity.

"I'm writing about the Fortnite competitions the players hold every Friday. The players are super into it. Andy even bought a second flat screen for the players' lounge and extra gaming equipment. It's intense."

"You've been talking about this story since training camp," I said. "I can't believe you convinced Garrett to let you do it."

"After last week's win, Garrett finally agreed. I'm so pumped. I've been playing Fortnite in my apartment to get ready."

"Calm down there, cowboy." Carleton laughed. "The players may not be that excited about you bothering them on a Friday afternoon."

Ryan looked down bashfully. "Yeah, I need to figure out how I'm going to get the players to talk to me."

"Don't you just ask them about it during open locker room?" I said.

Ryan kicked his foot on the rubber track surrounding the field.

"The players basically ignore me. If they need something, they just shout 'Intern' at me. I don't think they know my name."

"I'm sure they'll be fine answering a couple of questions about a video game," I said.

"We'll see," Ryan muttered.

We followed the players off the field. Ahead of us, Seth walked with Monster Calves, their helmets dangling from their fingers. I watch them banter back and forth. Then Seth turned back to find me. Our gazes met. His hazel eyes twinkled, and I smiled softly.

"So, what do you think?" Ryan asked.

"Think of what?" I shook my head, trying to reorient myself.

"What do you think of me going into the players' lounge now? Should I get them on their way to lunch?"

"I'm probably not the person to ask. Remember, I've never been in the locker room."

"I know, but you know the players better than I do."

"You'll be fine," I said reassuringly, but my thoughts were still on Seth.

We stopped in front of the locker room. "Here goes nothing," Ryan said and entered the code into the keypad.

The cafeteria was eerily quiet. A few sales managers and assistants were scattered at tables, watching ESPN on the mounted televisions. None of the players were going through the buffet lines. On Fridays, the players and coaches liked to order fried chicken and biscuits from a neighborhood restaurant and eat in the locker room.

I handed a plastic plate to a server behind the hot food line.

"Roasted vegetables and grilled chicken, please."

"Sweetie, your tray is vibrating," she said, handing me back a full plate.

It was Ryan. "What's up?" I asked.

"I need reinforcements ASAP!" Ryan's voice was rife with desperation.

"Are you serious? Or is this a practical joke?"

"I'm serious. It's a code red. The guys won't talk to me. They keep saying that they don't give interviews to interns. But if you help me with the interview, they'll do it."

"Ryan, you know I'm not allowed in the locker room. I'm sure the same goes for the players' lounge."

"I was thinking maybe Johnny would make this one exception," Ryan pleaded. "You could enter through the cafeteria. The players will all be dressed. No inappropriate encounters between coworkers. Please, will you ask him?"

"I don't think it will do any good."

"Blake, I'm begging you."

"Fine."

I hung up and called Johnny. Voice mail. I tried again. Same. I sent Johnny a text. No reply. Reluctantly, I dialed Garrett's number. It was a foregone conclusion he would say no. Garrett was the ultimate rule follower. But at least I could tell Ryan I exhausted all the options.

"Hi, Garrett, I've been looking for Johnny. Have you seen him?"

"He's in a meeting with ownership. Why do you need him?"

"Ryan's working on that Fortnite story, but the players are being hard on him, saying they don't give interviews to interns. They told him that I should help him. But I know I'm not allowed in the lounge."

"Technically, you're not allowed in the locker room. The lounge is a different area. I really want to post this story. I teased it on social media and the fans went crazy. This is going to get hits."

I was stunned.

"So, what should I do?"

"You should help Ryan. Ask a few questions and then leave. You don't need to be in there for more than ten minutes."

Within seconds, Monster Calves swung open one of the double doors at the back of the cafeteria.

"Welcome to our humble abode."

The room was exactly how Ryan described it—a total man cave. Three overstuffed, brown sectional couches surrounded two large flat-screen

TVs. There was a pool table in the back corner and several computer bays against the adjacent wall.

When I walked in, the players didn't notice. They were either playing video games or watching from the couch, their feet in slide sandals and their legs comfortably spread wide.

"Hey, assholes, you should stand when a lady enters the room," Monster Calves said, ceremoniously announcing my presence.

A few players awkwardly half stood, then fell back into the couch. Seth, who was perched on an armrest, jumped to his feet.

"It's about time they took the chains off you. I was telling the intern we would only answer his questions if you were the one asking."

"I'm flattered," I said, blushing. "But I'm bending the rules by being here, so we should probably do this quickly."

"The rules? Whose rules?" Monsters Calves asked, chugging Muscle Milk.

"It's sort of a team rule," I stammered.

"Sounds like a Johnny-jerk job." Monster Calves burped. "This is our room. We can invite whoever we want in here."

"OK, then," I said. I raised an eyebrow at Ryan, who stood behind me, bracing himself against the pool table nervously.

"We take Fortnite very seriously. This talk will take more than a couple of minutes. Come sit here and I can tell you more." Seth sank into the couch and patted at the seat next to him.

As I sat down, our arms brushed. Skin to skin. The warmth of his body next to mine sent a bolt of heat through my veins. I inhaled the fresh laundry smell of his white T-shirt and felt my head go light.

I could not sit this close to Seth. It was sensory overload. Too much heat. Too many pheromones. And what if Johnny walked in? What would he think? I scooted over a couple of feet and crossed my legs, attempting to regain a semblance of professional composure.

"How does this all work?" I asked. My voice was squeaking more than enunciating.

"We started these competitions during training camp for team bonding. It's important to bond with your coworkers," Seth said and winked.

Seth was flirting. Overtly. And it was lighting up my insides.

I moved closer to him and let myself indulge in the energy pulsating between us. We began to talk like we were alone on the couch, teasing and laughing in effortless banter. After what seemed like a couple of minutes, I checked the recorder I had been holding and it showed we had been talking for almost a half hour.

"Wow, I lost track of time. I need to go to Coach's presser," I said and pushed myself up from the sofa.

"I wish you didn't have to go," Seth said, his eyes shining bright as he looked up at me.

I beamed back. My cheeks tingled from smiling for so long.

"You were amazing," Ryan said as we walked back into the cafeteria.

"Hardly. I was just making conversation." I suddenly felt self-conscious about the blatant flirting that had just taken place. There was no way Ryan hadn't noticed the long glances and blushed cheeks.

"It helps when the players like you," Ryan said.

I arched an eyebrow.

"Come on, Blake. Seth couldn't take his eyes off you. You should embrace the attention."

"Right now, I'm going to embrace basically being in the locker room."

"Blake, you did one better. You were in the lounge. Things are looking up."

Ryan was right. Going into the lounge was a big step in the right direction. Getting access to the locker room was imminent. I could feel it in my bones. I could also still feel the lingering effects of Seth. His bewitching eyes and lusty smile left my body warm and effervescent.

Fifteen

On the Prowl

I pulled a couple of gossip magazines out of my satchel as we waited for the players to board the flight for our first road trip of the regular season. I flipped to my favorite section: *Who Wore It Best?* Two movie stars wore the most fabulous pair of knee-length, chunky-heeled, black boots. I sighed enviously.

"Don't tell me Britney Spears did something stupid again?" Ryan smirked.

"No, I'm obsessed with these Prada boots. I have to find a cheaper version."

I carefully tore out the page.

"I don't know why you like reading that garbage," Ryan said, pulling out a *Sports Illustrated*. "Johnny has been giving me his *SI*s each month. Now, this is a real magazine."

"I read and write about football all day, every day. My mind needs a break," I said, turning the page to *Celebs Are Just Like Us*.

"They better win tomorrow," Ryan said.

"Yeah, starting 2–0 would be huge."

"No, because they can't lose after my Fortnite story. If they lose, Garrett and Johnny will never let me do something like that again. They'll say I was a distraction."

"Welcome to my world."

I glanced to the front of the plane as the players began to file through the galley. Alyssa stood proudly and greeted each player personally, often with a made-up nickname.

"Looking good, Andy 'Miller Time' Miller."

I leaned closer to Ryan. "Do you think she's hooked up with a player?" I asked.

"Definitely," he said, watching her intently.

Alyssa patted a rookie linebacker on the back and then caught Ryan's eye. She pressed her acrylic nails to her lips and blew Ryan a kiss. His face turned a deep magenta, matching the color of Alyssa's nail polish perfectly.

. . .

The buses turned into a winding drive lined with large palm trees. Johnny stood up, braced himself against his seat with one hand.

"All right, people. We're doing things a little differently this trip. Instead of staying in town by the stadium, we are going to be at this beautiful beach-front resort," he said, pointing out the window to a sprawling hotel surrounded by vibrant, manicured lawns.

The bus stopped at the hotel entrance, where valets waited.

"I highly recommend enjoying all this resort has to offer. Walk over to the golf course. Relax by the pool. Go to the beach. Wade your feet in the Atlantic Ocean. This is as close to a vacation as you will get during the season."

"Good thing I brought my Speedo!" Hal howled.

"Hal, my friend, you're too much man for a banana hammock." Johnny snorted in laughter.

I followed Johnny off the bus, trying to shake the visual of Hal from my head and lamenting that I didn't pack my own swimsuit.

The hotel lobby was an endless sea of white marble with stairs cascading down to a lower-level bar and dining area that overlooked the verdant lawns and connected lagoons. As I walked to the check-in desk, I spotted a boutique off the lobby.

At the entrance, a mannequin posed in a sleek leopard dress. Another wore a white, crocheted bikini and matching crochet cover-up. The clothes looked expensive, but my wardrobe still seemed drab in comparison to what women like Emily wore to work.

"Can I help you with something?" asked a saleswoman in a tropical midriff top that revealed luscious caramel skin. She spoke with an accent that added to her exotic allure.

"I'm looking for a swimsuit. Nothing too fancy."

The saleswoman quickly pulled a few selections from the rack. "These would look beautiful on you. You have the body for them."

I held up two sets of string bikinis and almost choked. Not only were they over $200, but they barely would cover my rear. Johnny would lose his mind if he saw me prancing around the pool in one of these. "I'm not sure these are right. I'm here on a work trip."

"This is what everyone wears in my home country of Columbia." She shrugged.

"Actually, can I try on that?" I said, pointing to the leopard dress in the entrance.

"Of course."

She whisked a couple of sizes off a rack and led me to the dressing room. I closed the heavy, red velvet curtain and turned over the price tag. Gulp—$450. I stepped into the dress and the silk liner caressed my skin as I inched it over my hips. It was as if the dress was made for me. It hugged me tightly while being tailored and polished in its cut and length. I stepped out of the dressing room.

"*Dios mio*! You look like a model," the saleswoman said, waving an arm adorned with chunky, colorful bracelets. "You have to buy it."

How could I not? How could I wear the cheap suit wrinkling away in my bag after trying on this?

"I'll take it," I said, handing her my debit card and vowing not to buy another piece of clothing until Christmas.

• • •

After a four-course dinner at a steak house near the golf course, Johnny directed our department back to the hotel lobby bar.

"They have the TVs on. We can watch the end of the college games. Drinks are on me."

The Bobbsey Twins bopped along, undoubtedly giddy to order a round of Jack and Cokes on Johnny.

"So, how come we are staying outside of the city instead of a hotel close to the stadium?" I asked them.

"Coach is trying to keep the players out of trouble," Carson said. "They love those all-nude strip clubs that Florida's proud to offer."

"Out here we are at least forty-five minutes away from downtown. The players can't sneak off to see titties and be back by curfew," Carleton added.

I could not help but smirk. "I have to agree with Coach. Hitting up strip clubs isn't a healthy or productive way to get ready for a game," I said with a passive-aggressive undertone.

The Bobbsey Twins went silent.

When we reached the lobby, Garrett stealthily slid into an elevator.

"That truffle mac and cheese is inducing a food coma. I'm heading up too," I said to the rest of the group.

"You can't wuss out like Garrett," Ryan said. His speech was slow and lazy after a long day of drinking and watching the OSU game. "Stay for a nightcap. Come on."

"Fine. One drink," I conceded.

We walked to the bar and I saw why Johnny wanted to be there. It was a total scene—the team's GM and the VP of Football Administration swirled whiskeys at a high-top table. Alyssa and her attendant sidekicks flirted loudly with the bartender. And three Jessica Simpson look-alikes sat at a banquette, their toned legs crossed and their cleavage on display in tight spandex dresses. They stared at Ryan and me as we approached the bar, looking us up and down in unison.

"I get the strange feeling we're under surveillance," I whispered to Ryan, nodding at the women behind us.

But Ryan didn't hear me. Alyssa was holding up a shot glass filled with frothy yellow alcohol and winking at him from across the bar. "Sugar, I got this lemon drop just for you," she said.

Within seconds, Ryan rounded the bar and was clinking shot glasses with Alyssa and the two other flight attendants.

I took a long sip of my vodka cranberry. There was no way Alyssa would seduce a man thirty years younger than her. Right? There was no way Ryan would risk his job and hook up with her. That could not happen. I watched as she pressed herself against him, her pink lips brushing Ryan's ear. Oh, it was happening.

A high-pitched voice startled me.

"What happens on the road, stays on the road," said one of the Jessica Simpsons, who had perched on the chair next to me. She was even more perfect close-up. High cheekbones and full lips accentuated her delicate face.

"My friend has had too much to drink," I said carefully. "I hope he doesn't get himself into trouble."

"Johnny isn't going to care. I'm sure he's seen way worse."

I blinked hard.

"You know Johnny?"

"Yes, my husband is on the team. Starting left tackle."

She was Monster Calves's wife.

"Wow, he really married up," I blurted out.

She lifted a French-manicured hand to reveal an engagement ring with a gargantuan rectangle diamond.

"He knows it. That's why he bought me this sucker."

"It's stunning," I said. "And sorry about the marrying up comment. What I really meant is that you're very beautiful."

"Well, the same can be said about you," she told me. "The guys have been talking about how pretty you are. Not in a done-up way. Just naturally pretty. I'm glad I got to see for myself."

I flinched with discomfort. For several months, I had gotten to know the players in the vacuum of the daily grind. We lived at the stadium during the season, arriving before the sun rose and leaving after it set. It was easy to forget the players had families to go home to at night. I certainly hadn't considered what their wives would think of me. I didn't even think I would be on their radars.

"You look like a deer in headlights." Monster Calves's wife laughed. "Did you think we didn't know about you?"

"I guess," I said softly.

She tucked her blonde hair behind one ear and looked me square in the eyes.

"If you thought you could pop up on the website, start traveling with the team, and the wives wouldn't notice, you're crazy. We notice everything."

She swirled her glass of chardonnay.

"Most of us google our husbands each morning. Some stalk the internet because they want to know what the media is saying about them. Some wives stalk their men because they want to make sure they aren't getting into trouble."

She took another sip of her wine.

"I'm not worried about my baby. He's the most loyal man I know. But other wives don't have it so good. Their husbands lie and cheat."

Her smoky eyes narrowed.

"Be careful of players playing you, and be careful of their wives hating on you."

I nodded meekly.

"Please tell the wives not to worry about me. I'm here to do a job and that's it."

"You seem like a sweet girl. I can tell by your smile. Just be careful. There are haters everywhere," she said.

I glanced back at the two other Jessica Simpsons, who were studying us raptly.

"Are they wives too?" I asked.

"No, those are my sisters. They live here. I grew up in Florida, went to college here. I never travel to road games. Most wives never do. We don't want to be distractions. Plus, the guys are busy the entire time. But I always come back here to see my family."

I relaxed slightly as the conversation shifted, and loosened my legs, which were crossed so tightly sweat dripped between my inner thighs.

"And heads up, you might want to check on your friend. He's leaving with a full-fledged cougar," she said and nodded toward the lobby.

Ryan and Alyssa were walking hand in hand. They stepped into an elevator and kissed sloppily as the doors closed.

· · ·

After a second nightcap, my head felt light and my body loose as I sank into the pillow-top mattress. My mind floated from visions of the Jessica Simpsons to Ryan's lipstick-smudged face.

When the hotel phone rang, I thought it was part of my dream. But the ringing didn't stop. I pried my eyes open and rolled toward the bedside table.

"Hello?" I muttered groggily.

"Did I wake you?" a man said, his voice familiar.

"Who is this? I think you have the wrong room."

"No, I have exactly the right room," he said. "It's Seth."

I sprang from my pillow, my pulse quickening.

"Seth. Why are you calling? I mean, what's going on?" It was after midnight. I had been nearly snoring seconds earlier. Now, my mind fired like I had drunk a double shot of espresso.

"I haven't been able to stop thinking about you. That was really nice yesterday. You and I talking together in the lounge," he said.

I settled back into my pillow and let his words soak in. Then, I pictured him on the other end of the phone, lying on his hotel bed in his boxers with his chiseled bare chest exposed. Seth had a way of igniting my body from head to toe.

"I really enjoyed it too. It was one of those pinch-me moments. I had to remind myself that this is really my life," I said.

"Was that because you love your job or because you loved talking to me?" Seth asked coyly.

"A little bit of both," I flirted back. "It's been my dream since I was a little girl to be a sports reporter. Now here I am, getting to interview pro football players and launch my career."

"I've watched your videos and read your stories. You're good and you understand the game."

"I've got a lot to learn. I can see that from watching Sheridan Lane and how smooth and insightful her reporting is."

"She's one of the best. She asks smart questions. The players notice those things. She also makes the locker room smell nice, which I appreciate." Seth laughed. "Hey, why aren't you ever in the locker room?"

"I'm not allowed," I said, feeling disarmed by how naturally our conversation was flowing.

"Not allowed? There are women in the locker room every day. Sheridan Lane, case in point."

"Yeah, but those women don't work for the team. Johnny thinks women who work for the team shouldn't see their coworkers undress."

"It's not like we are walking around naked. We are wearing towels. You might catch a glimpse here or there, but only if you're looking."

The image of Seth changing at his locker made me bristle and blush. "The locker room thing is a pain. It makes doing interviews a lot more difficult. It's also embarrassing because I have my own set of rules, like having to ride my own bus."

"Are you kidding me?" Seth said, sounding genuinely shocked.

"Johnny doesn't want me to distract you guys on game day."

"That's such garbage. Johnny can be a real turd."

"Wait, what?" It was my turn to be shocked.

"You heard me. Johnny sucks. He only cares about star players—guys he can pitch to ESPN—guys who make him look important. The way he sucks up to Devonte is disgusting. Even Devonte gets annoyed by it."

"I'm surprised. I thought the players liked him."

"We tolerate him. Getting media features is important. It promotes our brand, gets us endorsements, makes us more valuable. We need Johnny for that. But I can't stand him. You should watch your back."

"I'm hearing that a lot these days," I mumbled.

"What'd you say?" Seth asked.

"Nothing," I said and shook my head into the phone. "I just realized that you've been asking all the questions. I want to hear more about you."

"Another time. I need to get some sleep."

"I understand," I said, trying to hide my disappointment. I was really enjoying getting to know Seth, and hearing about his dislike for Johnny had made him even more attractive.

"Blake, one last thing," Seth said. "Let's not tell anyone that we talked. You never know how someone will react."

"I totally agree. It's our secret," I said.

"Our secret," he whispered back and hung up.

I closed my eyes and pulled the covers tight. Everything about my conversation with Seth had felt so right. The ease, the honesty, the humor—all bound together by an undeniable sexual attraction. But from the far reaches of my mind came a voice cautioning that it was all wrong. I shouldn't be flirting with a player late at night.

Then again, what was right and wrong on this team anyway? Strip clubs were sanctioned team bonding. My boss commented on my body. Ryan was sucking face with the flight attendant. My head was so scrambled I couldn't make sense of any of it. One thing was clear—I wouldn't be falling asleep anytime soon. My body pulsated with the thought of Seth.

Sixteen

Lights, Camera, Prime Time

My suitcase tumbled down the luggage piled under the bus and landed back at my feet.

"Do you need some help?" a chipper voice asked.

It was the team's kicker, his green eyes bright and wide. He was far more rested and awake than I was.

"I thought I could store my bag and hold my latte at the same time. Clearly, my plan failed."

"Let me. Between my wife and five daughters, I'm very well trained at helping with bags."

"Thank you. Bonus news is that I didn't lose a drop of coffee, which I sorely need right now."

"A big night last night?"

"I had one drink too many." I grimaced, walking to the stairs of bus number four.

"I would say I know the feeling, but I don't. I've never had a sip, unless you count communion at church." The kicker followed me into the bus.

I was too shocked by his presence on the Blake Bus to respond. For the first time since I started the job, the Blake Bus was departing at the same time as the other buses because of the long distance to the stadium.

The police escorts couldn't circle back for the staggered departures, so we were all leaving together.

"I think you're supposed to be there," I said, pointing to the bus idling at the front of the drive.

"It shouldn't matter," he said and slipped his arms through the straps of a gray Nike backpack.

Johnny sat in the first row, a stack of newspapers occupying the seat next to him. When he heard the kicker's voice, he dropped the *Florida Times-Union* and popped to his feet.

"Whoa. Whoa. Whoa." He put his hand on the kicker's shoulder. "You're not on this bus. All players are on buses one through three. You need to go to the bus in front of us."

"Johnny, what difference does it make? I'm just going to sit and read the good word."

The kicker patted the Bible secured in an outside pocket of his backpack.

"The media here isn't going to bother me. You should know as well as anyone they aren't interested in talking to a kicker."

Johnny pointed his bald head in my direction.

"No, it's her. She's not supposed to be riding with the players. Team rules."

The kicker rolled his eyes.

"Johnny, I've played in this league twelve years. I think I can handle riding in a bus with a lady," he said. "But whatever you say."

My face flamed with embarrassment. I slid into a seat next to Hal and looked down at my computer bag, allowing my hair to drape across my face and shield me because I was pretty sure everyone in bus number four—every media personality, TV and radio producer, scout, and member of my department—was staring in my direction.

Hal patted my knee, and we rode in silence to the stadium.

· · ·

I avoided talking with anyone until we got to the press box, where I had no choice. Garrett slid behind me as I set up my laptop station. I assumed he was relishing my humiliation. Johnny had smacked me down to the bottom of the pecking order. That had to have been satisfying to Garrett.

"Blake, you have to put what happened on the bus behind you." Garrett pressed his black-rimmed glasses firmly against his nose. "We have a big day ahead. It's game day and I need you focused."

I nodded silently.

"And, Blake, if Devonte has a really big game, let's get you a one-on-one postgame interview with him."

My head jerked up. "Are you serious? That would be amazing."

"Our fans can't get enough of him. If the Network is interviewing him one-on-one, so should we. We need more original video content," Garrett said matter-of-factly.

Just when I thought I had Garrett figured out, he proved me wrong. Garrett wasn't conniving, chauvinistic, or vindictive like Johnny. Garrett's world revolved around clicks. If it produced clicks, it was good. If it didn't garner clicks or detracted from work, it was bad.

It didn't help that Garrett was innately antisocial and awkward. But he didn't discriminate. He was generally indifferent to everyone.

I sat back and looked at Garrett with a different lens. We weren't going to be friends. Garrett wasn't interested in making friends at work. But I understood his motivations better, and that gave me peace of mind.

"Thank you for this opportunity, Garrett. I won't let you down," I said.

With a renewed pep in my step and a little extra time to kill, I wandered to the media dining area. Alone at a corner table, Ryan hung his head over a plate of runny scrambled eggs. I spooned yogurt and fruit into a bowl and sat next to him.

"You OK, my friend? You're dangerously close to face-planting into your bacon."

Ryan looked up with bloodshot eyes.

"I'm really pissed at myself right now."

"What happened last night?" I said, leaning closer. "With Alyssa."

Ryan rested his head on a bacon-greased hand.

"I only remember bits and pieces. We kissed. I know that much. I took my shirt off. And I'm pretty sure I passed out after that. Because I woke up in the middle of the night with my jeans, belt, and socks still on."

"It's nothing to be proud of, but it could have been much worse," I said, patting his slumped shoulder.

"I'm so embarrassed. I'm embarrassed to see her. And I'm terrified Johnny will find out."

"I hate to break it to you, but a few people saw you guys get into the elevator together. I wouldn't be surprised if Johnny already knows."

Ryan dropped his head, his uncombed hair grazing the ketchup on his plate.

I stacked my bowl on his plate and placed them on a cart behind the buffet.

"Come on, big guy. It's time to buckle the chinstrap."

I got through my pregame duties at a measured pace, relishing the extra time afforded me from the early bus departure.

"Good job on getting the slideshow up," Garrett said.

"The extra time this morning really helped."

He pursed his thin lips.

"We need to talk to Johnny about the bus schedule. Things ran a lot more smoothly this morning with you getting here early."

"That would be really helpful, Garrett," I said, leaning back and stretching my arms. For a few seconds, I closed my eyes and listened to Johnny schmoozing the media sitting near our row in the press box.

"There's the man, the myth, the legend," Johnny said, clapping an ESPN writer on the back. "Great story on Andy."

It was the first time I had heard Johnny's voice since the episode on the bus. It made my skin prickle in disgust and anger. He was starting to repulse me *and* make me mad.

"All right, team. Get ready to rumble," Johnny said as I opened my eyes. He stood at the end of our press box row, fists pumping below his chin like a boxer.

He pounded the Bobbsey Twins' knuckles aggressively before crouching down next to me. I avoided making eye contact. Outrage still fumed inside me. Instead, I kept my eyes locked on my computer and halfheartedly extended my fist.

Johnny wiggled his fingers in an exaggerated blowup motion and leaned close to me.

"BB, that's a nice dress. But it looks like you're cheering for the other team. I'll forgive you because you look so good."

I straightened in my seat. *Shoot. Shoot. Shoot.* How could I not realize a leopard dress would make me appear like a traitor when the opposing team's mascot was a cheetah? I could only imagine what coaches and players thought when they saw me on the sidelines before the game.

"Should I change?" I asked. I was bouncing between feeling disgusted by Johnny's comment and embarrassed by a wardrobe gaffe.

Johnny's eyes narrowed.

"If we are losing in the second half, you should change."

"OK," I said and turned away from him as quickly as possible.

Out of the corner of my eye, I watched Johnny clutch Ryan's shoulders and lean over him.

"I hear you're a man now." Johnny howled in laughter. "Way to go, son."

I was speechless. Did Johnny just congratulate Ryan on hooking up with Alyssa? I shook my head in confusion. Since when did Johnny find hooking up with coworkers on a work trip acceptable?

I couldn't help but think that if the situation had been reversed—if I had hooked up with a male flight attendant—Johnny would have publicly shamed me and then fired me. With Ryan, Johnny was praising him and pumping his fists.

Fury flamed in my belly. I couldn't look at Johnny or Ryan. I knew it wasn't Ryan's fault. He hadn't influenced Johnny's reaction. But he embodied the infuriating double standard. My nostrils flared with each breath.

I stared at my computer and thought about what Garrett had said earlier. I needed to find a way to shelve my anger and concentrate on the game. For the sake of my interview with Devonte, I had to stay focused.

. . .

With the game scoreless at the end of the first quarter, there was little to update and post on the website. I did not mind the slower pace, but my interview with Devonte hinged on him having a spectacular game, so I silently pleaded for him to haul in some highlight-reel catches.

Quite the opposite happened. Three minutes into the second quarter, Andy threw an interception that led to a Cheetah field goal. With the Cheetahs leading 6–0 at the half, Andy stared in disbelief at the scoreboard as he jogged to the locker room.

"They're playing like a bunch of slappies out there. Coach was pissed as hell," Johnny barked when he returned to the press box after halftime.

"Should I go down and change?" I asked Johnny reluctantly.

"Not now, Blake. I don't have time to deal with your cheetah dress," Johnny growled.

I shook my head in silent annoyance.

Whatever Coach Bush said to the team at the half worked. In the third quarter, Andy threw over the middle to Devonte, who made two defenders miss and ran thirty yards for a touchdown. On OKC's next offensive possession, Andy flung the ball deep in the back of the end zone. Devonte outjumped the defender, flipped over his back, and scored his second touchdown of the game.

Johnny bolted from his seat and placed both hands on my shoulders. "Blake, this dress might actually be our lucky charm."

With a win secured in the fourth, Garrett divvied up duties.

"What about the one-on-one interview with Devonte?" I asked.

"Let's do it," Garrett said. "I will talk to Johnny after the press conferences."

I couldn't suppress the smile stretching across my face.

When Devonte took the podium for his presser, Sheridan asked if the defense gave him different looks in the second half. Devonte half laughed.

"No, the defense didn't do anything different. I just said to Andy, 'Give me the ball. I'll make a play.' So, he gave me the ball and I did what I promised. I made plays."

Sheridan nodded in satisfaction. It was a money quote, and she knew it.

After the press conference ended, Boss and I rushed to the locker room. Carson ushered in reporters.

"Open locker room has started. Out of courtesy to our players, please wait until they've put on shirts to begin interviews," he said to a TV anchor before allowing the door to slam in my face.

Boss stepped in front of me and told me, "Looks like I'll need to go in there first."

He knocked on the locker room door, and like a bouncer at a hotspot nightclub, Carson cracked open the door.

"I need to shoot open locker room and talk to Garrett," Boss grumbled. The door flung open and Boss disappeared into a sea of buzzing reporters.

I stood outside and waited. A few team scouts wheeled their bags past me, heading to the bus. I smiled quickly and looked back down at my phone. I was scrolling through my emails when I smelled Sheridan's tuberose perfume. She was flanked by her photographer and Jeremiah.

"Are you waiting on someone?" she said, tucking a tuft of brown hair behind her ear.

I looked up, feigning surprise. "Just going through an important email."

"It never stops," Sheridan said and knocked on the locker room door.

Carson opened it grandly, genuflecting slightly, saying in a fake British accent, "May I present Lady Sheridan."

Sheridan rolled her eyes. "You're ridiculous. Blake, go ahead."

"I'll wait out here," I said quickly.

Carson straightened his posture. "Yeah, Garrett and Johnny are talking about your interview. Someone will come out in a little bit and let you know what's going on."

Sheridan balked. "Why can't Blake just come in and talk to Johnny directly? Why does she have to wait outside?"

Carson deflected Sheridan's gaze to me, causing her to pivot and all four of them—Sheridan, her photographer, Jeremiah, and Carson—to stare intently at me, waiting for an answer.

I felt my palms sweat against the legal pad I was clutching.

"Well, um, I'm not really supposed to be in the locker room. It's, um, a team rule."

"Is it because you're a woman?" Sheridan asked pointedly. "Because that's workplace discrimination."

I was too ashamed to acknowledge that she was right. Instead, I stood there with everyone staring at me and said nothing at all.

Carson interjected, "Actually, Sheridan, this has nothing to do with gender. This is because Blake was called by HR for inappropriate dress. So, HR doesn't want her in the locker room."

Sheridan raised an eyebrow, unconvinced, and walked past him into the locker room, her photographer and Jeremiah trailing behind her.

"What the hell was that?" I hissed at Carson. I was on the precipice of losing it. So much for shelving my anger; I was fuming again.

"I couldn't throw Johnny under the bus, or the whole team for that matter. Sheridan could get on that women's rights high horse and do a bogus discrimination story on us. Seriously, I did the right thing."

"You threw *me* under the bus and made me look like an unprofessional floozy."

"Johnny did say you shouldn't have worn this dress today. It looks like you're cheering for the opponent. So, it's not that far off. Trust me. I was in the right," he said and let the door slam.

I stood motionless in disbelief, staring at the closed locker room door. I wanted to go in there and start screaming at all of them—Johnny, the Bobbsey Twins, even Ryan. There was only so much humiliation and shame a person could take.

Reporters trickled out of the locker room, and I did not even pretend to be busy. I just stared at them with my fists balled, ready to combust.

When Sheridan exited, she linked arms with mine.

"Come on," she told me. "We are interviewing Devonte at my set on the field."

Her photographer trotted behind us.

I started to process what was about to happen. "We are going to do an interview together?" I asked in disbelief.

"Yes. I want to do a dual interview on the Network," she said and handed a stick microphone to her photographer.

My eyes widened at what was unfolding before me. We approached a raised desk with the Network's logo that had been set up next to the field. A production assistant handed me a lavalier mic while her photographer clicked his camera into a tripod and adjusted the light stands.

My head was racing. Why was Sheridan including me in her interview? What was I going to ask Devonte? What did Johnny think of all of this?

"Close your eyes, take a deep breath, count to five," Sheridan said calmly. "You're going to be great."

A few seconds later, Johnny emerged from the tunnel with Devonte at his side. Johnny looked like a chihuahua trying to keep up with a gazelle, his stocky legs scampering to meet Devonte's long, graceful stride.

"All right, ladies, we've got five minutes. Literally," Johnny said, ushering Devonte to his spot at the end of the desk.

Sheridan cued the photographer to count us down and opened the segment, introducing Devonte and then me as the team's lead reporter. She asked the first question and after Devonte answered, nodded toward me.

The indignation preceding that moment dissipated in an instant. I felt secure and emboldened under Sheridan's wing.

"Devonte, you mentioned after the game that you approached Andy during halftime and told him to get you the ball. You promised you would make a play. Tell us more about this conversation."

Devonte grinned and looked up from the microphone he held. "You know, I'm a quiet guy. I don't say much on the field. When I talk, my teammates listen. Andy listened. He started looking for me and I started making plays."

Sheridan winked at me, signaling her approval. I almost melted. Interviewing Devonte with Sheridan Lane for the Network. Actually, I felt as if I *were* melting.

· · ·

"Did the interview air on the Network?" Ryan asked me.

I set my laptop on my tray table and plugged in my memory stick.

"It must have run during the bus ride to the airport because my phone was blowing up. I got tons of texts from friends who saw it."

"You realize you're famous now. So big-time," Ryan cooed.

"It was the coolest experience I've ever had. It totally validated my dreams of wanting to be a reporter just like Sheridan. It was all so natural and fun."

"Is Garrett putting the clip on the website?"

"Yes, Sheridan's photographer said they would send Boss the clip tonight. And to think, the day had been total hell until that point. It's funny how quickly things can change."

"You're telling me. I was a wreck about last night. But Johnny didn't care a bit, and Alyssa is acting completely normal, like nothing ever happened."

"Sounds like the best-case scenario," I said flatly. I was still annoyed with Ryan but much less so after my interview with Sheridan. It was hard to be mad at anyone right now. I was brimming with elation.

As the players exited the plane, I turned on my phone, my fingers fluttering as I scrolled through the congratulatory texts. Then, a new message appeared.

Come to the club. You look hot.

It was from a number that I didn't recognize. I felt a foot nudge mine as it passed my aisle seat. It was Seth's brown suede loafer. I peered up, and he pointed to his phone.

So much of me wanted to ride this euphoric high into the night. My body ached to press against Seth's muscular chest and dance with him until dawn. But the ramifications gnawed at my conscience. I would be risking my job, my connection to the Network. I had come too far to jeopardize that, especially now that I had Sheridan looking out for me.

Tempting . . . rain check?

Seth typed as he walked down the aisle. *I want nothing more. TTYL.*

Seventeen

Boots on the Ground

The rattle of coffee cups stirred me. I heard Mom's voice. Then Dad's.

"I'm worried about her. She hasn't had a day off since the season started. She's burning the candle at both ends, working until midnight and then waking up early to be at the stadium at dawn."

"Honey, that's football. You pay your dues, put in your hours."

I buried my head under my pillow. I had survived my first four weeks of the regular season on little sleep and lots of Twizzlers. It was not the healthiest existence, but I'd seen worse. Like the defensive line coach, who considered a king-sized bag of potato chips to be his sustenance for the day. He walked from his office to meeting rooms to film rooms shoveling sour cream and onion chips into his mouth and leaving a trail of crumbs in his wake.

"Blake, I made you a latte," Mom chirped from the staircase.

"Coming," I said and threw back my fluffy, white duvet.

It was the first week of October. While the air still was warm, there was a slight crispness to it, signaling the end of summer. I stepped into an old, sleeveless blue sundress. It was time to invest in some fall work clothes—so much for the cheetah dress being my last purchase until Christmas.

As my wedge sandals clomped against the wooden stairs, Mom rushed my latte to the microwave to warm it up.

"Thanks, Mom. I was so tired this morning I decided to sleep in."

She carefully placed the steaming coffee mug in front of me.

"You needed it. You leave each morning before sunrise and come home well after sunset. I've been worried about you."

I encircled the warm coffee mug in both hands. "You don't need to worry. Working late is just part of the job. Something always comes up. Like last night, Garrett wanted me to rewrite a story about Coach Bush for the *Gameday Magazine* the team hands out at home games. I didn't finish the story until after midnight."

Dad set down the business section. "I told your mom that's life in pro football. But I am glad to see you getting caught up on your sleep."

"You will also be glad to know that with Johnny out all morning, today should be low-key."

Mom handed me a bowl of granola, saying, "I'm not sure the league knows how to do anything low-key."

. . .

Mom had a point. There was nothing low-key about a pro football season, but there was a much slower pace on Tuesdays. It was the players' off day, meaning they did not have to practice, but many often came to the stadium to treat an ailing body part, lift weights, or watch film, none of which the media could cover. Instead, all coverage was directed to community appearances, usually held Tuesday afternoons.

It often was an easy, feel-good story about a player and the team doing good, a PR stunt in Johnny's eyes. The community appearances were some of my favorite stories, a chance to see the players unguarded, watch them laugh, play, and help those in less fortunate circumstances.

I skimmed the release for Marcus's appearance that day. *Star Quarterback to Guide and Mentor Inner City Children: Oklahoma City rookie quarterback Marcus Dixon will lead children at a local YMCA through 60 minutes of exercises and then share an inspiring story.*

The story was a total layup. Pro quarterback with local ties inspires young children to be more active and dream big. I had the story outlined by 10:00 a.m. and meandered into the break room for a bottle of water.

Emily stood over a box of kolaches. A stack of sparkling David Yurman bracelets jingled as she pointed to the plump pastries.

"You're too skinny to eat these, but I've got a booty to feed," she told me.

I shook my head. "For the record, I've been here so late and been so desperate that I've eaten leftover kolaches for dinner."

"That's tragic," Emily said, before taking a dainty bite.

"I know. I had indigestion for days."

She dabbed the corner of her mouth with a waxy napkin.

"Sorry, I didn't mean to offend you with the skinny comment. What I meant is that you have an awesome figure."

"No offense taken."

"Don't be so bashful. You should flaunt what you've got. Everything you wear is so innocent, except for that sassy leopard dress you wore on TV. That dress had the players talking you up big-time." Emily winked before taking another bite.

I couldn't help but wonder if Emily had heard anything about me and Seth. Since the Cheetah game two weeks earlier, we had texted each other nonstop.

When I woke up, I had received the text, *Morning, sunshine. I'm thinking about you*, to which I replied, *I'm thinking about you too. I think about you too much!*

I was nervous someone would see our texts. The team claimed to monitor phones it issued to players and personnel. But Seth had assured me he was texting from a secure number, his Bat-phone, as he called it. He explained all players had secret phones for business they didn't want the team to know about.

I smoothed my loose dress, which looked more like a burlap sack next to Emily's shiny black pants and black stiletto heels.

"There's actually something I've been wanting to buy," I told her, thinking about the knee-high boots from the magazine. The page I ripped out still was in my satchel's zip pocket.

"How about we break out of here at lunch for a quick shopping trip?" she suggested.

The idea of leaving the stadium during lunch never occurred to me. I usually worked at my desk, eating from the cafeteria's to-go container.

But that day I had nothing pressing, no reason to stay chained to my cubicle.

"Let's do it!"

Emily's aqua eyes flickered.

"That's what I like to hear. I sold a suite yesterday and deserve something fabulous."

An hour and a half later, I strutted into the stadium in my newest purchases. A fitted sweater dress hugged all the right places, and the knee-high black boots added the perfect amount of work-appropriate sex appeal.

"This feels like the scene from *Pretty Woman*," Emily said as our heels clicked through the concourse. "You look amazing."

I tossed my hair behind my shoulders.

"To be honest, I've never felt so glamorous," I said, stopping in front of the cafeteria. "Thank you. I had a lot of fun today."

"Me too. The players are going to crane their necks when they see you."

There was only one player I cared about impressing—Seth. I had worn my new clothes, hoping to run into him before I left for my story. "I'm going to grab a snack in the cafeteria. Want anything?" I asked.

"Nah, I've got an early dinner with my man."

As giddy as I was about my new clothes, I was equally excited about my burgeoning friendship with Emily. While we combed through boutiques, I quickly learned that Emily's love language was fashion—and sharing her expertise on it. She pulled armloads of clothes for me, ogling over some, dismissing others, and extolling the importance of accessories. Our conversations remained surface level, speaking in generalities about the team and our jobs.

"It's definitely a lot of work. There's some curveballs I didn't expect," I told her when she asked me about traveling for road games. When I asked Emily about her impressions of the organization, she shrugged her shoulders.

"It's a job. It's paid the bills for the last two years, but I won't be doing it forever."

Neither of us asked the other to go deeper and share more, but we laid a foundation for building trust.

The cafeteria door slammed. A raspy voice began to hum the Nancy Sinatra song, "These Boots Are Made for Walkin.'" Scooter, the cornerbacks coach, walked toward me.

"Summer Breeze, I'm going to start calling you Boots from now on," he said, removing his bifocals and hanging them on the neck of his gray sweatshirt.

"Boots. I'm down with that nickname," I said.

"Well, those boots suit you well."

"Thanks, Coach!" I said, emboldened by his compliment and my new nickname.

I met Boss and Garrett outside the locker room. "You look different today for some reason," Garrett said.

"It's those fancy boots she's wearing." Boss pointed at my feet.

"Maybe." Garrett frowned.

"Garrett, I didn't know you were joining us," I said, redirecting the conversation.

"I'm writing a feature on Marcus's mother who overcame breast cancer. It is the perfect tie-in to our Breast Cancer Awareness game this Sunday, and it has potential to be award-winning content for the site," he said proudly. "I want to interview Marcus without other media catching wind of my information. The car ride is the perfect place."

Marcus stepped out of the locker room, handsomely dressed in a navy team polo and khaki pants. He and Garrett wore the exact outfit, but it couldn't look more different on them. The shirt hung off Garrett's lanky frame, while Marcus's swelling biceps threatened to rip through the sleeves.

The third-string quarterback with a soft smile tugged at his collar. "Hey, man, we're twins."

Garrett's mouth twitched before giving way to a giant grin.

• • •

When Marcus entered the gymnasium at the YMCA, the children leaped from their seats and erupted into screams.

He jogged to the podium, high-fiving children along the way.

"Hi, my friends! It's a beautiful day here at the YMCA. I'm so happy to be with you. Believe it or not, I sat right where you are ten years ago. I used to play rec sports where I grew up not far from here."

The children listened with their eyes wide and attentive. Marcus told them about the importance of physical activity and the lessons he gained through playing sports.

"Now, are you ready to play?" he shouted. The children jumped up and cheered wildly. Marcus beamed as he raced the children around cones and helped them jump over blocks.

I watched him encourage a young girl with thick glasses who was shying away from the drills. This was what made athletes so important, I thought to myself. Their capacity to inspire people from all walks of life. This was when athletes were at their best.

As the event wound down and the YMCA staff directed the children to folding tables for fresh fruit and granola bars, I approached Marcus. Perspiration glistened on his smooth forehead.

"This is the best part of being in pro football—making a difference. Don't get me wrong, I enjoy throwing touchdowns. But this gives me a different kind of satisfaction."

It was the perfect quote for the perfect ending to my story.

Eighteen

A Clutch Performance

A rare, early October cool front had blown into Oklahoma City, and tailgaters were relishing every bit of the perfect football weather. The parking lots were completely packed by 9:00 a.m. with fans clutching beers and debating the strengths of their 3–1 team.

It was a crucial game, a divisional game against Los Angeles. A win would put OKC atop the division as the team headed into the most challenging stretch of the schedule.

I skipped through the concourse in my new boots, slowing my gait in front of the locker room in hopes of seeing Seth.

He had not asked me to meet up since the night of the Cheetah game, but we continued to text with reckless abandon. I was pushing the boundaries of the team's policies, communicating this much with a player. But there had been no physical contact between us and most of our texts qualified as PG-rated, like:

Seth: *What are you doing right now?*

Me: *I'm out to dinner with my friends.*

Seth: *I wish we were eating out together. It's another boring grilled chicken dinner in the hotel ballroom.*

Me: *Why do you guys stay at a hotel before home games?*

Seth: *To keep players out of trouble and focused. We have team meetings. Officer Frosted Tips checks curfew at 11.*

Me: *That's no fun.*

Seth: *I know! I need your company!*

At that point, I apologized for being on my phone and excused myself from dinner, telling my friends I needed to handle a work emergency. It was an excuse they had heard a lot this season.

I had hardly seen my friends since I joined the team. I worked late nights and weekends, so I had missed catching up over happy hours, celebrating at birthday dinners, or traveling for weddings. I also could sense we had a lot less in common these days. They worked to pay the bills while focusing on their relationships and dreaming of marriage. I was working around the clock, trying to build a career.

We were navigating different stages in life. Planning a wedding shower that I couldn't even attend didn't appeal to me right now. If I had free time, I wanted to cuddle in my bed and give my full attention to Seth. My full cellular attention, that was.

When I got home that night, Mom and Dad were reclining in armchairs and giggling at a romantic comedy they'd found on TV.

"You're back early," Mom said, taking a sip of tea. Dad lifted a bowl of popcorn. "Come sit. I popped the buttery kind that you like."

"I'm beat. Big day tomorrow. See you in the morning," I said, racing upstairs to my room. I kicked off my shoes, jumped into bed, and checked my text messages.

Seth: *So, what does Blake Kirk like to do? Outside of covering football.*

Me: *Read. In first grade, Charlotte's Web transformed my life. I cried for Charlotte's death and for my own mortality. Ever since, I've been a voracious reader.*

Seth: *Wow. That was deep.*

Me: *I'm a nerd at heart.*

Seth: *That's what makes you so amazing. You're incredibly smart and incredibly beautiful.*

Me: *I'm blushing. Let's change subjects.*

Seth: *I don't want to change subjects. I like talking about you.*

Me: *What do you like to do? Outside of playing football.*

Seth: *The guitar. I taught myself to read music and play when I was 13. My friend's mom played a Bob Dylan cassette in her car during carpool. I became obsessed.*

Me: *Color me impressed. And surprised.*

Our exchange continued until we dozed off with our phones in our hands. Despite not getting much sleep, I had woken up giddy for what the crisp October game day held in store.

"What a glorious day!" I said, waving to Officer Frosted Tips, who stood outside the team's locker room.

"This here, young lady, is what they call football weather. It's so nice, they're rolling open the roof."

"I've never been to a game here when the roof is open."

"They only do it once, maybe twice a year. Some coaches think the open stadium isn't as loud. You lose the homefield advantage. I think this is how football is supposed to be played."

The locker room door flew open.

"Hey, Boots," a cornerback said as he trotted past me.

"Like your new nickname?" Officer Frosted Tips smiled.

"Love it!" There was something about being called Boots that made me feel like I belonged. The players and coaches were treating me like I was one of them. No matter how much Johnny boxed me out, I had a team nickname to call my own.

. . .

Garrett sat alone at the end of our row in the press box. I set down my laptop and leaned over the empty seat between us.

"Any sign of Ryan? I didn't see him on the field," I said.

"Nope," Garrett said without turning from his computer.

"That's strange. He usually gets here extra early before home games."

"You know what's also strange? Your new nickname. What's up with that?" Garrett said with an edge to his voice.

"One of the coaches started it. I guess it stuck."

"It's not very professional," he said and folded his arms.

It hadn't occurred to me that the nickname Boots could be regarded as unprofessional. There were so many unethical situations transpiring on the team, how could I define what constituted professional work-place behavior?

Last weekend, I had ridden an elevator with a prostitute hired to give a player a quickie at the hotel before dinner. Johnny routinely commented on reporters' chests and butts in our department meetings. The nickname Boots seemed harmless in comparison.

"It's definitely not business decorum, but I think it's all in good fun," I said. "Like how the players all call Ryan 'Intern.'"

Almost on cue, a message from Ryan appeared on my phone: *Shit. Just leaving Stillwater. Went to the game last night and slept through my alarm. Will miss the first quarter. Can you cover for me? Shit. Shit. Shit.*

I glanced at Garrett, who was back to obsessing about the Game Day page, and quickly typed, *It's OK. I've got your back.*

I set down my phone and made a mental checklist of Ryan's pregame assignments. It was a good thing this was a home game and I was not screeching in an hour before kickoff on the Blake Bus.

"Unacceptable!" Garrett said, pounding his fist against the desk. "Ryan is having car problems in Stillwater. He won't be here for a couple of hours. Blake, can you handle his assignments?"

"Of course."

For the next couple of hours, I moved like Bo Jackson hitting a hole on the way to the end zone. Lightning fast and unstoppable.

Halfway through the first quarter with LA up a touchdown, Ryan slinked quietly into the press box with his head hanging low. White shirttails hung over his wrinkled, navy suit—his only suit, which he either had forgotten to launder or left wadded in his car all weekend.

When he saw Johnny's seat empty, his eyelids closed in momentary relief. I smiled sympathetically as he began the walk of shame down our row.

"Nice of you to join us, Ryan," Garrett said, his dark eyes storming with anger.

Ryan stared at his worn penny loafers.

"Being late to a game is a punishable offense. I'll discuss the consequences with Johnny after the game. Right now, I need you to get to work," Garrett said. "And fix your hair."

Ryan patted the mangled mess.

"Garrett, I'm really sorry. It's a long story, but I know I messed up," he said.

"Stop talking and start working," Garrett snarled.

Ryan blinked back tears as he opened his laptop. He had created this mess, but I hated seeing a good friend languish. *This too shall pass*, I scribbled on the notepad between us.

"Thank you," Ryan mouthed.

Ryan, Garrett, and I worked in silence, none of us saying a word until the start of the fourth quarter. With the team down a touchdown, it still was unclear what our story lines and assignments would be.

"Garrett, what are you thinking about for postgame?" I asked.

"Not sure. Let's give it a few more possessions," he said as we watched Andy kneel in the huddle.

Andy stood up and clapped. The offense hustled to the line of scrimmage. It was a play-action pass. He ran to his right and sensed pressure. Instead of going through his progressions, he panicked and threw a wobbler to the tight end. LA's cornerback read it perfectly, intercepted the pass, and took it back for a touchdown.

The crowd collectively stared at the field, stunned in disbelief. In a matter of seconds, the team was down fourteen points, and Andy was clutching his ankle, writhing in pain on the turf. While players from both teams took a knee, Seth warmed up on the sidelines, dropping back three steps and throwing tight spirals.

"Just when I thought this day couldn't get any worse," Garrett grumbled. "All postgame reports are on standby until we hear from Johnny on Andy's status."

When Seth trotted onto the field, I scooted to the edge of my seat. After our night of texting, I felt more connected to the team with him in the game, more invested in the outcome.

On first down, Seth dropped back and hit Devonte for a 39-yard gain. Six plays later, Seth scored on a quarterback draw to get the team within a touchdown. My heart welled with pride as he jumped into Monster Calves's outstretched arms.

With renewed life, the defense made a stop. Seth retook the field with four minutes on the clock, the game squarely in his hands. He marched the team into LA territory, converting on every third down. With less than a minute to play, he connected with Devonte in the back of the end zone. The fans screamed wildly as Devonte jumped into the stands behind the end zone.

"Do you think Coach will go for two?" I whispered to Ryan.

"No way. I'm sure he'd rather kick and take his chances in overtime," Ryan said.

But on the field, Seth held up two fingers and the offense huddled around him.

"Holy shit. He's lost his mind," Garrett spat out.

Seth took the snap. LA brought pressure. Seth scrambled to his right. A broken play. I gripped the sides of my seat. Seth spun and scrambled back left. He threw a dart to the middle of the end zone and hit a wide-open Devonte for the two-point conversion. Instinctively, I leaped from my seat and clutched my heart.

"Holy shit," Garrett said, shaking his head. "We've got our story. Blake, hurry down to the pressers."

Johnny dutifully took his place on the edge of the stage and announced, "The team is four and one and in first place in the division. Coach Bush will now take questions from the media."

Coach hunched over the podium and lowered the microphone.

"Quick update on Andy. He's got what looks like a high ankle sprain. It's getting looked at right now. We'll know more tonight. He's our starting quarterback. But if he can't go, we feel good about our number two. Seth battled today. I'm real proud of him and all our guys for their effort. It was a big win for this team."

Sheridan's hand shot up.

"You started throwing deep when Seth went in. The offense sparked. What changed offensively with him under center?"

"Our backs were against the wall. It wasn't the time to run the ball. We felt comfortable letting Seth run play-action pass. Seth found Devonte a couple of times for some big plays."

"What made you decide to go for two?" Sheridan blurted out again.

"Seth was in command of the game. He was in a rhythm. As a former quarterback, I know how that feels. I liked our chances on going for two right then and there. And it worked out."

Satisfied, Sheridan sat back down and let other reporters have their turns.

"Coach's presser is now over. Up next, quarterback Seth Barker."

A few minutes later, Seth walked proudly to the podium. My body fluttered at the sight of his wet, tousled hair and green-flinted hazel eyes. He looked polished and relaxed in a gray V-neck sweater and blue-checkered button-down shirt.

Reporters fired away questions. The media chuckled in unison at Seth's witty answers, and I tossed back my head, dizzy with delight.

• • •

Emily flung her Louis Vuitton tote bag on the ground in my cube and folded her arms.

"Are you seriously working all night after a win like that?"

I rubbed my eyes, which ached from staring at a computer screen for the last eleven hours.

"I don't have a choice. We have tons of content to post."

Garrett had handed out a steady stream of assignments after the pressers. While he didn't give me any one-on-one interviews, I wrote all the top stories, while Ryan transcribed and handled the grunt work. Of course, Ryan assumed these duties with little complaint, knowing the worst of punishments was yet to come.

"That's totally lame. I'm going home to change before I meet the guys at the club. You should come when you're done."

"I wish I could, but I will be here past midnight."

"Girl, that's when the party gets going. Coach gave the players tomorrow off. It's getting lit tonight," Emily said, sticking out her bottom and pumping it in the air.

I leaned back in my chair and giggled.

"Tempting, but I have to pass. I'm really tired."

"That's an even lamer excuse. You do realize that I was sent here because a player is requesting your presence. I'm not sure who. But my man told me to make sure you come tonight."

My cheeks flushed. I imagined Seth wrapping his arms around me and holding me tight as we surrendered to the night. There was nothing I wanted more. But the consequences would be far too severe. If I wanted to be with Seth, I had to wait until at least the offseason. That's what I kept telling myself.

"Emily, I would get into a lot of trouble if I went with you."

"Really? I told you those sexpot assistants in scouting are going to the clubs all the time. No one seems to care."

"My position is different. I cover the team and travel with them. I can't risk it."

"This place is so effed up. Different standards for different people," Emily said and picked up her purse. "There's a guy in that locker room who's going to be really disappointed."

I texted Seth. *Wish I could go tonight. Too much work. You played awesome!*

He texted back. *You're breaking my heart! It won't be the same without you.*

I closed my eyes. As much as I wanted to be with Seth, I had made the right decision. Really, I had no other choice.

Nineteen

Heartless

"Mondays are a lot more fun when you're winning," Johnny said, clapping his hands against his desk. "Four and one, baby. Leading the division. That's what I'm talking about."

The Bobbsey Twins pumped their fists in the air. Our department was gathering in Johnny's office for our regular weekly meeting. After the previous day's win, excitement permeated the stadium. The coaches played their music a little louder that morning. Scouts high-fived over breakfast tacos in the break room. Even Garrett smiled at me when I walked by his office.

The only person utterly dejected was Ryan, who was quivering in the corner of Johnny's office, chewing on his nails as he awaited his punishment for arriving late to the game.

Johnny lowered himself into his leather desk chair.

"Everyone knows that Andy has a high ankle sprain. He's going to miss a few weeks. Seth will start on Sunday. Then we have the bye week."

Johnny leaned forward, his eyes scanning the room. "For nosy media asking about when Andy is coming back, just tell them we'll know more after the bye week. We aren't going to play into their talk of a quarterback controversy. Andy is our starter. Seth is taking his place this Sunday. End of story."

We nodded obediently.

"A little bit of housekeeping. Garrett, you can take Kimmie off the cheerleading page on the site. She's off the squad. She went to the club with the players last night. Fired," Johnny said with his best Donald Trump impersonation.

I gulped. That very well could have been me. If I had caved to Emily and danced the night away with Seth, the team would be erasing *me* from the site while I cried in my parents' house over blowing up my career before it even started. It was a bitter reminder about the parameters of my relationship with Seth.

"All right, we are done here. Everyone out, except Ryan," Johnny said.

I looked at Ryan, half expecting to see a puddle of urine pooling at his feet. His hands trembled as he steadied himself against a chair in front of Johnny's desk. I shut the door and cringed empathically.

. . .

"It's the ultimate VIP experience, the premiere way to entertain clients. There's the catered buffet, fully stocked bar; even the cheerleaders come to say hello," Emily said, laying on the charm in a sales pitch call.

I was totally distracted. It had been two hours since Johnny's morning meeting and no word from Ryan. I imagined him rocking back and forth under his desk, sucking his thumb. Or worse. Fired.

"Come to the stadium for a tour. I personally will show you the amazing view from this suite," Emily paused, dipping into a throaty voice. "And the view of me isn't bad either. OK, great. See you on Friday."

I minimized the stats page I was updating and wandered to Emily's cubicle. Photos from LSU sorority parties, family hunting escapades, and team events covered the blah fabric walls of her cube.

"I never would have pegged you for a hunter," I said, studying a photo of her in a camouflage jumpsuit, leaning against a jeep with three young men inside.

"I grew up in small-town Louisiana. You shoot to eat."

She pointed at the men in the jeep.

"And I had three big brothers. I had no choice. I was going to deer blinds as soon as I could walk."

"No wonder you're so tough."

"Yeah, they roughed me up some. I'm grateful for that. It's what makes me good at this job. I never back down from a fight."

"You certainly know how to sell."

"I work what God gave me," Emily said with a shimmy.

I couldn't help but laugh as her cleavage jiggled back and forth.

"Hey, want to grab dinner one night this week?"

"Are you asking me on a girl date?" Emily said, leaning back in her chair.

"I thought it would be fun to get to know each other better."

"I've never been on a girl date before." Emily paused. "Let's do it. How about dinner at my place on Saturday? We can watch the LSU game."

"Great!"

There was so much I wanted to ask Emily: how she and Devonte started dating, why the team allowed it, what she thought of Seth. I walked back to my desk, daydreaming about what Emily's apartment would look like. Maybe bathed in pink.

Inside my cube, my phone rattled against my desk. Texts from Ryan:

> *Johnny came at me hard. Yelled at me then sent me down to clean up shit in the locker room. Literally shit. An assistant coach drank too much coffee and didn't make it to the toilet in time.*
>
> *I'm on probation for the next month. Any slipup and I get the pink slip. Johnny's exact quote.*
>
> *This is my last chance and I'm not going to let anyone down. Most of all myself.*

I was stunned. And it was not because a coach pooped on the locker room floor. Ryan was late to the game because he partied at his alma mater, and the consequences were manual labor. I expected Ryan's punishment to be more severe. I was happy for Ryan because it was clear Johnny believed in him and wanted to give him a second chance. But I couldn't help but wonder what my punishment would be for making the same mistake.

I texted back, *A lot to discuss. Especially about poop-gate. Gross.*

Ryan responded. *It was like a crime scene until the carpet cleaners got there.*

Maybe Ryan's punishment was worse than I thought. I chuckled to myself and texted back. *As you said, this job can be a shitstorm.*

· · ·

Fashionable twentysomethings held dog leashes in one hand and wine glasses in the other outside the café on the ground floor of Emily's apartment complex. The newly constructed stucco and glass building sat near the heart of the city, blocks from trendy restaurants and stores.

A few of my high school friends lived nearby. Guilt gnawed at me for not reaching out to them. But they didn't understand how much my life had changed since I started this job.

I pressed the button for the seventh floor. When the doors opened, I followed Taylor Swift's voice to Emily's apartment and knocked loudly.

"Coming!"

Emily flung open the door, wearing a pink Adidas tracksuit and white platform sneakers.

"I was picking things up and needed a little Tay Tay to help me clean. Come on in," Emily said and motioned for me to follow her inside.

Emily led me to an all-white marble kitchen that looked like it had never been used.

"Wow, your place is beautiful, so fresh and modern," I said, eyeing the Lucite chairs at the kitchen counter that looked like they were floating.

"Thanks," she said and removed a bottle of Pinot Grigio and a charcuterie platter from the refrigerator. "I'd be lying if I said I cooked a lot here. I order most of my food from the café downstairs."

She pointed to a couple boxes of crackers. "Do you mind opening those and putting them on a plate? I'll grab us some glasses."

As I arranged the crackers, I glanced around Emily's apartment. Almost everything was decorated in white. White leather dining room chairs accompanied a white marble table. A white angular sofa faced a white lacquer media console. Even the pillows and throws were white.

"Your furniture, the whole vibe—it's so fancy," I said.

"Doesn't it feel like a winter wonderland? Devonte's decorator helped me," Emily said, filling the wine glasses.

"Does Devonte live nearby?" I asked and followed her to the couch.

"No, he lives in a McMansion out in the burbs. His two brothers live with him. During the season, I stay out there a couple of nights a week. Usually Sundays after games and Mondays before his day off."

Emily took a long sip of Pinot Grigio.

"During the offseason, I basically live there. Sleep isn't much of a priority, if you know what I mean," Emily said, licking her full lips.

"Are you close with his brothers?"

"Oh yeah. They're great. One of them is on Devonte's management team and the other runs his foundation. He wanted to take care of them, but he also wanted them to earn their keep. To their credit, they've worked hard."

Emily twirled her long blonde hair at the nape of her neck and secured it in a loose bun, allowing a few perfectly curled tendrils to fall loose around her face.

"Does their mom live here too?" I asked.

"No, she's still in Jersey. It's more complicated with her. Devonte helps her a lot. He wants her to move here and get away from her exes. But she won't do it. She keeps getting sucked into destructive relationships. It's really sad."

There was so much I wanted to learn about Emily. The questions kept tumbling out of my mouth with no end in sight.

"What about your family? They must think it's so cool that you're dating a famous football player," I said.

Emily pulled in her legs tight, curling herself into a ball.

"My relationship with Devonte is a huge source of tension with my family."

"I'm sorry. I had no idea."

"My family comes from rural Louisiana. There was one high school in my town and the seniors got to vote on having a segregated prom. My class voted yes. I'm not trying to make excuses for my family," Emily said, looking down at her knees. "My parents can't understand why I would want to date a Black man. They think I can do much better."

Her voice trembled with anger.

"They'll cheer like hell for LSU football, a team that's mostly Black. But when it comes to me dating a Black player, they won't allow it. It pisses me off."

"How does Devonte handle that?"

"It upsets him, for sure. But he says he's used to people like my parents."

Emily leaned back and closed her eyes. When she opened them, her gaze was softer, almost wistful.

"Just thinking about him makes me happy. He's really the sweetest man. He treats me like a princess and has the most tender side to him."

"I can't believe your parents don't want you and Devonte together," I said, still shocked by this revelation. If I was in Emily's shoes, my parents would have invited Devonte over for steaks after our first date.

"I've thought about cutting my family out of my life, but I can't bring myself to do it," Emily said and blinked back tears. "There's so much hate out there. I see Devonte deal with it on a daily basis. It kills me to know that my parents are some of the biggest haters of them all."

I squeezed Emily's hand sympathetically.

"I'm so sorry, Emily. This all must be really painful."

"It actually feels good to talk about this with someone who doesn't judge our relationship."

"I am always here if you want to talk. No judgment."

Emily leaned toward me. "All of this about my family stays between us. You can't say anything."

"I promise to keep it confidential."

I looked up and asked the question that had been burning inside me for weeks. "How do you keep your relationship with Devonte a secret?"

Emily let out a small laugh. "Oh, all the coaches and players know we're dating. They just pretend nothing is going on when we're inside the stadium. Somehow most of the staff and media are clueless. I guess that's a good thing, since technically I could be fired for it."

"I'm surprised the coaches and people like Johnny don't care."

She shrugged. "Maybe they turn a blind eye because Devonte's happy and he's having an All-Pro season. Or maybe I'm too removed from their daily lives since I work over in sales."

"You've mentioned the women who work in scouting. What's their deal?" I asked.

"There's two of them. Both young and pretty. They work in the dungeon of the scouting office, so no one ever sees them. It's a sucky job. They make millions of files on all the players being scouted. In their free time, they plot how to hang out with the players and coaches. They always end up at the club after games, grinding on some player. It's embarrassing."

"Why doesn't HR do something about it?"

"Those girls work strictly for football ops. Unless a coach, the GM, or Johnny complains, then HR isn't doing a thing. HR leaves football ops alone."

"I'm surprised Johnny hasn't said something. That isn't his style."

"That's because Johnny is too busy letting these girls rub up against him."

My mouth dropped open in shock.

"You've got to be kidding me. Johnny's dancing with coworkers at the club?" I said, shaking my head in disbelief. "I can't go in the locker room to do my job and he can dance with assistants at the club. That makes no sense."

Emily looked at me squarely.

"It's not fair, but it does make sense. You work directly for Johnny. He doesn't want to have any connection to a reason why a player didn't play well in a game. You're too much of a liability for him."

"I give up. These double standards are impossible to navigate."

"That's why you've got to just live your life," Emily said, curling her legs behind her. "By the way, I've heard that Seth's been crushing on you."

My eyes widened. How did Emily know?

"Oh, it's nothing. We just text," I said nonchalantly.

"That's how things started with Devonte. He got my number and we started texting. Be careful with Seth, but I'm sure you know that."

My mouth dried. I did not know that. And for some reason, I did not want to.

"I'll be careful," I said softly.

· · ·

It was three hours before kickoff and Ryan was working on his laptop in the press box when I set my satchel in the seat next to him. "Well, look who's here bright and early."

Ryan's thick hair was perfectly coiffed and his suit neatly pressed.

"Too much is on the line for me to mess this up. I even stayed in last night and made myself a pasta dinner. I wanted to come in fresh and rested for game day."

"You look it. I, on the other hand, am moving a little slow. Too much wine with Emily last night."

Ryan's head recoiled in surprise.

"You hung out with Emily? What did you guys talk about?"

"Girl stuff that's none of your beeswax."

"Fair enough. I'm just surprised. I didn't know you were friends."

"What are you two hens clucking about?" Johnny chirped as he walked down our row. "And yes, Ryan, I called you a hen. You like to cluck with the best of them."

"Ryan was telling me about his pasta recipe."

I shot Ryan a glaring look, a warning not to mention Emily.

"As I said, Ryan loves to cluck."

Johnny gave my shoulders a long squeeze and I fought the urge to gag.

"I heard something about Johnny last night and can't look at him the same," I whispered to Ryan.

"Really? What?"

"Tell you later. I need to go get the photo cards from the field."

"That's totally unfair," Ryan said, shaking his head. "You can't dangle juicy tidbits out there and then walk off."

"Watch me."

Kanye West's "Heartless" blared from the field. I walked through the tunnel and saw Seth warming up at midfield. My pulse quickened as he dropped back, his long, muscular legs flexing and extending in motion.

Most of the city would be watching Seth take the field. They'd root for him, criticize his play, imitate his throws in the backyard. But only I had wished him sweet dreams the night before. I was the only person he called his good luck charm.

I found Monte crouched on the sidelines, his camera angled at Seth.

"Any good ones?"

Monte popped out the card reader.

"Your basic warm-up shots. But there's a great close-up of Devonte and Seth fist-bumping. Would be good as the cover to the slideshow."

"Thanks, my friend. See you after the first quarter."

I stood up and caught Seth eyeing me. He wiped his hands on the towel tucked into the waist of his pants and smiled wide. Every part of me wanted to run across the field and hug him. Instead, I gave a discreet thumbs-up and skipped off the field.

On the elevator ride up to the press box, I thought of Emily's warning: "Be careful with Seth."

What did she mean by that? Was he a womanizer? He had been the starting quarterback at Florida. I could assume he slept with half the Gators cheerleading squad, even though the thought made me nauseous.

Really, what pro player didn't have a past? It was almost part of the job description. But there was something about Seth that set him apart from the other players I'd met, a kindheartedness and vulnerability that he shared with me.

After I had gotten home from hanging out with Emily, Seth had called because he was too nervous to sleep. He said he'd started a handful of games the previous season, but that had been a year ago. The team was playing much better football now and there was a lot more pressure on his shoulders. I told him to trust himself. He had pulled off the most improbable win last week. He could do anything. He thanked me for comforting him and said just hearing my voice put his mind at ease. He said there was something about me that always made him happy.

I clutched the photo card in my palm and prayed for a win.

The first two quarters had me walking on air. Seth brilliantly orchestrated the offense. He spread the ball around, hit his tight ends in space, and connected deep with Devonte. OKC entered the half with a ten-point lead and the crowd on its feet.

"Wow, Seth is making a case for himself as the starter. Andy might be 'hurt' for a while," Ryan said, tossing air quotes around "hurt."

I gazed at the field with pride. "Yeah, he's been awesome today."

When the team retook the field for the third quarter, I grabbed a pair of binoculars from the Bobbsey Twins and watched Seth kneel in front of the huddled offense. As he dumped the ball to the tight end, the crowd fell silent. Devonte was lying on the other side of the field, clutching his knee.

I gasped. The head trainer and the team's orthopedic surgeon sprinted to Devonte.

"Eff me," Ryan mumbled.

My eyes darted to a press box TV for a replay. There was Devonte, his leg buckling as he cut across the field.

Players from both teams lowered to one knee and trainers lifted Devonte onto a gurney. The fans clapped solemnly, paying their respects to the receiver in what felt like a funeral procession. Devonte waved meekly as the flatbed cart carrying him exited the field.

No one in the press box spoke. I grabbed the binoculars again and studied Seth. His face was stricken, his eyes dazed. The offense took the line of scrimmage like an inner tube that had leaked air, sagging and deflated.

Seth got the snap and handed off to the running back. Fumble on the exchange. A defensive end jumped on the loose ball for the turnover.

"This is not good," Ryan said with a clenched jaw.

Seth walked to the bench on the sidelines and threw down his helmet. I ached to go down there, to have him see me, but now wasn't the time.

Johnny marched into the press box. He grabbed the press box PA phone, slamming it against his desk before picking up the receiver.

"Attention. Devonte has a knee injury. He has been ruled out for the rest of the game."

"No shit, Johnny," yelled a crusty beat reporter from his desk. "What are the doctors thinking? Dislocation? Tear?"

"He's getting looked at now. We'll know more tonight," Johnny said, forcing out a measured tone. Then he balled his hand and pounded the desk.

A few minutes later, an ESPN writer shouted, "Johnny, I've got an agent saying it's a torn ACL."

Johnny inhaled sharply. "You know I don't speculate on injuries."

He crouched between the Bobbsey Twins and whispered, "ACL. Done for the season."

The rest of the game was a blur of disasters. Ryan and I looked at each other, stunned as the clock ticked to zero with OKC down four points.

"I can't believe we just blew that game," I said, shaking my head in disbelief.

"Seth totally lost it," Ryan said. "After Devonte went down, he fell apart."

My stomach dropped. For some reason, I felt responsible. Like I didn't say or do enough to encourage him the night before.

"I need to talk to you guys," Garrett said. He'd been so quiet at the end of our row I forgot he still was there.

He bent down between me and Ryan. "We're getting tons of traffic on the site. Fans want updates on Devonte. I want to capitalize on this. But Johnny is very strict when it comes to injuries. We don't release information until Coach holds a presser with an official diagnosis."

I clicked on an ESPN story. "But it looks like his agent is confirming Devonte tore his ACL."

"I know. That is what makes our site look foolish. We can't post anything until Johnny has talked with Coach about how he wants to proceed."

I thought of Emily. She was probably with Devonte at that very moment.

"Garrett, I have a source who could get us great quotes."

Garrett shook his head.

"It doesn't matter. Johnny won't let me run the story."

"So, what do we do?" Ryan asked.

"We are going to provide basic coverage of the game. We will mention that Devonte got hurt, but we won't give specifics about the injury. Once we have the green light from Johnny, we can write a more comprehensive story. My hands are tied. It's all we can do."

I packed up for the press conferences in silence, my emotions twisting and turning. I could only imagine how upset Seth was about his dismal performance. And poor Devonte, his All-Pro season derailed by a devastating injury.

I exited the elevator and saw red stilettos pacing the marble floor in the stadium lobby. Emily looked at her phone and then shoved it into the back pocket of her slim-fit jeans.

"Emily, are you OK?"

"No, I'm not," she said, her voice cracking. Tears and mascara streaked her tan face. "I'm waiting for one of Devonte's brothers to take me to the hospital. No one is telling me anything. I'm so scared for him."

I wrapped my arms around her.

"I'm sorry. At least you know that Devonte's in good hands with excellent medical care. You'll feel so much better when you see him."

"You're right, but it doesn't make this easier," she said, wiping her face with the top of her hand.

"I have to run to Coach's presser. I will check on you later."

I slipped into the auditorium just as Coach took the podium.

"The first thing is that Devonte has a knee injury that's being evaluated right now as we speak. He did not come back to play, so it's a big concern. That's all I know."

"Coach, any thoughts on if this injury is season-ending?" an ESPN reporter shouted.

"He's getting an MRI now. We will know tonight. I'll take questions about the game."

"What did you think of Seth's performance?" Sheridan asked, speaking over several reporters.

"I thought he came out in the first half and threw the ball well. He made plays and took control of the offense. The second half, we just self-destructed. Devonte's injury may have played a part in that. I will have to go back and look at the tape."

"Will Seth be starter moving forward?"

"Sheridan, we're off next week and we're going to focus on getting this team healthy during the bye. What I do know is that we are a 4–2 football team with a lot of talent."

Johnny stepped toward the podium. "That's it for Coach. Seth will be next."

On cue, Seth walked into the auditorium. I cringed as he hunched over the microphone and braced himself for the media's torture.

"It wasn't my best game. That was on me."

"How much does Devonte mean to this offense?" a beat reporter asked.

Seth looked up with sagging eyes. "He's the heart and soul of this offense. We are going to miss him."

Seth turned and walked out of the auditorium. I was overcome with the need to see him, talk to him, hold him. I grabbed my phone and quickly typed, *I'm sorry about today. How about I come over later?*

I was crossing the line, dipping my toe into a fireable offense. In that moment, I didn't care. Seth was aching, and I ached to comfort him.

Seconds later my phone vibrated. *I need to be by myself.*

My heart seized. For the first time since we met, Seth didn't want to be with me. I tried to tell myself he wasn't rejecting me; he was angry about the game. But a louder voice said I was headed for heartache.

Twenty

A Certified A-Hole

I woke up at 4:00 a.m., my mind churning over Seth's aloof text. I checked my phone, longing for a sweet message. Nothing. I probably was overreacting. Seth played an abysmal game. He had every right to sulk alone.

Restless, I switched on my bedside lamp and opened my laptop. Every sports site led with headlines about Devonte's torn ACL. I read through the stories, which included quotes from "sources close to Devonte" saying the receiver was out for the rest of the season. On the team's website, a story about the team's loss topped the featured news. There were no quotes or sourced information about the injury, only the company tagline that "more information will be forthcoming." Garrett was right. Johnny's policy on injury updates was making our website look foolish.

I cracked my wood blinds. It was too dark outside to run, but I needed to pound out my frustration. I laced up my running shoes, packed my work clothes, and headed to the stadium.

I scanned my badge and walked through the dimly lit concourse. The gym was completely dark and quiet. No rap songs blaring or players bench-pressing racks of weight. I hopped on a treadmill in the far corner and popped in my earbuds.

After a mile, I relaxed into a steady pace and allowed my endorphins to lighten my mood.

"Hey there, Boots," I heard a twangy voice say. Panicked, I hit the emergency stop button.

"Sorry, didn't mean to scare you," Coach Bush said, stepping onto the machine next to me. He turned on the attached TV monitor and changed the channel to a fishing show on the Outdoor Network. His bright white running shoes began to plod along the slowly moving belt.

"Hi, Coach," I said with a wave. I stared at our reflections in the glass-paneled wall in front of us. Coach, the man Johnny worked tirelessly to protect, was power walking next to me, humming along in shorts a size too small and watching a deep-sea fishing show. Never had a man seemed more ordinary and prominent at the same time.

After three miles, I slowed the belt to a crawl and disconnected my earbuds.

"Girl, you've got some wheels. You could show the players a thing or two," Coach said.

"Running clears my head. It's like therapy," I said between gasps of air.

"Ain't that the truth?" Coach said, punching the incline button as his machine tilted upward. "You play a lot of sports?"

"Yes, sir. I played volleyball in college. I was a defensive specialist—libero is the technical term."

"I bet you were fast around the court," he puffed. "You should run in my race here this summer. It's a charity thing for veterans."

"It would be an honor," I said and made my way from the gym to the cheerleaders' locker room. It was just past 6:00 a.m. Still no word from Seth, or anyone for that matter.

I sent Emily a text. *How are you?* She called immediately.

"Blake, thank God. I need someone to talk to," Emily sniffled.

"Are you OK? What happened?"

"No. It's about what's not happening. No one is telling me anything. I went to the hospital last night to be with Devonte. He was so happy to see me. We held hands. He just wanted me to sit with him. His brother and his agent were talking with doctors and surgeons and calling other doctors and surgeons. Then they told me I had to leave. I went home and stayed up all night, waiting to hear from someone."

Emily hiccupped back a sob.

"Not a word. Until this morning. He texted me that he's getting on a private plane and flying to Alabama. He's having surgery today and won't be back for two months."

"He must be going to see Dr. Allison."

"Yeah, that's the one."

"He's the most famous orthopedic surgeon in the world. Every top athlete goes to him. That should make you feel better."

"What would make me feel better is being with Devonte. They should have let me stay and say goodbye in person. If I was his wife, they would have let me stay."

"Emily, I really don't think this has anything to do with you personally. His agent, brothers, the coaches—they all wanted Devonte to get the best care."

Emily inhaled into the phone.

"Maybe. I just don't like being cut out of his life like that."

"I'm sure you can visit him after the surgery. Devonte will really need you then."

"The best therapy he can get is my TLC," Emily said with a glimmer of sass.

"Now that's the Emily I know and love."

I looked down at my computer satchel.

"Hey, would you mind if I used the information about Dr. Allison today in my story? I won't mention you. The source will be totally anonymous."

"Anything for you, girl."

I hung up with Emily and immediately texted Garrett, *Got inside info on Devonte. He's on a plane to see Dr. Allison.*

Garrett texted back. *Who's your source?*

Me: *Can't say but completely reliable.*

Garrett: *I will ask Johnny . . .*

Two seconds later.

Garrett: *Johnny says no. Need to wait for team announcement.*

I thought, if I couldn't break this story, I needed to pass it along to someone who could. Sheridan. It was early, but not too early for a reporter covering pro football.

Sheridan answered after the first ring.

"Blake, good morning. You're up bright and early."

"I have time-sensitive news for you. Devonte is on a private plane as we speak, headed to see Dr. Allison in Alabama. If all goes as planned, he will undergo surgery later today."

"Who told you this?"

"A close friend of Devonte's."

"Why aren't you reporting this?"

"Team policy. Johnny doesn't report injury news until the team releases an official statement."

"Are you sure you don't want to break the Allison news personally? Put something out there on Twitter?" Sheridan asked.

"Johnny would fire me on the spot."

"I see," Sheridan said. "I'll get off and call Devonte's agent now to confirm the details. Thanks for the tip. I owe you."

. . .

Johnny leaned back in his chair and propped his feet on his desk. I took my usual spot against the wall next to Ryan and checked my phone as the rest of the department filed in. It had been three days since the game, and still nothing from Seth. My mind told me things between us were over, but my heart was holding out hope for a message to appear.

Johnny cleared his throat, and I shoved my phone in my back pocket. "As you guys know, today is the last day of practice during this bye week. The players get Thursday through Sunday off. Just like the players, our department needs to recharge the batteries. I've talked to HR. Because of all the weekends you've worked, they've agreed to give you Thursday and Friday as comp days. Let's finish out the week strong, enjoy time with our families and friends, and come back ready to grind."

Johnny smiled and the department burst into applause, the Bobbsey Twins rising to their feet for a standing ovation. Even Garrett broke into a grin.

It had been three months since I had enjoyed a free weekend. A week earlier, I would have been cheering for the time off and fantasizing about Seth. Now, I resigned myself to sitting at home for the next four days, stewing over what went wrong.

Johnny knocked his championship ring against the desk to regain our attention.

"As I tell the players, stay out of trouble. I hold this department to a high standard."

"You got it, boss!" the Bobbsey Twins proclaimed in unison.

"Also, I want to call out Blake. Her hard work on the website hasn't gone unnoticed. Her stories and videos have drastically upped our page views. And the team is rewarding her with an office."

My jaw dropped. "Really?"

"Yes, little lady. You'll be moving into the open office near the ownership suite on Monday."

I proudly stepped away from the wall. When Johnny had called my name, I had expected him to grant me locker room privileges. He repeatedly told me I was close to earning them. But getting my own office was almost as exciting. It was more than the double monitors and flat-screen TV that came with the closed-door space—it was the validation and support that underscored the gesture.

"Johnny, thank you. This is a huge honor."

"Keep up the grinding, BB," Johnny said and stood up. "All right, meeting adjourned. Remember, family practice is in thirty minutes."

"I almost forgot about the players inviting their families today," I said to Ryan as we filed out of Johnny's office.

"Yeah, there are some hot wives that I've been hearing about. It should make practice a lot more entertaining." Ryan smiled.

"Geez, the Bobbsey Twins are rubbing off on you," I said, shaking my head. "Before we go to practice, let's check out my new digs."

We walked past the owner's suite, and I pushed open the door to an empty office.

"This is bigger than I expected," I said.

"Someone on this team really likes you," Ryan said, leaning against the wall-length credenza.

"What do you mean by that?"

"I'm not saying you aren't doing great work. Page views are up. But around here that isn't enough. You have someone looking out for you, speaking out on your behalf."

Who could that be? It certainly wasn't Johnny. Tension lingered between us since the bus incident and cheetah dress debacle. I was doing my best to play his game—abide by his ridiculous policies, laugh at his offensive jokes, and remain outwardly upbeat. The only possible ally who came to mind was Coach Bush. But why would he care if I got an office?

"Someone looking out for me—is that a good or a bad thing?" I wondered aloud. There was something unsettling about being singled out at work, even if it meant scoring a big office.

"It's a good thing. I wish I had that," Ryan said and glanced at his watch. "I'm heading to practice. I'm writing a story about the families coming today and want to talk to some of the wives before things get going."

"I'll see you down there. I want to freshen up first."

As I swiped on a fresh coat of lip gloss, I pictured all the beautiful wives standing on the sidelines. I twisted open my black eyeliner, carefully lined my lower lashes, and brushed on extra coats of mascara for a more dramatic look. I picked the lint off my tight black pants, which I had paired with a long, gray sweater and my black boots. I checked the mirror one more time. Chic and sporty. Just the look I wanted to achieve for family practice.

A golf cart puttered behind me on the concourse. I moved closer to the wall to let it pass.

"Boots, hop on," Johnny said, screeching to a halt.

I slid into the seat next to him. "Don't mind if I do."

Johnny turned toward me. "There's something I wanted to talk to you about."

My body instinctively stiffened.

"Boots, don't look so scared. It's good news. I've got two backstage passes for the Jackson Ways concert here on Saturday. I don't like country music, but I know you do. Want to go?"

"Are you kidding me? Yes!" I squealed in delight.

"I'll let Jackson's manager know. He wanted me to get some local celebs and good-looking ladies backstage. You can bring one of your hot friends with you. Makes for better photos and social media."

I suppressed a snort. There was always a rub with Johnny. He could never bestow an act of genuine kindness. I swallowed back my annoyance and reminded myself of the payoff. I was getting two backstage tickets to see Jackson Ways and Johnny would be nowhere in sight.

"Well, this day is shaping up nicely," I said. "First, an office. Now, backstage passes to see Jackson Ways. Thank you, Johnny."

Johnny waved off my gratitude. He stomped on the gas pedal and we zoomed out of the stadium.

On the fields, the players were warming up with their position groups. Women wearing sleek workout attire and oversized sunglasses looked on while children in miniature jerseys dashed between them and the fringes of the field to wave at their fathers.

"It must be so fun for the kids to see their dads in action," I said as we screeched to a stop.

Johnny took two iPhones from the front console and clipped them to his waistband.

"Family is important to Coach. He knows how much the wives and kids sacrifice during the season with their dads never home. Coach makes it a priority to hold Family Day during the bye week."

Johnny nodded at two women in black spandex leggings showcasing their perky round rears.

"If you ask me, this is more of a pissing match between which wife has the best body and the biggest ring."

I followed Johnny into the practice area and watched him ooh and aah over the wives and their children. He stopped and kissed the cheek of a tall blonde with porcelain skin who held twin toddler girls on each hip. She set them down and they began to tug at their number 9 pink jerseys.

"Off. Off," one girl pleaded.

"No, sweetie. We are wearing these for Daddy. He's so proud you're here."

My knees buckled. Number 9 was Seth's number. I backpedaled to the iron gate surrounding the field, gripped one of the rods, and choked back a rising tide of bile. Seth had a wife and kids, and for some masochistic reason, I could not take my eyes off them. My clammy hands began to slide, and I felt myself falling into a dark abyss.

"Blake! You look like you're about to faint," Ryan said, throwing my arm over his shoulder and propping me up.

"I don't feel so great. I'm going into the training center," I said, turning before he could respond and running as fast as my boots could take me. I flipped on the lights in the bathroom and steadied my hands against the sink. When I looked in the mirror, I almost didn't recognize myself; my skin had paled to a ghostly white and my eyes were ashen gray.

"How could you be so stupid?" I yelled at my reflection. "You actually believed he was falling in love with you."

Tears streamed down my face, followed by unbridled sobs. I felt like such a naive fool. I had let my guard down and had fallen hard for a player. I had allowed myself to believe that our souls had connected over long, intimate conversations.

I had listened to him recite song lyrics and thought he had written them just for me. He had said that I was the first person he wanted to talk to in the morning and the last one he wanted to wish goodnight. He had been that person to me. Now, I knew it was all lies. He fucking had a wife. The truth was Seth was married with kids and I was his girl on the side.

Who fucking does that? Who seduces an innocent person while being married? A certified asshole, that's who.

Pain gripped my heart. My body felt vapid and empty. I hiccupped for air. As much as I wanted to, I could not cower in the bathroom. I needed to face my new reality. A reality where Seth was married to a Nicole Kidman look-alike and I had been played by a player.

Twenty-One

Tequila Nights

"He's such an asshole!" Emily said, holding up her margarita glass and motioning to the server for another round.

"That's what I keep telling myself," I said and took a long sip of tequila-infused goodness. "I feel so stupid for falling for him."

It had been just over twenty-four hours since the family practice, and my wounds still gaped and stung. Seth had shattered my heart. Now I was trying to piece it back together and make sense of what had transpired with him.

I replayed our conversations in my head and dissected every word and gesture. Had there been hints or threads to pull that would have exposed his narcissistic and deceitful ways? Or had I been so attracted to him, so wrapped up in what I believed was a genuine connection, that I had blindly trusted and fallen hard? I imagined both to be true, but there was nothing I could do to change the past.

Still, I was disappointed with myself for being naive and gullible, and I was furious with Seth for being a two-timing liar. I cursed him for putting on a boyfriend-like charade. I daydreamed about screaming at him for betraying me and his wife. In the car, I sang at the top of my lungs to Carrie Underwood's "Before He Cheats," pumping my fists as she bashed her ex's headlights with a baseball bat.

I called Emily to vent, and she immediately suggested drowning out my pain with girl talk and tequila. So far, it was working.

"Blake, you really can't blame yourself. Seth never wears a ring. Also, I should have told you straight up," Emily said and daintily licked the salt from her glass so as not to smudge her lipstick.

"What do you mean?" I asked.

"That night you came to my place. I told you to be careful of him. I figured you knew about his marital problems. Seth's always got a side hustle. When his wife finds out, she usually kicks him out and threatens to leave him. Then they get back together."

I choked back crushed ice.

"That's so messed up. Why would she want to stay married to a husband who cheats on her?"

"Because, in the end, she doesn't want to give up her happily-ever-after family. Or her Range Rover and Gucci diaper bag. And she's probably deluded herself into thinking it's just a phase. He'll stop when he's done playing."

"Do you think he started texting me after she had kicked him out?"

"That's exactly what happened. He got caught sucking face with someone at the club and wifie sent him packing. He was living in a hotel until last Sunday. After he played that crappy game, he went crawling back, begging for her forgiveness and wanting her TLC."

"How do you know all of this?" I said, dipping a chip into a bowl of guacamole.

"Most of my info comes from Devonte. But I'm also cool with the wife of one of the receivers. She started out as a baby mama. None of the wives invited her to anything. Andy's wife flat-out ignored her and didn't ask her to any of the family events. So, she was an outcast, like I am. After she got married, the wives finally started asking her to all the team stuff. She gives me the gossip."

"Why is Andy's wife the social director?"

"She's married to the starting quarterback. The QB runs the offense, and his wife runs the social scene. Andy's wife is always talking trash about Seth and his wife."

"Geez, there's a lot of backstabbing," I said and took another long sip of my drink. "I guess I should count my lucky stars that things with Seth ended before anything really happened. I mean, we never even kissed."

"Thank God. You deserve much better. You're such a catch. You'll be dating someone in no time."

"I really don't have time to date. The season is way too demanding," I said.

"Everyone needs some lovin' or at least some eye candy," Emily said with a wink.

"Speaking of eye candy, would you like to be my date to the Jackson Ways concert on Saturday? I have two backstage passes."

"Can't. I'm going to Alabama!" Emily squealed.

"That's awesome! How's Devonte doing?"

"He's in pain. He's bored. But the doctor said everything went great. We've been on FaceTime, but it isn't the same. I miss him so much. Today he surprised me with first-class plane tickets. I leave tomorrow night."

"It's going to be a great weekend," I said, squeezing Emily's hand across the table, grateful to have found such a loyal friend.

· · ·

Ryan waited outside the gates of an old low-rise apartment complex, a cowboy hat riding high atop his forehead. I rolled down the cab's back passenger window.

"Howdy there, partner. I heard there was a buckaroo wanting to go to a concert."

"My lady, you heard right."

Ryan clicked the heels of his black cowboy boots.

"And I took a page out of the Boots's book and decided to wear a pair myself."

I had thought long and hard about who I wanted to invite to the concert. I had considered reconnecting with an old friend, but that seemed more like a chore than fun. It would entail discussing why I had grown distant from our mutual friends and explaining the demands of my job.

I thirsted for a night to let loose—get lost in the music and alcohol—and forget about Seth. Who better to do that with than Ryan? He lived for a boozy, carefree night.

The cab turned onto the main thoroughfare leading to the stadium and bumped to a stop. Brake lights illuminated the half-mile stretch leading to the stadium entrance.

"I thought we were getting here early enough to beat traffic. Apparently, we're not the only Jackson Ways fans in these parts," I said.

"Geez, this is as bad as game days."

I pulled a couple of twenties out of my wallet. "I'm OK walking if you are."

"Yep," Ryan said and hopped out of the car.

"Come on, we need to book it to will call," I said. "Someone from Jackson's management team is supposed to meet us there at 5:00."

"I still can't believe we are going backstage to meet Jackson freaking Ways," Ryan said, nipping at my heels as we weaved through concertgoers and vendors.

"This is a zoo. I have no idea who I'm looking for," I said and sidestepped through the maze of lines approaching the will call booth.

We finally reached a clearing in the plaza. Parked in that sliver of open space was a four-seat golf cart with palm trees painted across the side and a miniature license plate with "Jackson" on it. A man with spiky, brown hair reclined behind the steering wheel, his cowboy boots resting on the dashboard as he typed on his phone.

"That must be our guy," I said to Ryan.

I approached the golf cart and caught the man's eye. He was young, not much older than me. And he was fit, biceps stretching the sleeves of his tight black T-shirt.

"You must be Blake," he said.

His baseball mitt–sized hand enveloped mine in a firm shake.

"I'm Slade. I'll be taking care of you tonight."

"Good to meet you, Slade. This is Ryan. We both work for the team," I said, looking at Ryan lingering shyly behind me. Ryan waved silently.

"Well, let's get you fine people to where the rum is flowing and the beer is chilling," Slade cooed.

"Sounds like paradise," I said, jumping into the back seat.

"You've got that right," Slade said. "Ryan, I take it you're a man of few words."

"No, sir. Just taking it all in. I could use a drink."

"I'm on it," Slade said, flipping on a siren affixed to the dash and stomping on the accelerator. Fans stepped aside as we motored past them to the back of the stadium. We turned into the lot usually reserved for players and coaches, which looked more like an overcrowded truck stop.

"Wow. There are more trucks and buses here than on game days. This is a huge operation," I said.

For three years straight, Jackson Ways had won Country Music Artist of the Year honors. His latest album had gone platinum seven times. His face was plastered across gossip magazines, linking him to romantic rendezvous with Hollywood actresses. He was country music's heartthrob du jour, and he was soaking up every minute of it.

Slade slowed down near the loading dock and turned off the siren.

"Jackson travels with a combined sixty-five buses and trailers. We've gone to seventeen stadiums on this tour. This is our last stop, and I'm warning you—it's going to get wild."

Slade stopped at a bus painted with a beach scene matching the golf cart and a life-size depiction of Jackson relaxing in a folding chair, his bare feet buried in the sand. An awning stamped with a beer company's logo extended from the top of the bus, and seven self-service taps were built into the side of the bus, below the awning.

"Here is our beer bus," Slade said and hopped out of the golf cart.

"Does Jackson travel on this?" I asked.

"No, it's more for show. They are his biggest sponsor, so we take the beer bus everywhere we go. We set it up for the crew and VIP guests like yourselves."

Ryan took a cup and filled it to the top.

Slade handed me a cup. "I was talking to some of the players backstage. They told me I could spot you by the tall boots."

"Yeah, these boots are my uniform. I bet half of the players don't know my first name. They just call me Boots."

"With a nickname like Boots, you'll fit in here just right," Slade said, gulping down a frothy sip of beer.

"So, how long have you been touring with Jackson?" I asked.

"This is my fourth year. I enlisted in the Marines out of school. After the military, I was working with a security consulting firm, and Jackson's people hired me to help with his detail. We became good friends and now I'm his right-hand man."

"What an awesome experience."

"It's exhausting. But I wouldn't change it for the world. And I'm thankful that tour bus can't talk," Slade said and pointed to a black bus with blacked-out windows and gold accents, "because she could tell some pretty crazy stories."

"I heard a few Miss Georgias have gotten personal tours of that bus, if you know what I mean," Ryan said, refilling his cup.

"Get a drink in you and you become the funny guy," Slade said, slapping Ryan on the back playfully. "Pace yourself. We've got a big night ahead."

We steadied our drinks and sat back down in the golf cart. Slade accelerated slowly into the stadium and waved at the officers guarding the entrance. We followed the concourse around to the greenroom, where security guards stood on either side of the double doors.

"Any issues since I've been gone?" Slade asked.

"No, sir. Still a long line for the meet and greet."

Slade nodded and ushered us inside. The stadium's greenroom had been transformed into a tropical destination. Gone were the bare white walls and drab florescent lighting. Instead, drapes featuring island scenes hung from the ceiling to the floor. Thousands of tiny white lights twinkled from the branches of the potted trees lining the room, and Jackson's music played in the background.

In the center of the room, on an elevated platform, Jackson nuzzled between two identical peroxide blondes in low-slung halter tops.

"Twins! Double the trouble!" he hooted, and a photographer snapped away.

"Jackson, you're the sexiest man I've ever seen," one of the twins professed.

Jackson pulled the twins in tight. "I have the most amazing fans on earth. I love you guys!"

The fans waiting in line to meet the country star clapped and wildly shouted, "Wahoo!"

Slade draped an arm around my neck. "There's no one who works harder for his fans than Jackson Ways."

"He definitely turns on the charm," I said, watching Jackson sign autographs for two middle-aged women in Wranglers.

"Wait until you meet him. He's more than charming. He makes you feel like the most important person in the room," Slade said.

I watched Jackson hug, high-five, tease, and talk with each of the hundred or so fans waiting to meet him. He exuded star power, and he knew it. But he kept his appearance unassuming and relatable. He played the part of the good old country boy perfectly. A T-shirt with cutoff sleeves exposed his freckled shoulders. Muscular thighs bulged from inside a pair of worn, fitted jeans. Light brown curls tufted out of an OKC baseball hat, his tribute to the city.

"You want to meet him?" Slade asked.

"Sure," I said, trying to sound cool and casual.

I followed Slade to the stage where the last group of fans posed with Jackson. He looked up from the camera and met my gaze. A broad smile spread across his face, crinkling the corners of his eyes.

Slade jumped onstage and nudged Jackson. "I've got a VIP who wants to meet you."

"Excuse me, folks," Jackson said to his fans and walked in my direction.

"I hear there's a very important person I need to meet," Jackson said in his melodic drawl, which instantly softened me, like the opening vocals of one of his slow ballads.

"Hi, I'm Blake Kirk," I said through a smile. "I'm not really a VIP. I work in the team's media department."

Jackson's eyes twinkled as he laughed. "Media department. That sounds important to me. Where are you sitting, Miss Kirk?"

"In the standing section, right in front of the stage."

"How about I upgrade you to the stage? You'll practically be part of the show."

"How can I say no to that?" My face glimmered with excitement.

"Good. Now you'll be close enough that I can see your smile," Jackson said, his eyes locking onto mine. My cheeks blushed and I looked down, overwhelmed by the attention.

It wasn't until Ryan loudly cleared his throat that I remembered I hadn't arrived alone.

"Uh, Jackson, there's someone I'd like you to meet."

Ryan lurched forward, sloshing beer out of a full cup. "Sorry about that," he said, rubbing the beer into the carpet with the bottom of his boots. "I'm Ryan. I work with Blake. I just want to say you're awesome. I've downloaded every single one of your songs. Your newest single is my favorite."

"Thanks, man. You're in luck. We'll be playing 'How to Love Her' tonight," Jackson replied, his eyes still fixed on me.

"That's awesome!" Ryan said too loudly.

"All right, Jackson, we'll let you finish up," Slade said, stepping in front of Ryan. "I'm going to take them to the tiki bar. Good luck out there."

Slade motioned for Ryan and me to follow him. I turned to catch one last glimpse of Jackson. He was autographing a poster with his large, loopy signature. Unexpectedly, he peeked up, his deep brown eyes flickering as they met mine.

As we walked into a dimly lit back room, Ryan nudged me.

"OK, that was crazy. Jackson Ways was flirting hard with you."

"Stop it! He was just being nice. Jackson probably does that at every concert."

"Who cares? Go for it. We only live once," Ryan said, extending his arms wide and inhaling the alcohol-infused air.

We followed Slade to a large bar under a thatched tiki hut. Local celebrities milled around us. I recognized a major league pitcher and his wife. A Heisman-winning quarterback-turned-TV-analyst was chatting up a leggy brunette. The current Miss Oklahoma paraded around in her pageant sash.

"Quite the scene," I said.

"It's like this at every stop, but it never gets old," Slade said, waving at a bartender in a skimpy white tank top.

"You mentioned some players from our team are here. Do you know who?" I asked, surveying the room for a familiar face.

"A couple offensive linemen and a quarterback. I hadn't heard of them. We get so many pro athletes backstage that it's hard to keep track of who's who unless it's Aaron Rodgers or Tom Brady."

My breath seized. Was Seth here? Did he bring his wife? The thought of seeing them sent waves of nausea up my gut. If they were backstage, I was leaving. I couldn't torture myself by hanging out with them all night.

"What do you want to drink?" Ryan said, leaning against the bar.

"A tequila and soda. Make that a double," I said.

I scanned the room, searching for Seth. Tucked in the dark shadows of fake palm trees, I spotted his tousled auburn hair. I craned my neck to get a better view. Seth tossed his head back in laughter, revealing a woman with impossibly high cheekbones and a stream of shiny, black hair. The Kardashian clone looked in my direction, and Seth followed suit. I straightened myself immediately, mortified that they caught me staring at them.

Anger shot through me. He'd already found a new side hustle. What an asshole.

"I'll take another," I said to the bartender.

"Thatta girl," Ryan said and tossed back his whiskey and Coke.

Instead of leaving because of Seth, I was getting drunk to forget him. The tequila would make him a distant memory and numb any vestiges of pain. Plus, I wasn't missing my chance to watch Jackson perform on stage.

Ryan and I clinked glasses, and I gulped down the rest of my drink. My body loosened from my temples down to my toes, and my anger began to melt. I ached to feel free. Free of Seth. Free of Johnny. Free to move to the music of the night.

"All right, guys, time to go to the stage." Slade waved at me and Ryan.

"Can I invite two friends?" I asked.

Slade shook his head. "Jackson only wants a handful of people on stage."

"Just those two guys."

I pointed to the two offensive linemen huddled by the bar.

"Isn't there another player here? The quarterback?"

"I don't care about him," I said.

"Fine. The big guys can come too," Slade conceded.

I walked to the corner of the bar. "C'mon, guys. You're coming with me. On stage."

"Wait, what?" The players' eyes widened with expectancy.

"Jackson invited me, and I invited you."

"Damn, Blake. You're a high roller."

Seth turned around and crinkled his brow in confusion.

"See ya," I said with immense satisfaction.

. . .

Jackson's stage was enormous, taking up the entire north end zone with a catwalk extending to midfield. The sold-out crowd waved glow sticks and chanted for his entrance.

Slade directed us to the wings of the stage, just in front of sound engineers operating massive equipment.

"You can see why it takes us two days to set up," Slade said. "Our goal is to draw in 50,000 fans and give them the experience of an intimate show. Jackson wants the people in the cheap seats to feel like they're close enough to touch him."

"It's unbelievable," I said, my voice drunk with excitement.

The lights went dark, and Jackson's band began to play one of his summertime anthems. A spotlight shone on the upper corner of the stadium where Jackson sat on a swing suspended from a cable. He sang the opening verses and zip-lined over the crowd, bringing the screaming fans to their feet.

"Hello, Oklahoma City! We are here for one simple reason: you people are here," Jackson said as a cable lowered him to the front of the stage. "I have an idea where I want to take you tonight. Will you come with me?"

Jackson turned toward the band and our eyes met. He pointed discreetly at me, sending heat waves rushing through my insides.

Ryan elbowed me. "He's singing this for you."

I was too captivated to reply. Jackson raced across the stage, crooning about a woman stealing his heart. I swayed, surrendering to the beat.

It didn't take long for me to forget about the sold-out stadium, the players standing beside me, or Seth's infidelity. Jackson's voice moved through my body as I fell into the rhythm of each song.

"Jackson's been looking over here all night," I heard one of the players say. "Country's biggest star has the hots for Boots."

I pinched my arm to remind myself it was all real. As the stage lights dimmed, a stagehand passed Jackson an acoustic guitar.

"Love is a powerful thing, my friends. When I fall in love, I fall hard and fast. I wrote this song about meeting the woman of my dreams. I'm still looking for her. She could be here among us tonight. If so, beautiful lady, this song is for you," Jackson said, lowering his head and beginning to strum.

His deep, smooth voice sent a hush over the stadium, and I realized I was with Jackson, willing to go wherever he took me.

. . .

Jackson leaped onto an elevated platform and belted out the final verse of his encore song. "Thank you, Oklahoma City. You're amazing! I love you guys!"

Slade draped his arm around my neck. "What did you think?"

"Incredible."

No wonder music stars didn't sleep at night. How could you, after riling up so much emotion and exhilaration?

Slade waved us through security, and we made our way back to the tiki bar. Standing just inside the door with his arms folded and a huge scowl draped across his face was none other than Seth.

"What the hell? Why did you guys ditch me?" he said to the players.

"Blake got us on stage," a player said.

"We had the best seats in the house. And Jackson was looking over all night, making eyes at her. It was unreal."

Seth recoiled. "At Blake?"

"Yeah, pointing at her and everything."

Seth looked at me, dismay contorting his face.

"Whatever. I'm out of here."

"Bye!" I said, waving from behind the players, and headed to the bar. I felt as if I were floating on air.

"What would you like?" the bartender asked.

"Two tequila shots," a voice crooned.

I turned around to face Jackson, my chest practically touching his well-defined pecs.

"You'll have to excuse the wet shirt; I usually shower after a show," he said, pulling at his soaked T-shirt. "But I didn't want to miss my chance to talk to you."

"No apology necessary," I said breathlessly.

Jackson reached around me for the shot glasses. "To tonight!"

I bit my lower lip. "To tonight."

We tossed back our drinks.

"I couldn't stop looking at you all night. Your smile. It's addictive."

I cocked my head flirtatiously. "I bet you tell that to all the girls."

"Nope. There's something about you. You have a way about you that's special," Jackson said and tossed back another shot.

Jackson clasped my hand with his and squeezed it tightly.

"I have to say hi to a few people. Will you join me?" he asked.

The room blurred, a haze of twinkling lights and loud voices. As we walked toward Slade, Jackson stopped and pulled me close. His arms encircled my waist, and he whispered in my ear, "Can I kiss you?"

I wrapped my arms around his neck and lowered my eyelids. His lips softly met mine. As he gently pulled away, my body instinctively bowed against him, aching for more.

"Should we go to my bus?"

"Yes," I breathed into his ear. The words tumbled out of me without caution. After three months of confinement, my body craved to be wild and reckless.

I clasped Jackson's hand, and we left the party, security guards and Slade following behind us.

"Do they come on the bus too?" I asked.

"They'll be outside making sure no one bothers us."

I followed Jackson into the black bus with blacked-out windows.

"I'm going to take a shower," Jackson said. "Make yourself comfortable."

I braced myself against a leather bench. The bus's bright lights and the haze of alcohol made it hard to focus, but I could still recognize the bus from photos in my gossip magazines. Jackson and an actress had snuggled on this very seat.

Jackson was a player. Not a football player like Seth. Jackson and Seth both played women. My subconscious understood that. But, for at least one night, I wanted to indulge in the game and get swept up in the dangerous desire of it all.

I walked toward the back of the bus, where Jackson had closed a curtain. From the edge, I could see him sliding down his tight, ripped jeans. My insides tightened. Emboldened by the tequila coursing through me, I pulled back the curtain and stepped inside.

"Is this your bedroom?" I asked, fingering a crisp white duvet.

Jackson stared at me, a fluffy towel wrapped around his waist and his tan, muscular chest slick with perspiration.

"If I'd known I was having company, I would have made the bed," he said, stepping toward me.

"It's fine just like this," I said, moving close enough to feel the warmth of his breath.

Jackson tenderly traced my cheek with his wide, calloused fingers.

"From the moment I saw you, I wanted to be close to you."

Jackson had probably cooed the same line to hundreds of women in the back of this bus. But in that moment, I believed him. I needed to believe him and feel special.

I closed my eyes and his lips caressed mine. As the tenderness gave way to hard passion, we fell to the bed. I pulled off my top and straddled my legs on either side of his waist. The room was spinning, and I was along for the ride. I leaned down and kissed him long and deep before making my way to the nape of his neck.

Jackson unhooked my strapless bra. I had no ability to fear or question what was about to come; my body was moving without my control.

My bare chest pressed against his, our skin hot and slick, and I surrendered to him.

We collapsed on the bed, the sheets damp against our limp bodies. Jackson turned toward me and gently smoothed back my hair. "Wow, Blake. I don't know what to say except that you're amazing."

The room was spinning. The passion that had just ignited my insides was subsiding, leaving in its place waves of queasiness from the alcohol.

I had no idea what to say to Jackson or what to do next. I had never had a one-night stand in my life, and already I was starting to regret this decision.

As I stared at the ceiling and tried to find some equilibrium, I heard voices clamoring at the front of the bus. I jerked upright.

"You're not supposed to be in here," a man said.

"I'm looking for my friend. I want to check on her."

It was Ryan.

"If she's with Jackson, I wouldn't go back there," the man said to Ryan.

I sat up and covered my chest with my hands. I suddenly felt vulnerable and exposed.

"Are you OK?" Jackson caressed my shoulder.

I rummaged through the sheets for my clothes and quickly dressed in silence.

"I need to go. This isn't like me," I said without looking at him.

"Blake, I thought tonight was incredible," Jackson said.

My head was whirling. The high of lust, adrenaline, and alcohol had worn off. I gripped the side of the bed, trying to tether myself.

"I need to go," I said.

I pulled up my boots and stepped outside the curtain. Ryan was standing in the kitchen with Jackson's security detail.

"Ryan, let's go," I said with my eyes lowered.

"Whatever you want."

Ryan followed me out of the bus.

· · ·

"You OK?" Ryan asked in the cab.

"I'm just tired," I said, staring out the window.

"I am sorry if I, um, interrupted things." Ryan stumbled over his words awkwardly. "You had been gone awhile and I was worried about you."

"You didn't interrupt," I said shortly.

"It's just you drank a lot tonight. You're usually taking care of me, so I wanted to watch out for you," he said.

"Thanks, Ryan. I appreciate it," I said and folded my hands in my lap.

My emotions were clattering against each other. Regret. Satisfaction. Fear. I couldn't make sense of them. Not now, at least. I needed to get home, take a shower, and wash the night away.

Twenty-Two

Walking the Line

Foam frothed out of my Starbucks lid as I darted down the hallway to my new office. I was cutting it close to the 8:00 a.m. start time of the department morning meeting.

I took a long sip of my latte, praying it would dissipate the haze of booze still clouding my head. More than a day had passed since the concert, and I still felt unsettled about sleeping with Jackson. I would close my eyes and imagine his chiseled chest pressed against mine, and heat would course through my body. Then, I would picture myself doing the walk of shame out of the bus and I would bristle with humiliation.

I plopped down in my chair and logged into my new computer. I had two minutes to get situated before I needed to be in Johnny's office.

"You look comfortable."

I sat upright, startled. "Good morning, Garrett. I didn't hear you walk in."

Garrett's dark eyes narrowed. "Perhaps you're still recovering from the weekend."

My breath seized. Garrett was pissed. Really pissed.

"The show was awesome, and it got a little crazy, I guess."

"Actually, you went very crazy. Johnny knows. Everyone on the team knows. There will be consequences."

Garrett turned on his heel and walked away.

Consequences. I sat paralyzed. Was this about me getting drunk? Or did it have to do with my tryst with Jackson? My stomach twisted anxiously at the thought of reliving the concert. I willed my legs to stand up and walk the twenty yards to Johnny's office.

The entire department had assumed their positions around Johnny's desk. I leaned against the wall next to Ryan.

"I don't have to tell you how important this game is. Sunday night, nationally televised. A lot is on the line," Johnny preached and paced. "And we have a situation to manage."

"A quarterback situation," Garrett interjected.

"Correct." Johnny frowned. "This information doesn't leave this room. The coaches want Andy to start, but he isn't ready as of today. They're game-planning for both players. But Coach won't announce anything until after Friday's practice. Our message is that it's a game-time decision."

"We'll keep the quarterback coverage basic on the site," Garrett said.

"I'd appreciate that," Johnny said, cracking his knuckles. "What do you have planned for the site this week?"

Garrett uncrossed his legs.

"I'm going to do a Q&A with a beat writer for a 'Behind the Steel Curtain' piece. Ryan is writing a story on a couple of our defensive players who played in college at Pitt."

Garrett's assignments did not include me. I bit my lip nervously. This must be part of my punishment.

"OK, meeting adjourned." Johnny paused and cleared his throat. "Blake, you stay."

My gut clenched. Johnny shuffled papers as people filed out. When the door closed, he looked me squarely in the eyes.

"Blake, I can't tell you how disappointed I am in you."

I swallowed hard.

"Johnny, to be honest, I'm not quite sure what I did wrong."

"Really? Let's start with you being drunk at the concert. Then there's your make-out session with Jackson Ways on his tour bus. You did this in front of players and coworkers, mind you. Now everyone in this building is talking about it. 'Did you hear that Boots knocked boots with Jackson

Ways?'" Johnny mimicked a high-pitched gossipy voice. His narrowed eyes shot daggers of ire.

I blinked away tears. What Johnny said was true. I had no defense. To make matters worse, I had turned into locker room gossip. It was embarrassing and regretful, but I still didn't understand how I had violated team rules.

"Johnny, I'm really sorry," I managed to say without crying.

Johnny's jaw hardened.

"Sorry isn't going to cut it. You made me and our department look bad. I have no choice but to suspend you without pay for the next three games."

Tears trickled down my face and I fought back the urge to sob. A three-game suspension. Johnny hadn't issued a punishment this harsh to anyone in our department. Not even to Ryan for drunkenly hooking up with Alyssa on a road trip or arriving late to a home game after a bender.

"Johnny, please, can we talk this through? I really don't want to miss the next three games," I pleaded.

"Blake, you should have thought about that before you acted like a drunk fool. Now, everyone thinks you're a floozy."

His cutting words slashed me like sharp knives. *Floozy.* That gashed me deep. Johnny had every right to be disappointed in me, but he didn't have to be cruel.

"Johnny, that's not fair," I said and wiped my tear-stained cheeks with the back of my hand.

"Don't you get started with me, young lady," he shot back.

I took a deep breath. Johnny had beaten me down, but I had to find the strength to reclaim some self-dignity. I clasped my trembling hands tightly in my lap and looked at Johnny square in the eyes.

"Johnny, I have watched coworkers drunkenly ogle strippers and hook up with a flight attendant, on team trips, mind you." My voice quivered but I kept pushing out the words. "You gave them fist bumps. How does the team get to punish me for a relationship I had outside of the workplace?"

"Don't ever question me or how I run my department!" Johnny shouted. "I gave you those tickets. Players were there. The concert was an extension of work."

My body still reeled with hurt, but now a fiery anger flickered in my belly. Words sparked off my tongue.

"Johnny, you gave me those tickets because you said Jackson wanted 'hotties' backstage. That didn't make the concert seem professional at all. What I did with Jackson should be my choice and should stay between Jackson and me."

"What you did was slut around like a cheap jersey chaser."

I gasped. Johnny had wielded his final blow, cutting me straight through the heart and extinguishing any fight I had left. I sat across from him immobile, too battered to move.

"I'm done with this conversation," he said. "Out. Now."

Once inside my office, I allowed the tears to stream down my face, my body trembling with each sob. I had been racked with conflicting emotions; now I could add rage to the list. Johnny had no right to degrade me over my sex life.

There was a soft knock on my office door. "It's Ryan."

I cracked the door enough for him to shimmy inside. "You're the only person I'll allow in here."

Ryan looked sympathetically at my red, swollen face. "What happened?"

"Johnny suspended me for three games. He heard I was drunk and making out with Jackson in front of the players. How did he even hear about it? You were the only one who knew I was on the bus, right?"

"Blake, I promise I didn't say anything. I think some guys were talking in the locker room," Ryan stammered.

"Ryan, you have to tell me what they said."

"I wasn't going to say anything because I didn't want you to feel bad. This morning, when I was storing my gym bag, I overhead the o-linemen tell Seth that you walked out of the after-party with Jackson. They heard you'd gone on his bus. And then Seth blurted out to the entire locker room that you had been knocking boots with Jackson on his bus."

I seethed. So, this was Seth's way of getting back at me for snubbing him at the concert.

"For the record, Seth is a cheating lowlife. But I will save that topic for another day," I hissed.

"A lot of the players think the same thing. They came to your defense and told Seth to shut his mouth," Ryan said.

"Wow, I can't believe the players defended me," I said.

"Blake, you are going to get through this. Everyone here loves you. And the players and coaches have much more important things to think about—like winning on Sunday night."

"It's just so humiliating to think that the team is discussing my sex life. What if Coach Bush thinks I'm a huge slut?"

"No way. He doesn't think that. Think about everything that goes on here. The scouting assistants hooking up with players and coaches. I had my situation with Alyssa."

"But it's different. I'm the only woman traveling with the team. The expectations are different for me. Look at the concert. Johnny wanted me to go and look pretty because that reflected well on him. But he was furious that I drank too much and left with Jackson. If Shania Twain had been performing and you had been in my shoes, he would have congratulated you at this morning's meeting."

"You have a point," Ryan said.

"I walk a tightrope. Look pretty but not sexy. Hang with the guys but don't act like them. And no matter what you hear or see, remain innocent. I fell off the tightrope, and now Johnny is punishing me."

. . .

I stood as far away as possible from the media contingency, my back grazing the practice field gates. I didn't have an assignment. Really, I had no reason to be at practice, except Garrett insisted I went in case Ryan needed help. I had no idea if anyone outside my department knew what happened. All I knew was I felt as if I were wearing a scarlet letter.

Hal looked my way and waved. I pretended not to see him, staring straight ahead as if lost in deep thought. I couldn't bear to face anyone. Not now, not after what happened in Johnny's office. When the final horn sounded, my shoulders dropped in relief.

"This team better be ready for Blitzburgh's exotic packages," Hal said in his overly loud and raspy broadcast voice.

"The bigger question is which quarterback will be reading those packages," Sheridan countered.

I grimaced. Had Sheridan heard about my suspension? The only thing worse than being punished by Johnny was disappointing Sheridan.

As Johnny gathered the media to review the team's schedule for the week, I slipped past the gates and headed for the stadium. I was incapable of engaging in pleasant chitchat. There was only one person I wanted to speak with. Emily.

Can you meet in the parking lot? I texted furiously.

C u in 5.

Perf.

I perched myself on the back bumper of her Tahoe. About fifty yards away, a silver Mercedes sedan sat where Jackson's tour bus had been parked.

I rubbed my eyes, seeking clarity. How could I earn back the team's trust? Where did my career go from here?

"Hey, girl!" Emily said with a disposition as bright as her spray tan. "You look like you need a hug."

"A hug and a new job," I said, blinking back tears. Just when I thought I'd cried them all, more leaked out.

"Whoa, whoa, whoa. What the hell happened?" Emily said, unlocking her car and directing me to the passenger seat.

I slowly inhaled the cool fall air wafting through the open window and told her every detail of the Jackson Ways saga.

"Holy shit. I thought my life was complicated," Emily said.

"What do you think I should do?"

"Remember, you're asking the girl who's committing the cardinal employee sin and is dating the team's star player. In my opinion, it's not fair that there's a double standard for you and Ryan, or even the Scouting Sexies, for that matter. They can get drunk and hook up with people employed by the team, and no one cares. Not fair. Secondly, Johnny has no right to control your love life. Period. End of sentence."

Emily handed me a tissue from her purse.

"I know you're right. It's just that there's this cloak of shame enveloping me, and I can't seem to step outside of it."

"You need to give that cloak a big kick in the ass," Emily said. "You can't let Johnny bring you down like this."

"To make matters more confusing, Jackson has started texting me. His assistant tracked down my number through the team. He feels badly about how things ended between us and wants to see me again."

"Giddy up!" Emily said.

"I'm not sure I want that. Don't get me wrong. I got swept away watching him mesmerize an entire stadium. When he looked at me, I felt like I was the most important person in the room. And the physical part was amazing. But Jackson Ways has a woman in every town. I don't want to be his Oklahoma City girl. I'm done with players."

"Speak for yourself," Emily said with a laugh. "But I get what you're saying. You have been through a lot with Seth and Jackson. You want someone who's down to earth."

"What I want is to pursue my dream of reporting on the sidelines. I need to get my head back in the game and figure out how to progress my career despite Johnny."

"That's my girl. Johnny will get his due in the end. I know it in my bones," Emily said.

I sat up. "Em, I wasn't even thinking. How was your weekend with Devonte?"

"A lot less exciting than yours. We watched movies and ate pizza at his hotel. He has to keep his leg in this giant machine. So, there wasn't much sexy time. But we had the best time laughing, talking, and snuggling. I miss him already."

"That makes my heart sing. Thank you for being such a good friend."

"Right back at you. I never thought I'd find true friendship in this place."

• • •

The timer rang and Mom opened the oven door to inspect her famous squash casserole. Cheese bubbled over delicate layers of yellow and green squash.

"I'm trying to make this healthier. I substituted yogurt for some of the cheese. Don't tell your dad. He'll claim he can taste the difference," she said, carefully placing the casserole dish on a trivet.

I still hadn't worked up the nerve to tell my parents about Jackson or the suspension. It pained me to think about their disappointment, especially Dad's. He had always taken such pride in my accomplishments. No one cheered louder when my high school volleyball team played in the state title game. For my last game at USC, he printed a jumbo-sized cardboard cutout of my face and wildly waved it from the stands.

Since I started this job, he would email friends and family links to my stories and videos. The idea of telling him I was suspended from work for a drunken one-night stand amounted to torture. That's why I needed to baby-step the discussion and tell Mom first. And there was no better opportunity than sitting in the same kitchen where she had consoled me so many times through heartbreaks and setbacks.

"Mom, there's something I have to tell you."

"This sounds serious," she said, sitting on the stool next to me.

"Yesterday, the team suspended me for the next three games," I said, looking down, my eyes flooded with embarrassment.

"Suspended you? What on earth happened?"

"You know the Jackson Ways concert I went to? Well, when I went, I drank too much. And I kissed Jackson backstage. And I went on the bus with him. And the players saw it all."

Mom folded her hands in her lap. Her silence weighed heavy in the air.

"I'm sorry if I've let you down in any way," I said, my throat tightening.

"Oh, sweetie, you haven't let us down. We are so proud of you and always will be. But I am a bit surprised."

"I know. It's not like me to drink and carry on like that in public."

Mom placed a warm hand on top of mine.

"I'd like to think that's not how I raised you to act. But mistakes happen. I'm more surprised that the punishment is so severe. It sounds like there are a lot of shenanigans that go on with this team without consequences."

"There's definitely a double standard for me. I'm trying to figure out how to navigate it. Deep down, I've known Johnny hasn't been fair to me. But I've been so grateful for the job and opportunity to be a part of a pro football team that I'd do anything to please my boss."

"You've worked day and night to please him."

"Well, this experience has been eye-opening. I need to figure out how I can do my job, do it well, and not let Johnny control me."

"That's a very good idea. Blake, I've been worried about you. You've been giving your heart and soul to this team. You've had no time for your family or friends, let alone a boyfriend."

"I just don't know how to tell Dad about all this."

Mom patted my hand. "Let me take care of that. Like me, he's going to be surprised, but he's not going to be any less proud of you. I promise you that."

"Mom, I don't know what I would do without you."

"I love you, sweetie," Mom said, holding up a fork. "Now, come taste this casserole for me."

I stabbed a thin slice of squash draped with cheese. "Heavenly. Your new recipe is perfect."

· · ·

The rest of the week passed slowly. I kept to myself at practice, which thankfully went unnoticed. The media was too busy preparing for Sunday night's prime-time game to socialize. I smiled politely and pretended to be just as busy even though Ryan had taken over the important stories and I was handling his grunt work.

On Thursday, I opened a Styrofoam to-go box overflowing with iceberg lettuce and nudged my keyboard aside. I stabbed a piece of grilled chicken and refreshed my screen. An email from the team's defensive coordinator with the subject "Boots" sat at the top of my inbox. I never received emails from coaches. Could this be about my suspension? I had prayed no one outside of my department even knew about it.

Come find me

No punctuation. No hint of what this was about. Was this my moment of reckoning with the coaches? Would they tell me I couldn't be trusted and they no longer wanted me around the players? My hand trembled as I closed the message.

I waited until evening when the hallways were quiet and made my way toward football ops. The Hall & Oates song "Maneater" played in the conference room. Now or never. I closed my eyes and knocked on the frosted glass doors. The linebackers coach inched open the door and smiled.

"Boots is here."

The defensive coordinator clapped and said, "Let her in."

The defensive coaches surrounded a large conference table, which was piled high with binders and iPads. The scent of dry-erase markers filled the room.

The DC leaned back in his chair and crossed his arms above his hard, perfectly round belly.

"Boots, I've got a favor to ask you. I'm trying to light a fire. Get that extra spark from my guys. Can I borrow a pair of your boots for a couple of hours tomorrow?"

I blinked in confusion.

"You need my boots?"

"We're preparing for an offense that runs a lot of split-zone bootlegs. I thought it would be funny to end tomorrow's meeting by pulling out your boots and shouting, 'Remember the Bootleg,'" the DC said, thrusting a fist in the air for emphasis.

I smiled awkwardly, unsure if this was a prank or joke. But the coaches stared at me expectantly, awaiting a response. I glanced down at my favorite black boots.

"Sure, I'll leave this pair in your office tonight and wear my running shoes home."

"Thanks, Boots."

The DC began to hum the melody of Nancy Sinatra's 'These Boots Are Made for Walkin', the rest of the coaches joining in with the lyrics.

Maybe the coaches didn't know about Jackson Ways and my suspension. Or maybe they didn't care. I started to close the conference room door, but a masochistic curiosity needled at me.

"I hope the boots help," I said, turning back around. "I wish I was traveling to the game to see the defense in person."

The DC removed his bifocals and nestled them in a head of thick gray hair. "Yeah, Johnny told me about that. I think that whole suspension thing is a load of bullcrap."

I cringed. It was mortifying to think about the coaches discussing my drunken escapade. But I also felt relief. I had some allies.

Twenty-Three

Back in the Saddle

The game-time anthem blared from the living room.

"Blake, the game is starting!" Dad called from his leather recliner. No doubt he was hunkered in for the night with a bowl of popcorn resting on his belly and a cold beer in hand.

"Coming."

I sank into the couch and propped my computer on my crossed legs.

"One of the few perks of being suspended is working from the comforts of your living room. It's a whole lot cozier than the press box."

"Can I pour you a glass of wine?" Mom asked from the kitchen.

"I wish. I need to stay sharp and take notes on the game. I'm driving to the stadium later to meet the team."

"You have to go there tonight?" Mom asked, pouring herself a glass of Pinot Noir.

"The media group needs help posting content to the site. I'm supposed to meet them around 2:00 a.m. to finish the postgame coverage."

"But I thought you were suspended without pay from the game?"

"Technically, I'm suspended from working the actual game and my compensation is reduced accordingly. But I'm still expected to do the rest of my job."

"That doesn't make sense."

"Johnny is making a statement. He is banning me from the most rewarding and exciting part of the job—the game. And he is punishing me with all the grunt work."

"It seems very childish."

"I know, but what can I do? Right now, I've got to play by Johnny's rules if I want to keep my job."

Johnny's rules. The two words that had tormented me for the previous three months.

A weekend off had finally given me the time and space to reflect on how dysfunctional my work culture really was. I ignored Johnny's comments about my body and endured his screaming rebukes because that was what I needed to do to keep my job.

In doing so, I was losing my sense of self. The integrity I prided myself on was devolving into loose standards measured against a toxic culture. It was why falling drunkenly into Jackson's bed had been so easy. I had yearned for a night of reckless abandon. If Johnny, Seth, even Ryan could act as they pleased, why couldn't I? But that wasn't me.

It was time to realign my moral compass and focus on my career. My goal was to land a reporting job on television in the next year. To accomplish that I needed to build my journalism portfolio and refine my broadcasting skills under Sheridan's guidance. I also needed to get in Johnny's good graces again. Unfortunately, his recommendation was crucial in moving up in the echelons of pro football media.

. . .

Dad turned up the volume of the broadcast as Andy jogged onto the field. The camera cut to the reporter standing on OKC's sideline:

"Andy Miller went down three weeks ago with a high ankle sprain. Coaches initially thought he would be out at least a month. This is a quick turnaround for the injury-prone quarterback. But Coach Bush said Andy gave them enough in practice to show that he's ready."

But Andy looked anything but ready. He stumbled through his drop backs and stepped gingerly on his plant foot. He couldn't get any zip on his throws and consistently wound up dumping the ball off to a running back or tight end.

By the end of the first half, OKC was lucky to be down 14–0. Considering how bad the offense looked, the damage could have been much worse.

Coach Bush stared ahead blank-faced as he jogged with the team to the locker room. The sideline reporter intercepted him in front of the tunnel.

"Coach, what answers do you have about Andy Miller's health after the first half?"

Coach's navy puffy jacket was zipped high to his neck and he looked as if he wanted to burrow down into the pillowy layers.

"Things haven't gone his way. There are adjustments we need to make. But Andy is a battler," Coach said, turning abruptly as Johnny scurried behind him, his long black peacoat flapping in the wind.

"Coach Bush was short on words tonight," Dad said, tossing popcorn into his mouth.

"What else could he say? Andy looks awful. He's not ready to play. They shouldn't have rushed him back."

"They aren't winning at Pittsburgh with either of these quarterbacks. You might as well take your licks with Seth and get Andy healthy," Dad said.

After sitting in silence through the halftime highlights, I finally mustered the courage to ask the question that had been needling my subconscious.

"So, what do you think of my suspension? Mom thinks it's totally unfair, but you haven't said much."

Dad stiffened. He was visibly uncomfortable.

"Blake, I really don't know what to think. I don't understand what you did wrong. But I also know there are two sides to every story. This might be how the league operates."

My brow furrowed. "You think Johnny was justified in disciplining me?"

Dad qualified as a mega fan of the team. He watched every game, listened to sports radio, and read the message boards, but how could he not take my side on this?

Dad pushed down the recliner's footrest and sat up straight.

"I'm not saying I agree with Johnny. What I'm saying is that pro football is the most powerful sports league in the world. It operates like the military. There's a strict chain of command that exacts order and a culture of supremacy. And league execs, Johnny included, have been damn successful running teams that way."

"Just because Johnny and front office guys like him have been successful doesn't mean that they're justified in their behavior," I pushed back.

"I agree with that. But I also see where they are coming from. They've been doing things their way for a long time, and they don't see it necessary to change."

"Yeah, Johnny calls it his 'old school ways.' Personally, I'm sick of it," I said.

"Well then, show that bastard what you're made of. Out-work everyone. Make your stories and videos go viral. Make him see how valuable you are to the team."

"Dad, it's not that easy. In case you forgot, I'm not allowed in the locker room. Johnny limits my access to the players. He won't let me publish injury updates, let alone break stories. How on earth am I supposed to produce viral content?"

"No one said it would be easy. But if you want this job, if you really want to be on the sidelines on Sunday nights, you're going to have to overcome this challenge."

"I'm not one to back down from a challenge," I said, "but beating Johnny at his own game is a daunting challenge to tackle. Pun intended."

"Blake, if you truly want to be the next Erin Andrews, you will find a way."

Dad leaned over and squeezed my shoulder. It was the same reassuring squeeze he'd given me since I was a little girl. After falling down on my fist bike ride, after losing a volleyball match, after breaking up with my college boyfriend—that squeeze was his way of saying, "You've got this."

"You're right. If I am going to make it to network TV, I've got to find a way of making the most of my job while also sticking to my guns."

"That's my girl."

Dad leaned back in his chair and re-glued his eyes to the game. OKC had driven to the red zone.

It was fourth and inches in the fourth quarter, and it seemed like the game hinged on this play. Andy took the snap and dove forward, extending the ball in front of him. A linebacker who was crouched like a tiger tracking his prey pounced. He punched the ball out of Andy's hand, scooped it up, and returned it for a touchdown and a 24–3 lead.

The camera cut to Andy splayed across the grass. He pounded the ground with a fist before pushing himself to his knees.

"You've got to be kidding me. I can't watch any more of this garbage," Dad said, walking to the kitchen with an empty popcorn bowl.

When the teams shook hands at midfield, no one looked more miserable than Johnny, who was following Coach Bush as he walked to his obligatory postgame interviews. The team took an ass whooping on the field. Now, Johnny had to make sure they didn't take one in the media.

"I'm going to get ready for work. I might as well get to the stadium early and get things done before the team returns."

"I can't imagine there's going to be much fanfare on the site after that game," Dad said.

"Nope. But I want to find a unique angle for my story."

It was time to buckle the chinstrap and get back in the game.

Twenty-Four

Photo Bomb

Muffled voices filtered down the dimly lit hallway. I peered out of my office. The coaches and staff bowed their heads as they towed suitcases back to their desks.

Garrett's computer satchel clunked against his leg as he plodded down the hall.

"Hey, Garrett," I said gently as he passed my door.

A skinny black tie drooped from his neck.

"Blake, it's been a long, shitty day. Let's just get our work done and forget the chitchat."

Part of me actually felt sorry for Garrett. He probably had been working for more than twelve hours and had to endure Johnny's wrath on a tense flight home.

"I got to the stadium early and finished transcribing the interviews you emailed me. I wasn't sure what stories you wanted me to write."

Garrett lowered his glasses and rubbed his eyes. "Johnny wants very little on the site about the game. Proof Ryan's game story and post it for him. You also need to shoot intros for the videos."

I raised an eyebrow.

"But I wasn't at the game. Isn't that going to seem strange to be shooting the videos from here?"

"Stand in front of a nondescript gray wall and act like you were at the game." Garrett sighed. "I don't want our fans to know that you weren't there. You have a following. They won't like someone else in the videos."

"I didn't think you'd want me on camera."

"Well, I do."

I went back to my office and pulled my makeup bag out of my desk drawer. I quickly dabbed bronzer across my face and coated mascara on my lashes. Fresh coffee dripped from the pots in the break room. For the first time, I was tempted to drink Coach Bush's sludge. Johnny's office was dark, which was no surprise. He usually worked from home after games, presumably because he didn't want anyone to hear his phone conversations with media.

I rounded the corner to Ryan's cubicle. His head rested on the keyboard and drool pooled at the edges of his mouth.

"Hi there," I said, nudging him.

Ryan pried open one eye.

"You don't have to stay here. I can finish up your work," I told him.

"Are you sure? Garrett had me running around like crazy today. I'm beat."

"I'm sorry I wasn't there to help. You really should go home."

"Thank you."

By the time I finished with the videos and website updates, it was almost 5:00 a.m. It didn't make sense to go home and return in a couple of hours, so I decided to make a pallet on my office floor with pillows from the break room and I promptly drifted off into a deep sleep.

. . .

My cell phone alarm jolted me awake just before 8:00 a.m. I had given myself extra snoozing time since Johnny had postponed our morning meeting to the afternoon. I fluttered my eyes, adjusting to the glow of the computer screen atop my desk.

Emily's signature perfume seeped under my door before I even heard her voice.

"Have you seen Blake?" Johnny asked.

Dread churned inside my gut.

"No, I haven't talked to her since Friday," Emily said.

"She should be here by now," Johnny said as his cell phone rang. "Excuse me. I need to get this."

When I realized I'd been holding my breath, I exhaled slowly and gripped the edges of my desk to stand up. Why was Johnny grilling Emily about me? What now?

I freshened up as best I could without turning on the overhead fluorescent lights. Lines from the corduroy pillows were imprinted on my right cheek. I rubbed them hard, willing them to go away.

After an hour of working in the dark, I gathered the courage to turn on my light and crack the door. Within seconds, I heard the jangle of bangle bracelets.

"Look who the cat dragged in!" Emily said, quickly shutting the door behind her. "My goodness, you look like shit."

"I've been here since midnight and only slept a few hours on the floor. I've actually been sitting at my desk with the lights off because I didn't want anyone to know I was here."

"By anyone are you referring to Johnny?" Emily said, crossing her arms. "He was in my face first thing this morning, asking about you."

"I heard. I have no idea what he's pissed about now."

"I'm sure you'll find out soon. How was your weekend?"

"My weekend was a much-needed break. I never thought I'd say this, but in many ways the suspension was a blessing. I got to clear my head and refocus."

"Did you hear again from Jackson?"

"Yeah, he texted me. He wants me to hang out with him this weekend when the team goes to Tennessee."

"And?"

"I told him that I was suspended from traveling to the game."

"What did he say?"

"He thought the whole thing was ridiculous. Jackson said his manager knows Johnny, and he was going to make his manager tell Johnny to end the suspension."

"Maybe that's why Johnny has his panties in a wad. He got scolded by Jackson's manager."

"I begged Jackson not to say anything. To be honest, I am done with Jackson Ways. I don't want to hear from him or see him again. In the week since I met him, all he has done is complicate my life."

"I get where you're coming from, but I keep thinking about the upside to dating him. You'd be an overnight celebrity. You'd get access to agents and TV execs," Emily said.

"You're assuming Jackson wants to date me and I want to date him. Jackson is looking for a fun night with no strings attached. I'm looking to prioritize my career."

"Not me. The day Devonte proposes is the day I quit," Emily said, cocking her head to one side emphatically.

"Why don't you quit now?"

"I need to pay my bills. I don't want to have to ask Devonte for money all the time."

"Do you think he'll propose soon?"

"I don't think so. We've talked about getting married. But he's not ready. Right now, he's concentrating on his rehab. And I respect that."

"That's great you're not putting pressure on him."

"He needs me loving on him right now, not begging for a ring."

"This is probably none of my business, but is it OK for him to have sex?" I asked.

"He hurt his knee, not his ding-dong. I know lots of ways to satisfy my man that are doctor approved." Emily winked.

"I'm sure you've got all sorts of moves." I giggled.

My phone rang, interrupting our schoolgirl-like laughter.

"It's Johnny." I grimaced.

"Hello, this is Blake," I said into the phone.

"In my office. Now," Johnny snapped.

• • •

Johnny swiveled to face me, his cell pressed hard against his ear, and motioned for me to close the door.

"Just make sure you've canceled all community appearances for Andy and Seth. They'll get pelted with quarterback controversy questions. Eaten alive by the media."

Johnny motioned for me to sit down. I realized I was gripping the back wall, staying as far away as I could from any flying shrapnel.

"Yeah, I read what that slappy wrote. He shit all over Coach. Don't give him credentials to the next game. That will teach him," Johnny said, pounding his desk with a meaty hand. "OK, I've got another fuckup I need to deal with now."

I gulped. I was the other "fuckup."

A dead silence filled the room as he opened an email.

"I thought after the suspension, this conversation would be over. But this morning, I received a perturbing link," Johnny said, angling the computer screen in my direction. "Some woman posted this photo on social media. It got picked up by local sites and is all over the internet now."

A photograph of me kissing Jackson backstage popped up with the headline "Jackson Ways Hot and Heavy with League Exec."

My stomach fell. Gossip about our hookup held an element of fiction on the team, the story changing with each retelling. The only people who really knew what happened on the bus were me and Jackson. This photo. Well, it was concrete evidence. There I was sucking face with country music's biggest star, and it was circulating the internet for the world to see. The team's owner, Sheridan, potential employers. All of them could look at me locking lips with Jackson and make their judgments—judgments that could impact my career. There was nothing I could do but absorb this crushing blow.

I swallowed back tears and searched for my voice.

"This is humiliating. I want nothing more than to erase this photo from existence. Since that's not possible, what can we do?"

"Blake, you've really fucked up," Johnny yelled. "I had to explain your fling to the coaches, GM, president, and ownership. It makes me look like I hired a celebrity-crazed prom queen. I wanted to fire you today. But our page views are the highest ever. Ownership thinks the publicity may be good for business. We've had more traffic on our site this morning than any Monday morning in team history. Mr. Morgan is fucking loving this." Johnny laughed maniacally. I flinched in my seat.

"To make things even more fucking complicated, I got a call from Jackson Ways's manager, who happens to be the most powerful music manager in the world. He said Jackson told him about the suspension. He wants me to end it so you can travel to Nashville this weekend and be Jackson's date at some charity event."

I looked up incredulously. "Are you saying you want me to go with Jackson to this party so you can get in good with his manager? Pardon my language—that is the definition of fucked up."

"I thought you'd be all over this. The way you were all over Jackson," Johnny said.

"That's not fair, Johnny."

"What's not fair, Blake, is the position you have put me in. I have worked my tail off to build relationships with powerful people like Jackson Ways's manager. I can't afford to jeopardize that. But I also need to send a message to this team that behavior like yours will not be tolerated. That's why I will be going to this charity event with you. I will be there to chaperone you, manage your every move, and make sure you don't embarrass yourself or the team again."

Ire overtook humiliation. What right did Johnny have to dictate my personal life and force me on a date?

"I would like to travel to Tennessee with the team, but I refuse to attend this party with Jackson Ways," I said.

"Oh, you're going. You're going to put on a tight dress, get your face made up, and take lots of photos all lovey-dovey with Jackson Ways," Johnny said. His voice hissed with anger.

I was about to bark back, "I will not," but I caught the words from escaping my mouth. It dawned on me that for the first time since I'd met Johnny, I held leverage over him. He desperately needed me to be his show pony at this charity event, to play the part of the sweet, pretty, docile employee so he could make his power moves.

As much as I wanted to spurn Johnny, I forced myself to swallow down the anger. I had to look at the bigger picture and find a way to use this leverage to my advantage.

"OK, Johnny, I will think about it," I said. I looked down at my wringing hands. I was too scared that if I met his gaze, he would see the insubordination percolating inside me.

"Whatever, you're going. End of story," Johnny said.

"Johnny, sometimes I think you hired me just because I'm a pretty face, not because I'm a talented journalist." The words popped out of my mouth. There were so many defiant thoughts clamoring inside my brain, fighting for airtime—I had to let something escape.

"That's exactly why I hired you. People love women football report-ers. Me included. But I don't think women belong on pro teams. You're proving my case with all your shenanigans and drama."

I bit my lip hard, so as not to let any more fighting words escape. It was time to retreat and regroup.

· · ·

I spent most of the day holed up in my office with the door cracked. Ryan messaged me to join him for lunch in the team cafeteria, but I lied and said I brought food, instead scavenging kolaches from the break room. The post had circulated through the stadium, and I was in no mood for conversations about Jackson Ways.

Messages streamed in from people who saw the photo. Friends excitedly asked for the juicy details. Media members asked for quotes. I replied to no one and sent all calls to voice mail. Emotional exhaustion overwhelmed me. My body felt boneless, like it lacked the infrastructure to operate.

"Knock, knock," Ryan said, sliding his head inside my office door. I shook my head silently.

"Blake, you have to come out of hiding. We have Coach's press con-ference in a few minutes," Ryan said.

I winced, thinking about gathering in the team auditorium for Coach Bush's weekly Monday address to the media. My friends in the media would undoubtedly ask me why I didn't travel to Sunday's game and, even more embarrassing, about my photo with Jackson.

"Ugh. That's the last place I want to be right now."

"I'm guessing this has to do with the photo of you and Jackson that's making the rounds."

"That and the verbal bashing I took from Johnny today. I don't have the strength to go downstairs and face everyone," I said.

"Put one foot in front of the other. The hardest step is the first one. But I know you can do it," he said.

I took a deep breath and pushed myself out of my chair. I followed Ryan to two seats at the back of the auditorium, far removed from the fray of reporters near the stage. A reporter I recognized from ESPN sat in the front row, her long, auburn hair meticulously framing her heart-shaped face and cascading down her green silk blouse. She tapped a coworker's arm and showed him a message on her phone. Jealousy streaked through me. I wanted to be in her position. Sitting at the front of the room, admired by colleagues at the top of their professions, wearing fashionable clothes. Instead, I cowered in a back row, avoiding other media members and wearing a wrinkled outfit that smelled like a kolache shop. Oh, and my boss was forcing me to go on a date where he would be chaperoning. That was the icing on the cake of my dream job that was devolving into a nightmare situation.

The room quieted as Coach Bush sauntered to the podium, Johnny dutifully following him.

"That's a heck of a football team we played yesterday. When you go into their place, you have to be pretty close to perfect. We were anything but that. Give them a lot of credit. They had a lot to do with why we played poorly. You can't turn the ball over like that and expect to win in this league," Coach Bush said. His face sagged under the weight of his drooping eyes.

"Coach Bush will take questions now," Johnny said to the room and pointed to the ESPN reporter.

"Will Andy start on Sunday?" she asked, flashing Coach Bush a mega smile.

"We'll look at him hard on Wednesday and see where he's at. But this is going to be a day-to-day thing."

"At 4–3, how would you assess this team almost halfway through the season?" Sheridan asked.

Coach Bush gripped the podium tightly, his thick knuckles whitening. "Our kids play hard. But we have a lot to correct on the mental and physical side."

As Johnny called the presser to a close, Sheridan darted up the auditorium steps toward her photographer. I lowered my head to my notepad, hoping to remain unnoticed.

"Blake, we missed you at the game," she said. "Lucky you to get days off during the season. And lucky you got to go out with Jackson Ways."

My cheeks flamed red.

Twenty-Five

A Hostage Situation

"Move to your right so the logo is over your shoulder," Boss said, waving me across the end zone in the empty stadium. "I'm going to shoot this from a distance. You look really tired."

"It's been a tough week," I said and took a deep breath before beginning my stand-up.

"Going into the ninth week of the season, Oklahoma City leads the division with a 4–3 record. But, as Coach Bush emphasized Wednesday after practice, injuries are a concern for this young team. Quarterback Andy Miller is still day-to-day after aggravating a high ankle sprain."

"How was that take?"

"I'm good with it if you are," Boss said, his right eye still pressed against the viewfinder, reviewing the shot.

Out of the corner of my eye, I saw Andy walk past the tunnel.

"Good. I need to talk to someone."

Johnny frowned upon me talking to players without his consent. He didn't want me privy to breaking information that he could feed to a media member in exchange for a favor—like telling a writer exclusive contract details about a player so the writer would hold a story exposing rifts in the locker room. But at this point, I had nothing to lose.

I intercepted Andy before he opened the training room door.

"Andy, do you have a quick second?"

"I have to get treatment. What's up?" he said. Dark stubble peppered his chin, making his doughy face look a little older and tougher.

"I wanted to get a little background info for a story I need to write tonight. Coach Bush said you're working hard so that you can get back on the field ASAP. What exactly are you doing to speed up your rehab?"

"I'm in the cold tub twice a day. They've got me doing electric stim and wearing a compression brace. Then there's the balance and strength work. I get to the training room at 5:00 a.m. and I'm here almost all day. The docs think I should be 100 percent in a couple of weeks."

A couple of weeks. That was breaking news. I had my story.

. . .

I raced to my office. "Miller Working Hard to Get Healthy." I began with Coach Bush's message from the presser, added specifics about Andy's rehab, and quoted doctors as speculating it would be two weeks until Andy completely healed.

I sat back and savored the finished product and then worked up the nerve to call Sheridan.

"Hi, Blake. What's up?"

"I'm calling because I just finished a story about Andy's rehab, and it includes some information about his return. Johnny isn't letting the media interview Andy right now, so these might be the only quotes he gives this week. I'm not sure Johnny will let me publish the story on the site. If he does, he might make me edit it. So, I wanted to send you an original version. That way you can see a sample of my work."

"Why exactly can't the team run the story?"

I inhaled slowly.

"Well, Johnny has a strict interview policy. I can only interview players with his approval. I got some of this information when I talked to Andy casually outside the training room."

"So, you were being a journalist," she said, with a sharp tone.

"I'm trying. I want to prove my reporting chops and build my resume.

But it's difficult given all of Johnny's policies. And, as you might know, I'm already on a short leash."

"I know about the bullshit locker room policy. There's no reason you shouldn't be in there. I'm guessing the short leash has to do with Jackson Ways."

"Yeah, it's a long story. The short of it is that I made some poor decisions in my interactions with Jackson. I really want to move forward from that and let my work take center stage."

"What goes on with Jackson Ways is none of my business," she told me. "My business is sports journalism. I've been doing it for over fifteen years. Women have fought hard for our place in the locker room, behind the microphone, and on the byline. We still have a long way to go. Johnny reminds me of that every day."

I nodded into the phone.

"The way we trump people like Johnny is with information," Sheridan continued. "Information is power. Today, you collected meaningful information. I know you're in a hard place about what to do with it. I want to help any way I can. I want to help you become a journalist, not just a mouthpiece."

"Thank you, Sheridan."

"No need to thank me. You gave me exclusive info after Devonte's injury. Now, it's my turn to help you. Email me the story. I will show it to my boss."

"That would be amazing."

"If you are building a resume, you also need to put together a reel of reporting clips. Keep that in mind as you do your video work," Sheridan said.

"I need more video content. I've mainly shot basic intros, aside from my hit on the Network."

"We'll get you on the Network again. Keep plugging away on your end, and I will see what I can do on mine."

"Sounds good."

I hung up and closed my eyes. Now for the call I'd been dreading. Johnny answered on the first ring.

"Blake, this better be important," he said.

"It is. I told you I would think about attending Jackson's charity party. I have thought about it. I will go if you publish a story that I wrote about Andy's injury. It includes some quotes he gave me about his rehab. And you have to grant me a one-on-one interview with Andy."

"Are you fucking holding me hostage?"

"I'm striking a bargain with you," I said measuredly.

"Fuck!" Johnny spit into the phone. "Send me the story, then I'll decide. But I'm done with your manipulative games, Blake."

I emailed Johnny the story, my heart racing as the message whooshed into cyber world. It pained me to think about linking arms with Jackson for a charity party while Johnny trotted along beside us. No part of me wanted to be physically connected to Jackson anymore.

But I wanted to use what limited leverage I had before it ran dry. An interview with Andy could get picked up by news outlets across the state, given his limited availability to the media. It was exactly what I needed to build my reel.

My computer dinged. An email from Johnny.

Story approved. Interview tomorrow.

I leaned back and propped my feet on my desk. I had scored a victory. A victory with strings attached, but a victory nonetheless.

Twenty-Six

Say a Little Prayer for Me

I slowly opened the creaky wooden front door and tiptoed to the kitchen, careful not to wake my parents. My stomach growled, angry that I abandoned a full plate of barbeque in the break room. I set my computer bag on the kitchen counter and raided the refrigerator. Leftover spaghetti with meat sauce filled Tupperware containers like gifts from the heavens.

I plopped down on a barstool with a heaping plate and pulled out my laptop to rewatch my interview with Andy. The video had gone viral. Even national networks had aired snippets of our exchange.

For the first time, I felt like a true journalist, instead of Johnny's mouthpiece. I had elicited significant information from the team's quarterback about his injury and mindset. My words had mattered.

I twirled noodles around a fork and glanced at my phone, which was vibrating next to me. A text from Sheridan: *Way to go, girl! We ran the interview on the Network. You killed it.*

My heart swelled with pride. This interview was garnering exposure and kudos from newsrooms across the country. Everything was working out as I hoped, except that I still had to attend the charity event with Jackson.

I cringed and forced myself to face his mounting texts. I had been ignoring Jackson for the last few days, willing his messages to disappear and for the invitation to the party to evaporate simultaneously. I just needed to get through this one night in Tennessee.

I pressed the first message. *How's my hot date? I'm flying to LA. My assistant Missy will holler for me. TTYL!*

The second message was from Missy. *Coordinating the details for Saturday. Sending 3 couture gowns to your hotel room. You look like a size 6. Please confirm. A limo will pick you up promptly at 5 pm.*

I had planned to wear an old prom dress that I had purchased at an outlet mall seven years earlier. A new gown didn't fit into my current budget. After splurging on my boots and the leopard-print dress, I had reevaluated my spending and begun using my paychecks to get ahead on my car note and student loans. It gave me immense satisfaction to see the seemingly insurmountable debt dwindle down to manageable figures.

Now that I was back on track, I didn't want to derail my finances by purchasing a dress just for a photo op with Jackson. But his management team was taking matters into their own hands, and Missy was securing me the latest designer fashions.

I rested my head in my hands. What had I gotten myself into? And more importantly, how could I get myself out of it?

. . .

"Boots, it's good to have you back," Hal said, patting my shoulder. He was standing in line behind me as we waited to board the plane for Tennessee. His floor-length, blue puffy jacket padded his overstuffed physique, making him look like a human marshmallow.

I assumed Hal knew a version of my suspension story since he knew everything about this team. But Hal, like most of my media friends, had respected my privacy and refrained from asking me about Jackson Ways.

A wintry breeze cut across the tarmac and I buttoned up my peacoat.

"Brrr. It's cold out here. Hal, you had the right idea with that big coat of yours."

Hal chuckled. "The forecast in Tennessee calls for sleet on Sunday, and there's no escaping the elements on the sidelines. I came prepared."

In the galley of the plane, Alyssa greeted me with a smile lacquered in light pink lip gloss.

"We missed you, honey," she said, extending a tray of sweet treats. "I got extra Twizzlers just for you."

Alyssa's soft tone put me at ease. She was not there to judge, just to reassure and provide an endless supply of candy.

"Thanks, Alyssa," I said and smiled at her appreciatively.

I found my usual seat, carefully removed my collection of magazines from my satchel, and wedged my bags in the overhead compartment.

"Now everything in the world feels right again," Ryan said, stepping over me to his middle seat. "Blake is back on the plane with her trashy magazines."

"Watch what you're calling trash," I ribbed. "It's called mindless entertainment. It's a reading genre."

"Make sure to pass that one back," Monster Calves said, lumbering past me in a distinguished gray sweater and white button-down combination most certainly picked out by his beautiful wife. "I gotta keep up with the Kardashians."

"You got it," I said.

I thumbed through a recap from the Emmys, and it dawned on me that the photo of me and Jackson kissing might be in this very magazine. My heart raced as I quickly scanned each page. When I reached the back cover, I exhaled in relief.

Now, I had to prepare myself for the onslaught of cameras and phones that would capture Jackson's every move on Saturday. I had to remain professional. No alcohol. Not even a drop. There could be no getting wrapped up in the Jackson mania of the night. I was there to do a job. Look pretty. Smile. Get out.

. . .

Rain pelted the windows of the bus as our police-escorted caravan rolled toward downtown. I leaned against the bus window and was taking in the city's skyline when a visceral groan bellowed from the back of the bus.

"Oh my God. It's Hal. Stop the bus! Stop the bus!" Johnny screamed.

Ryan and I bolted upright and turned around, gripping our seats as the bus lurched toward the curb.

Johnny forced an arm under Hal's shaking body, yelling, "He's having a seizure!"

Hal's torso jerked back, his head bouncing against the headrest. His eyes rolled back so far all I could see were the whites of his eyeballs. Hal's twitching legs kicked Johnny as he tried to lift Hal from his seat.

Dr. Lott, the team's orthopedic surgeon, ran to the back of the bus, pushing Johnny into his seat. The doctor straddled Hal with his legs and clamped his arms around Hal's chest. He heaved him into the aisle and lowered his body onto the floor of the bus.

"Move back. He needs CPR!" Dr. Lott yelled.

I clutched Ryan's arm and searched for my own breath. No one on the bus was speaking. Fear collectively gripped us as the doctor interlaced his hands and began strong, rhythmic compressions on Hal's chest. A meek shade of blue paled Hal's skin, and I realized this was what dying looked like.

Voices clamored outside the bus.

"An ambulance should be here soon," a police officer from the escort told the bus driver. "I alerted the other drivers about what's going on. I told them they could go ahead. The hotel is just around the corner. But the coaches want to wait here. They're worried as hell."

Dr. Lott's biceps flexed as he alternated between compressions and mouth-to-mouth breathing.

"How much longer can he give CPR? The ambulance needs to get here now," I pleaded to Ryan, whose hands were clasped as he prayed for Hal.

"He's breathing!" Dr. Lott yelled over the sirens blaring in the distance.

Tears slipped down Johnny's cheeks. Watching him cry was almost as surreal and shocking as the previous five minutes.

Within seconds, paramedics bounded through the aisle. They slid a backboard under Hal's limp body and carried him off the bus. Dr. Lott followed, detailing the situation with a steady voice as paramedics placed Hal on a stretcher.

"This man is lucky you were here," the paramedic told Dr. Lott as they talked outside of the bus.

Coach Bush ran from the lead bus toward Dr. Lott, his navy tie loose around his neck and flapping against his shoulder. "Is Hal going to be OK?"

"He's breathing. But we need to take him to the ER for tests. It looks like your doc saved his life," the paramedic interjected.

Coach Bush blotted the sweat on his forehead with his tie.

"Thank God."

Several coaches filed out of the first bus and gathered around Coach Bush. Johnny walked briskly past my seat, his head lowered, and joined them.

"Seein' Hal like that, it made me think that coulda been one of us," Coach Bush said. "It's no secret this job ain't good for your health."

"Coach, the good news is that Hal is breathing on his own and in good care," Johnny said, wiping away his tears and removing any vestiges of vulnerability.

Coach Bush shook his head.

"Let's get to the hotel. I want the chaplain to lead us in prayer before team meetings."

I turned from the bus window, my forehead red and cold from being pressed against the glass.

"Coach Bush seems really shaken up," I said.

"These coaches deal with insane amounts of stress. They don't sleep and they eat junk all day. What happened to Hal must hit close to home," Ryan said.

I thought about Hal's body stiffening against the bus floor, his eyes rolled back into the sockets.

"We just saw our friend die and come back to life," I said. "I don't think any of us will ever be the same after seeing that. Even Johnny."

. . .

I hung up the gold-sequin Tom Ford halter dress I had decided to wear to the party. The limo would arrive in two hours to pick me up. I needed to fix my hair and makeup, but my body begged to curl up and take a nap.

I pulled back the duvet and sank into the hotel bed. Hal's guttural groan roared between my ears. How could I strut along as Jackson's arm candy after witnessing Hal's near-death collapse? There was no way Johnny could go through with this charade.

As I fought to open my drooping eyes, my phone rang.

"Hi, Blake," Sheridan said breathlessly. "I'm running through the airport but wanted to catch you ASAP."

"Did you hear about Hal?" I asked.

"The Network called me a few minutes ago. Thank God he's going to be OK. What a horrible scare," Sheridan said. "I hate to switch gears so abruptly, but I'm about to board my plane and have something urgent to ask you."

"OK."

"I usually have Hal join me on the field for a pregame report. You know, to give the inside slant. Since he's in the hospital, I suggested you do it. The Network thought that was a great idea. You can touch on what happened to Hal, recap your Andy interview, and give us your takes on the game."

"Yes! Oh my gosh, thank you for this opportunity, Sheridan. I won't let you down."

"You'll do great. The important thing is to arrive early. It's a noon game, and the Network wants you to start your hit first thing. We have a lot to cover. Let's meet on the field a little before 8:00 a.m."

"You've got it."

"I'll call Johnny. You should call him too. You know that he doesn't like any curveballs," Sheridan said.

"Sounds like a plan," I said, my eyes suddenly wide and alert.

I hung up with Sheridan and immediately called Johnny. His phone went directly to voice mail. I tried several times more and no answer.

I decided to send him a text.

> Me: *Sheridan asked me to fill in for Hal on the Network tomorrow. I wanted to let you know that I will be going to the stadium early for that.*

> Johnny: *You should be asking me permission. Not telling me what you're doing.*

Me: *I figured you would be OK with it.*

Johnny: *I need to think about it. Find me in the morning.*

Me: *Send me talking points. I promise I will follow them. Are we going tonight?*

Johnny: *I can't go after what happened to Hal. And I can't trust you on your own.*

Me: *We are canceling on Jackson???*

Johnny: *I have no choice. I have to find a radio sideline reporter. Coach has called a team meeting. I have too much shit to deal with right now. And I don't trust you for fuck's sake.*

Me: *Do I need to contact Jackson?*

Johnny: *No. I'm calling his manager now. I'm so pissed. You got me into this fucking mess. It's all your fault.*

For once, Johnny's vitriol didn't pierce me. I was going on national television in the morning. And I was off the hook with Jackson. I said a prayer for Hal and sank back into bed.

Twenty-Seven

Tits McGee

I combed the tight curls rolling down my shoulders and glazed them with extra-stiff hairspray. It took an hour, two hairstyling YouTube videos, and cursing out my curling iron to achieve a style that vaguely looked like Erin Andrews's. But I was pleased with the outcome.

I stuffed my makeup essentials into my computer bag and glanced over the talking points Johnny had emailed me the night before. Feeling over-prepared was the only thing keeping my nerves in check. It was just before 7:00 a.m., which meant I had an hour until I needed to meet Sheridan on the field.

The ride to the stadium wouldn't take any more than ten minutes, but I had no idea when Johnny had scheduled the bus. He had noted in his email that the Blake Bus would make an early loop from the hotel to the stadium and to be ready in the lobby. I decided to play it safe and drink my coffee next to the windows facing the circle drive.

After twenty minutes, a venti latte, and a scone, I got antsy and texted Johnny. I stared at my phone and watched the minutes crawl. No reply.

Johnny made it clear that I was not allowed in the players' breakfast area, but at that point I had no option. I took the elevators to the second floor and followed the smell of bacon to a small ballroom. Inside, players wore headphones as they stared down plates of omelets, fruit, and bagels. No one spoke and no one noticed my entrance. They were in game mode.

I found Ryan eating French toast at a table with RJ and the scouts.

"Have you seen Johnny? I need to leave for the stadium ASAP. My bus hasn't arrived and he's not answering my texts."

"He's in the corner talking to Lenny. Must be something serious because they've been huddled up for a while," Ryan said, pointing across the room.

Johnny's back was to me, but I could tell he was irate from his hand motions. His meaty, balled-up fists punched at the sides of his gray pin-stripe suit. Lenny, the player operations coordinator, who cherished the formalities of his job, stood with his legs apart, deeply grounded into the ballroom carpet, earbuds firmly affixed to both ears.

My stomach did somersaults as I approached them. Already I was nervous about my spots on the Network and now I had to face Johnny inside the forbidden ballroom.

Lenny saw me and tapped his earpiece, and they both turned to face me.

"Sorry to interrupt. I wanted to check on my bus."

"Your bus isn't coming. Lenny couldn't change the schedule on short notice," Johnny quipped.

I straightened myself and met his steely gaze.

"Why didn't you tell me? I've been waiting in the lobby for a half hour."

"I just found out." Johnny stared back without blinking.

"How am I supposed to get there?"

"Put on your big-girl pants and call a cab. Aren't reporters supposed to be resourceful?"

"Johnny, I thought you were OK with me doing this?"

"Blake, you have a way of making things a lot more complicated. Right now, I don't have time to deal with you and your reporting dreams. In case you forgot, our radio sideline reporter almost died yesterday, and our replacement sucks."

I swallowed back the indignation, refusing to let his hurtful words wound me. Not today.

As I waited for a taxi to arrive, I texted Sheridan. *Mix-up with my transportation. About to catch a cab. Should be there right at 8.*

She replied, *K.*

I took a deep breath and tried to regroup. I was determined not to let Johnny sabotage this opportunity. I worked too hard. I sacrificed too much.

The bellman waved an old Lincoln into the circle drive.

"That's your car, young lady."

I piled my bags into the back seat.

"Nissan Stadium. As fast as you can."

"Going to the game?"

"I'm working it."

Rain spit against the windshield of the car as we crossed the river and approached the outer lots of the stadium. Tailgaters wearing powder-blue ponchos huddled under tarps and warmed their hands over simmering grills.

"Gonna be a sloppy one," the driver said.

I opened my wallet and found a twenty stuffed in the billfold. I hadn't anticipated paying for my transportation and rarely paid for anything on team trips.

"Sir, do you take credit cards?"

"Just cash. You need me to take you to an ATM?"

"I've got a twenty. How close can you get me?"

"Right about here," the driver said, pounding his brakes and stopping the taxi next to a wall of concrete barricades.

"Isn't there a limo line that can get us closer?"

"It's all the way on the other side of the stadium. Your meter is running out."

It was probably a half mile to the stadium. If I ran, I could be there in ten minutes. I buttoned up my peacoat and handed the driver the crumpled twenty.

The cold rain stung my face. I buried my head in the collar of my coat and ran. My rolling bag sloshed through puddles and muddy water splattered across my black boots. I didn't care—I had to make it to the field in ten minutes or less.

Tailgaters shouted as I passed them, "Run, Forrest, run!"

My once perfectly curled hair began to fall limp around my face.

Even if I made it to Sheridan on time, I would look far too disheveled to go on camera.

My feet throbbed as I entered the stadium's main concourse, and I pulled out my phone. Two texts from Sheridan:

Where are you????

Did the first hit without you. Second hit in 30 min. Are you coming?

My fingers fluttered. *I'm sopping wet. Will get fixed up and be there ASAP.*

I hurried into the bathroom. I looked worse than I had imagined. Wet hair matted against my forehead. Long gone were the perfectly curled tendrils. Instead, ratted clumps sat against my shoulders. Makeup streaked across my red, windblown face.

I squatted under the hand dryer and furiously combed out the tangles in my hair. It certainly was not ideal, but with a headband my hair looked decent. I smudged my makeup back in place and swiped on a coat of red lipstick. *Heading to the field*, I texted Sheridan.

Having tech issues because of the weather. Not sure they're coming back to us for a while. I'll update you soon.

My shoulders slumped in disappointment.

. . .

By the time I trekked halfway around the stadium to the press box, it was three hours until kickoff. Johnny was holding court at the breakfast buffet, reminiscing about a dinner at Jimmy Kelly's Steakhouse.

"We took over the private room. Kevin Costner came in to say hi. He was in town for some movie. The atmosphere was unbelievable. And you can't beat their steaks and cornbread cake," he said to a reporter.

I slinked behind Johnny to our department's assigned row and located my workstation. Ryan was typing diligently at the station next to me.

"Do you want me to get the photo slides today with the weather so bad?" he asked.

Ryan's team-issued puffy parka hung on his chair.

"Since you have the gear for it, that would be great. I can keep the stats for you."

"Deal," he said. "Oh, Johnny was looking for you."

"Do you know why?"

"Nope. He was pretty pissy this morning because the radio station sent one of their new guys out here to call the game," Ryan said, lowering his head. "I told Johnny you should do it."

"Thanks, Ryan," I said, patting his hand gratefully.

"You'd be really good."

"That is awfully kind."

"Just speaking the truth."

As I finished posting the latest injury report, Johnny tapped me on the shoulder. "I need you to come with me. There's something I want you to see."

I followed Johnny to his station. His long black coat billowed behind him as he walked, and he was breathing heavy. It was as if he were Darth Vadar marching me to an evil droid for torture. We got to his laptop, and he motioned for me to sit down. Then a smile crinkled across his face.

Maximized at the top of the screen was the headline "Jackson Ways Spotted with Buxom Beauty." Below the headline was a photo of Jackson with his arm wrapped around the waist of a woman with cleavage spilling out of a low-cut black gown. My fingers shook as I scrolled down the article:

> *Country music's most eligible bachelor was squeezing more than limes into his Coronas last night. Jackson Ways was spotted cozying up to a beautiful, buxom brunette at a charity event to benefit his foundation.*

I scrolled back up to the photo. There was Jackson with his megawatt smile, cheek to cheek with a woman who looked like she'd walked straight off the Victoria's Secret runway. It didn't bother me seeing Jackson with another woman—no part of my heart pined for Jackson. I had been dreading going to that very event. But something inside me cracked when I saw the photo. Johnny's delight in mocking me was too much to bear. He had set me up to fail—not just that morning with the Network, but since the day I took this job.

Tears trickled down my face. I dabbed them with the top of my hand.

"I thought you should know that Jackson has moved on to bigger and better things," Johnny said and cupped his hands below his chest as if he were holding a pair of large breasts.

I couldn't bear to look him in the face. I couldn't give him the satisfaction of seeing the tears stinging my eyes.

"You're always looking out for me," I mumbled.

"Yes, that's why I told Sheridan you'll no longer be joining her on the Network today. You have too much on your plate."

"You did what?"

"You're far too shaken up to report right now. It's better if you focus on the website."

Anger jolted through me. I reached for Johnny's laptop. My hands were operating without my control. An electrifying vitriol was pulsing through my nervous system, piloting my every move. I slammed the laptop shut, my fingers intent on flinging it across the press box when Johnny intercepted me. He snatched the laptop from my clutches and held it against his chest like a shield.

"Blake, you better watch yourself," he hissed.

I glared at Johnny and envisioned myself spitting on his championship ring. Tremors of wrath quaked my core. But teeing off on Johnny only would play into his hand. He would proclaim I was emotionally unstable and prone to erratic behavior, and he would insist that was why he had to take drastic measures to keep me in line. I knew his tactics.

If I wanted to get back at Johnny, I would have to be deliberate and thoughtful. I gripped the edge of the table and pulled myself up.

"Yes, sir," I said, pivoting on my heel.

· · ·

With all that had just unfolded, I felt much less invested in the significance of the game. The team was desperate to snap their losing streak and secure a division win. All I could think about was enacting revenge on Johnny.

"Andy is playing like crap," Ryan said, waking me from a haze of introspection.

"Yeah," I said, although I had hardly paid any attention to the play on the field. I looked at the scoreboard. OKC trailed by thirteen points as the clock ticked down to halftime.

"His mobility is awful. But Coach can't pull him. You can't jerk starting QBs in and out of a pro football lineup. That's bush league. No pun intended," Ryan said.

"I wish they'd put in Marcus. He's such a nice guy," I said.

Ryan looked at me quizzically. "Maybe at the end of the season if they have nothing to play for, but let's hope that's not the case."

"Right now, this team is very hard to cheer for," I said and went back to typing.

. . .

At the start of the fourth quarter with OKC down by twenty-four points, Garrett barreled down the press box.

"I want very little on the website after this shit show of a game. No sidebar stories. No video interviews. Just a few bites from the pressers and maybe a couple of plays. Blake, get cleaned up and ready to shoot the video intros. They need to be short and sweet. The digital footprint of this game should be as small as possible."

I nodded, already accustomed to this strategy after a loss.

With a few minutes left on the game clock, I stuffed my laptop into my satchel and followed the media into an auxiliary room, where a podium was set up for the press conferences. Sheridan sat in the front row, scribbling notes on a pad. I took a seat directly behind her.

"I'm sorry about this morning. I hope I didn't put you in a bad place with the Network," I said.

She turned around, her Burberry raincoat glistening with wet drops.

"Today was a mess with the weather. We will get you on before another game."

I leaned closer. "I just want you to know that I was basically sabotaged today."

"I had a feeling JC was meddling. We'll talk later."

Johnny walked to the podium and raised the microphone to his mouth.

"Coach will take a few questions. As you know, Hal, a good friend of the team's and our beloved broadcaster, was hospitalized yesterday. He will remain at the hospital here as he recovers. We will continue to provide updates on his condition."

Coach Bush lumbered to the podium, his face drooping with defeat.

"We got our butts beat today. Plain and simple. It started when we walked on the field. We got outplayed. We got outcoached. We were just totally dominated."

"How would you assess Andy's play?" Sheridan asked.

"I'll have to go back and look at it. There was a dropped ball and lots of penalties, so it's not all him. There are other people involved."

"Do you think his ankle affected him today?"

"I don't know, Sheridan. That would be a question for Andy."

"Do you feel like Seth would have given you a better chance to win today?" a local columnist asked.

"Andy is our starting quarterback. Our starter gives us the best chance."

"Two more questions!" Johnny shouted. I stared straight into his narrowed gaze. It was time for my voice to be heard.

"Has the team taken a big step backward?" I said before Johnny could call on another reporter.

Johnny's head whipped around and his eyes bulged. I sat up taller in my seat, refusing to back down from the moment. My words bounced like charged atoms across the energized room.

Coach Bush cocked his head and looked at me as if he didn't recognize me. I held my breath. My question violated one of Johnny's golden rules. Never ask Coach a question in a press conference unless it has been preapproved. I knew my question enraged Johnny. His fists had balled into ticking bombs capable of pounding through the wall behind him. But I was not sure to what extent I had irked Coach Bush.

Coach cleared his throat. "It's definitely our worst performance of the year. We got our tails kicked. Anytime you get your tails kicked, you're taking a step backward. We have to go back home and go to work. We have a heck of a lot of football to play before we finish up this year."

"We are done. Andy is next," Johnny said, abruptly signaling for Coach Bush to follow him out of the door.

"Great question," Sheridan said, giving me a thumbs-up.

Andy hobbled to the podium minutes later, shifting uncomfortably from side to side as the media began their questioning.

"How was your ankle today? Was it bothering you out there?" a beat reporter asked.

"The ankle felt good. I still have some timing issues. I'm going to look at the film, get in the training room, and go from there."

"How frustrating was this game for you?" I asked confidently.

Andy glanced up from the mahogany podium and rubbed his chin.

"Yeah, Blake, it was frustrating. It's a game that's very frustrating because they didn't do anything unusual or special. We didn't execute. You can't drop passes. You can't miss open throws. We had way too many negative plays."

Darts shot from Johnny's eyes, piercing me as I typed the quote on my laptop.

"That's it," Johnny barked.

"That was short and sour," a columnist grumbled.

While the last of the media filed into the team's locker room to get quotes from the players, I plugged earphones into a digital recorder and began transcribing the press conferences. Since I couldn't go into the locker room, I figured I might as well be productive until Ryan and Boss were done interviewing players.

Through Coach Bush's languid drawl, I heard the door slam loudly. I closed my eyes, pretending like I was lost in the recording piping into my ear. Johnny's black Bruno Magli oxfords padded against the nub carpet.

"What the hell are you trying to pull?" Johnny said, ripping the buds out of my ears.

I stared at him in disbelief, unsure whether to be scared or outraged but completely confident of what I had to do next. I discreetly hit the record button on my recorder and let Johnny continue.

"You don't ask questions. How fucking hard is that for you to understand, Blake? Your job is to make the team look good. You don't break news or even make news. You write flattering stories. You look cute in videos. You smile and nod during press conferences. Really, it's very simple."

"I'm sorry, Johnny." But I didn't feel an ounce of remorse.

"You know, you're lucky to have this job. I wanted to fire you for slutting around with Jackson Ways. But for some reason people like you on the team."

Johnny jabbed my arm hard with his elbow.

"How did that story about Jackson and Tits McGee make you feel? I bet pretty stupid."

"Yeah, it did."

My hollow expression belied the adrenaline building inside me. I peeked down at the recorder to make sure the red light still was on.

"In case you haven't noticed, this team is on a losing streak. People are on edge. Fuckups won't be tolerated. The stunt today just might get you fired. Got it?"

"Got it."

"I knew hiring a girl to work for me would cause too many problems. Coach Bush thought you'd be good for the team. Hell, he even insisted you get your own office. But you're a liability. I've got to worry about you hooking up with players. I've got to worry about you distracting coaches with your stupid-ass boots. I've got to charter you your own fucking bus."

"Johnny, you didn't seem that worried when you wrote me that note saying how good I looked in my white pants. That note you signed 'JC' in your signature chicken-scratch handwriting—I filed it away for safekeeping."

"Fuck you, Blake. I will kill your career before it's even started."

All I could do was smile. Johnny had revealed his true character. I quickly pressed save on the recorder.

Twenty-Eight

Spin Job

We flew back to Oklahoma City in silence. Even Alyssa whispered as she took our dinner orders. The quiet backdrop accentuated Johnny's voice piping through my earbuds as I listened to the recording.

"You look like you're grimacing in pain. Everything OK?" Ryan asked.

I desperately wanted to tell Ryan, but the stakes were too high.

"It's torture reliving this game," I said.

Ryan nodded.

By the time the plane began its bumpy descent, I was finished with my work. All that remained was posting transcripts and videos to the website, which would take less than thirty minutes. The weightier task was deciding what to do next with the recording. I saved it on a memory stick for backup, clutching the stick hard in my palm, feeling the gravity of my decision.

. . .

Coffee brewed in the break room. I poured a cup and grabbed a bottle of water.

"What are you doing here so late? It's almost two in the morning," I said, handing Ryan the steaming Styrofoam cup.

"The coaches asked me to help with running some stats," Ryan said, stretching his arms high, revealing sweat stains ringing the armpits of his white shirt.

"Why are you here?" he asked.

"I've got a lot on my mind. I'm too wired to sleep. I'll probably work ahead on my story for the Gameday Magazine."

"Let me know if you want me to walk you to your car."

"Have I told you that you're the best?"

I settled into my office chair and kicked my feet up on the desk. My eyes blurred as I stared at the red light flashing from the memory stick plugged into my computer.

Johnny had relished setting the rules for engagement and belittling me at every twist and turn. It was time for me to even the playing field.

. . .

It was 5:00 a.m.—my self-imposed deadline to press send. Nerves gripped me. I stared at my mouse, unable to click it. I needed to clear my head. I grabbed the spare workout clothes hanging from the back of my door and went downstairs to the gym.

The special teams coordinator was walking on a treadmill watching the History Channel. His right knee buckled inward with each step, the result of two surgeries and over a decade of bone-crushing hits as a player in the league.

"Hey, Boots. Guess I'm not the only person psycho enough to be down here on no sleep."

"I'm hoping this wakes me up."

"It did the trick for me. Excuse me. Nature calls," he said, shuffling toward the door, leaving the treadmill running.

I shook my head and set my treadmill to a fast jog.

After showering and changing into a clean dress, I almost felt refreshed. Upstairs, Styrofoam cups and binders littered the coaches' offices. Their meetings had begun. It would be quiet on this end of the hall until Coach Bush addressed the media in the afternoon.

My hands shook as I unlocked my computer and opened the email I had been drafting since 3:00 a.m. A deluge of emails flooded my inbox, all with the same subject line: "League VP Harasses Media Maven."

I shook my head in confusion. The story sounded strikingly like my situation with Johnny, but I hadn't shared Johnny's rant with anyone.

I clicked on the story link. A photo of Johnny and me on the sidelines of the season opener appeared. I gasped.

> *Pro football is vicious, even if you're playing on the same team. Johnny Cook, a PR VP in Oklahoma City, verbally smacked around his employee Blake Kirk. Kirk, a media personality for the team who has been linked to Jackson Ways, took it like a champ. Click* here *to listen.*

I sat motionless. How had this story gotten out? Who had leaked it? And why?

"Holy shit balls!" Emily screamed, slamming my office door. "What the hell happened in Nashville? The craziest story came across my feed this morning."

I steadied my thoughts and peeled my eyes from the computer.

"I just read it. I don't know what to say. I'm too shocked," I stammered.

"What went down between you and Johnny?"

My mind was racing, my thoughts scrambled.

"The trip was a disaster. Hal almost died. I missed my Network hits. I got harassed by Johnny. I reached my breaking point. I couldn't take his abuse any longer. I fought back the best way I could. I asked questions in the postgame pressers. After everyone left the room, Johnny went ballistic on me."

"How did the conversation go viral?"

"There are cameras and recorders running in the media rooms all the time. Someone must have leaked the conversation."

"Was that someone you?" Emily asked, arching an eyebrow.

"No," I said and looked down at my boots, which were still caked with mud from the day before. "I had planned to. I spent all morning try-ing to work up the nerve to email the audio to a few sites. But I couldn't do it. I was too scared of the repercussions. I was too scared I would get found out and blackballed from the industry."

I assumed most media outlets wouldn't have the courage to expose Johnny. Journalists needed him too badly. He was their pipeline to inside scoops on the team and their gateway to the players and coaches. Crossing Johnny could mean losing that access or worse—career suicide. His connections ran deep.

"My plan had been to email it to a sports blog. A site that doesn't need Johnny's access or connections and relies on anonymous leaks. I created a fake email account and sat all morning with my hand hovering above the mouse, debating whether to hit send. I was planning to do it after my workout."

"You do realize that Johnny's going to the chopping block over this," Emily said, pretending to slice her neck with her French-manicured fingers.

"You think so? Johnny is too entrenched here. He's a fixture in the league. He'll get a slap on the wrist and hopefully a wake-up call about how unfairly he treats people, especially women. But I seriously doubt he loses his job."

"I don't know, Blake. That might have been the case if the convo had stayed internal. But it's all over the internet. It's a PR disaster for this team. Someone has to take the fall."

Emily cracked open my office door. The sound of deep voices and heavy steps carried down the hallway.

"It's the Morgans," she whispered. "Father and son. Shit's about to go down."

Twenty-Nine

Meeting the Morgans

At 8:01 a.m., Garrett sent an email to our group canceling the morning meeting with Johnny. I exhaled in relief and summoned the strength to look at my phone, which had been vibrating nonstop for an hour.

> Mom: *Sweetie, I saw you didn't come home. I'm worried about you.*
>
> Ryan: *holy shit*
>
> Sheridan: *Call me ASAP.*

Sheridan answered on the first ring.

"It takes a damn good story to make headlines on a Monday during the football season. You're front and center. How are you holding up?"

"I'm pretty shaken."

"I'm sorry you're going through this. Has the team indicated how it will handle the situation?"

"Not that I know of. The Morgans are meeting now."

"I'm sure they are talking to the league office. This is about more than

Johnny being a dick. How the team handles his behavior could be a referendum on the league's sexual harassment policies."

I sat up in my chair. I hadn't thought of the bigger implications of the media scrutiny of Johnny's tirade. It had all been personal. Johnny berating *me*. Johnny belittling *me*.

"You think the story could have that much impact?"

"I do. There's indisputable audio evidence of harassment that's gone viral. It will be impossible for the league to ignore this."

"Is sexual harassment that big of a problem in pro football?" I asked, shrinking back into my seat.

"Sexual harassment is a systemic problem that's amplified in pro football. Things have gotten better in the last few years. There are more women working in front offices. More females speaking out about harassment in the workplace. But on almost every team, there's a Johnny—a power monger who thinks he can say or do whatever he wants."

"Really?" I said naively.

"Blake, you've been in this industry a few months. Men have been running the league for decades. Some don't know any better. They think they're being nice when they say your ass looks hot on the sidelines. Some do know better and believe they can get away with those comments because of their position."

"I can't imagine anyone harassing you. Everyone respects you too much."

"There was a time when I was a cub reporter and a coach sent me naked pictures of himself," she said. "I felt so ashamed. Like *I* had done something wrong. He cornered me one night and said if I slept with him, he could get me a promotion at my station. I said no and I never told a soul. I feared if I said something, he would get me fired. I've always been proud of my reporting and my integrity, but I do regret not speaking up about what that coach did."

"It's really hard to speak up when you feel vulnerable and ashamed," I said.

"I know. That's why I did what most twenty-three-year-olds would do. I marginalized my feelings and told myself to toughen up. Don't get me wrong, you need thick skin to be a journalist, but no one deserves to be harassed like that," Sheridan said.

"For so long I've dreamed about covering pro football. I had no idea what I was getting myself into when I took this job. It has really tested my character," I said.

"There's nothing better in sports journalism than covering this league. I live for reporting on the intricacies of the game—the play calling, the schemes, the talent evaluation," Sheridan said. "I also love telling meaningful stories about the men underneath the pads. And I've made special friendships along the way. But paving a career as a woman covering football means making a lot of sacrifices.

"I'm almost forty years old and single with no children. I have prioritized my career over everything else. I work weekends and holidays, covering games rather than celebrating Christmas with my family or a boyfriend. I've seen peers get demoted from their anchor desks after returning from maternity leave. Network heads liked their replacements better. I'm not complaining. There are also many advantages to being a woman in the industry. I'm just saying that balancing this career with being a wife or mom is very challenging."

"Sometimes I wonder if I'm cut out for it," I said, thinking out loud.

"Personally, I think you have the chops to make it at the highest level. Still, I want to be honest with you about what this job entails."

"Thank you, Sheridan. You're an amazing mentor."

"You don't need to thank me. Just prove me right. We need more women like you on the sidelines. That's why I want to get you looped in with the Network ASAP."

"Are you sure? Even with everything that's going on?"

"TV hits may not be the right platform because there would be expectations for me to ask you about Johnny, and you're going to need time to craft your message on that," Sheridan said and paused.

I could hear a microwave beeping and a television humming in the background. I had assumed Sheridan was at her office, but the sounds of home filled the silence in our conversation. Picturing Sheridan in her kitchen, heating up a cup of coffee, made our talk feel even more personal and intimate.

I realized that I had only thought of Sheridan in the context of her success as a reporter. She was so polished and accomplished that it had seemed impossible that she could have struggled with self-doubt and humiliation in her career. But she had, and she had persevered and climbed the ranks because in the end she believed in herself and that her words mattered. It made me respect Sheridan that much more.

"How about this," Sheridan said. "You can write a story about what Coach needs to do to turn around the season. You can do a web video to accompany the story. Your name is a draw right now. Let's capitalize on that."

"Yes! I will start working on the story as soon as we get off," I said and felt myself smile.

Then, I messaged Mom. *I'm OK. Going to be a long day. Had a big blowup with Johnny. It's being handled.*

I pressed send and my phone rang almost instantly. Mom. I sent her to voice mail. It was time to focus on Sheridan's assignment.

I opened a new document and began to outline my piece. The writing would be the easy part. The tougher task would be to convince Boss to shoot and edit a video for me during his lunch break. I was about to pick up the phone to beg him shamelessly when my office line rang. It was the team's general counsel.

I cringed.

"Hello, Karen."

"Blake, I was made aware of the story that came out today along with the audio recording. I would like to meet with you momentarily," she said.

"OK," I said nervously. Karen's cutting tone immediately put me on edge.

"Out of curiosity, have you spoken to anyone about this incident?"

"Emily. She came into my office earlier this morning. Oh, and I just talked to Sheridan Lane."

"I see. Did you give her an interview?"

"No. We spoke as friends. But reporters are bombarding me with calls. I haven't answered them. I wasn't sure what to do."

"Good, good. Come to my office in ten minutes."

I closed my eyes and tried to slow my racing heart. I got the sneaking suspicion that Karen wanted nothing more than to vise-grip my mouth and keep me quiet. She probably also wanted to shake me down to see if I was filing a lawsuit.

The thought of suing had crossed my mind. Surely, I had grounds to file sexual harassment charges against Johnny. However, taking legal action could get messy and the team could drag my tryst with Jackson and possibly my flirtations with Seth into the proceedings. The whole thing might ostracize me from the league and jeopardize my career.

I needed to figure out what I wanted out of this ASAP. When I had recorded Johnny's rant, my goal was to expose his disgusting behavior. But there was more at stake now. The league office was involved, and the national media was digging into coverage. I needed to use this platform to somehow empower other young women working in professional sports.

. . .

At 8:57 a.m., I crossed the hall and lightly tapped on Karen's door.

"It's Blake."

Although Karen's office was about ten feet from mine, we never spoke. She worked behind the scenes, mitigating crises. Meeting with her usually meant something was very wrong.

"Blake, I appreciate your cooperation as we work through this delicate matter," Karen said and pointed me to a chair across from her.

Everything about Karen was sharp. Her black hair was cut into an angled bob that swept against her shoulders. She had a pointy nose, razor-thin lips, and piercing dark eyes.

"We regret that you've been put in this situation," she continued. "I have spoken to Mr. Morgan, and he thought it would be best if we all sit down together. You can tell us in your own words what transpired with Johnny."

I smiled meekly. Karen was stone-cold unnerving—the ideal team attorney. I was struggling to find my footing around her.

"It is imperative that we get the facts straight before we proceed," she said and shuffled documents into a file folder.

"OK," I managed to say.

Karen straightened the sleeves of her gray blazer and tucked the file folder under her arm. I followed her out of her office and tried to give myself a pep talk. I was *not* in trouble. I was *not* the person in the wrong. Johnny was. I was going to stand up for myself and stay strong.

When we reached the wood-paneled entrance framing Mr. Morgan's office, Karen turned a stately brass doorknob.

"Blake, after you."

As soon as I stepped inside, one of Mr. Morgan's assistants popped up from behind her desk. She looked about my mom's age, sporting the same poofy, short hair with bangs. I imagined Mom doing her job. She would love nothing more than chatting with the players and coaches as they waited for meetings. The thought of it made Mr. Morgan's fortress of mahogany and leather feel a little less intimidating.

"He's expecting you," the assistant said brightly, opening an interior set of doors.

"Please, do come in," Mr. Morgan bellowed in his aristocratic drawl. He sat at a grand wooden desk adorned with scrolled legs and decorative carvings. Behind him hung an oil painting of a muscular chestnut horse. To his right stood his son Whittaker.

Karen handed Mr. Morgan the file folder and then perched on a wingback chair with her legs tightly crossed at the ankles. I sat by myself on a tufted leather couch and stared up at the horse.

"You're looking at one of the most agile thoroughbreds to gallop this earth," Mr. Morgan said to me. "Rigger won me the Kentucky Derby seven years ago. That day at Churchill Downs ranks up there with the birth of my children."

Mr. Morgan looked at Whittaker and winked.

"But we're not here to talk about horse racing," he continued. "We're here because we have a situation on our hands. A very troubling situation."

I nodded, sensing it was not yet my turn to speak.

"This morning we spoke with the commissioner. We also met with Johnny," Mr. Morgan said.

"We heard Johnny's side of the story," Whittaker interrupted. "Now, it's your turn. What happened between you two? And how in the hell did that conversation end up on the internet?"

Whittaker's voice prickled with petulance. The Morgans had hand-picked Johnny to head media and press relations when they rebuilt the team. Johnny was their confidant. He had been the Morgans' loyal media henchman and protector for over twenty years. Their instinct was to defend him. This would be an uphill battle.

"Mr. Morgan, I promise you that I was *not* responsible for leaking that recording. I have no idea who was. In all transparency, I did record the conversation with Johnny. I thought long and hard about sending it to sports sites, but I was too scared. I was too scared that the leak would be traced back to me and that Johnny, you, or ranking league officials would kill my career before it started."

The room fell silent. I looked down at my clasped hands, which were squeezed so tightly that my thumbs had turned the same shade of burgundy as the leather-bound books decorating Mr. Morgan's shelves. I had to keep going. If I stopped now, I might never work up the nerve again to state my case.

"As for what happened between me and Johnny—well, that's complicated. From the day I started, Johnny made it clear he didn't trust me. I couldn't tell if it was me personally or if it was because he was nervous in general about having a woman around the players and coaches."

"Johnny doesn't trust anyone," Whittaker cut in. "That's what makes him so good at his job. He's kept the team and my family from being burned by the media with that paranoia."

"I recognize that, sir. In that regard, Johnny is very good at his job. But it doesn't mean he was a good boss. Johnny enacted separate rules for me. He created unfair double standards. He duped me into going to an all-nude strip club and then wouldn't let me in the locker room because he didn't want me to see the players shirtless."

"Well, Blake, I did see his point on some of those rules," Mr. Morgan said. "It was new for us having a female around so much. And you gave him reason to question your intentions, carrying on with Jackson Ways like that. Johnny said it made him think that you were doing this job to date celebrities. I understood his perspective. Although, I was in hog heaven when ratings and page views soared because of you and Jackson." Mr. Morgan chuckled.

My throat tightened. I had expected the Morgans to bring up Jackson Ways. No doubt, Johnny had planted that seed so that they would question my character. Still, addressing the tryst with the Morgans was more humiliating than anticipated.

"Mr. Morgan, I have made mistakes during my tenure with the team. I regret my interactions with Jackson Ways. However, that fling doesn't justify the way Johnny treated me or how he yelled at me during the leaked rant."

"Where are you going with this, Ms. Kirk?" Mr. Morgan asked pointedly.

"Sir, Johnny's behavior toward me has been inexcusable and unjustifiable, and there is audio proof that isn't going away. It's making the rounds on social media and national news. It's evolving into a social commentary on the league. To get ahead of this, you need to own it. Use this opportunity not just to condemn Johnny but to be a trailblazer and hire females for high-level football ops positions. Why not a female assistant coach? Make yourself a hero for women fans. It will buy you a lot of media goodwill."

"A hero for the women." Mr. Morgan snorted in laughter.

Karen cleared her throat. "I concur with Blake on this. Hiring a female front office executive would serve this team well internally and externally. As you may know, current reports show that women make up almost half of the league fan base," she said. I turned and smiled at Karen. She did not smile back, but stone-cold Karen was growing on me.

Mr. Morgan leaned forward on his desk. His grin had reconfigured into a tightly drawn line and his bushy white eyebrows pinched deep creases in his forehead. "Well, maybe it is something we can consider," he said and reached for the folder Karen had left on his desk.

"Before we deviate off course, it should be known that the league is reviewing Johnny's behavior. We are helping officials conduct interviews and comb through emails." Mr. Morgan paused and glanced at a document, which I assumed was related to the investigation. He scowled and looked back at me. "You should also know that the team has suspended Johnny for the time being."

My eyes widened. The Morgans had suspended Johnny. In the league, that was typically a baby step to firing someone. I tried to imagine Johnny receiving the news. Had he cried? I remembered the awkward vulnerability of watching him shed tears during Hal's resuscitation.

"What does this mean for me moving forward?" I asked.

"We will hire an interim replacement for Johnny. You can continue doing your media work," Mr. Morgan said.

"As long as you don't try any legal funny business," Whittaker blurted out.

"You mean a harassment lawsuit?" I responded.

"Yes, he does mean that," Mr. Morgan said sternly.

"I want you to know that Johnny left a trail of documented evidence in his wake. If I wanted to sue, it would be easy," I said and let the bitterness of my words hang heavy in the air like stout cigar smoke. "But I don't want to do that. What I want is for the team to treat women who work here fairly and equitably. *And* I would like you to put in a good word for me with the Network."

"I promise to sing your praises to the Network, if you promise not to sue," Mr. Morgan said.

"And you'll address the workplace culture here," I added.

"That too." Mr. Morgan nodded.

"Then, we have a gentlemen's, or should I say gentlewomen's, agreement," I said.

"Very good." Mr. Morgan stood up and extended his hand. I hoped this backroom handshake truly marked a turning point for the team.

Thirty

A Girl Can Dream

"Knock. Knock. Special delivery." Emily tapped on my office door at 12:24 p.m.

I cracked open the door.

"Girl, you know my bootie needs more room than that," she said, nudging the door wider with her bottom as she balanced two Styrofoam containers in both hands. "Since you aren't leaving this room, I brought lunch to you."

"Thanks, Em. I really appreciate it."

She set down the containers on my desk and pulled up a chair.

"Well, you've got to eat. And I'm dying to hear what happened this morning."

"I will give you the CliffsNotes version. Johnny has been suspended. The league is investigating him. And Mr. Morgan is supposed to help me get a job at the Network. Something along those lines."

"Shit," Emily said, dipping a fry into ketchup. "That's intense."

"The team is going to review Johnny's emails and gather more statements as part of the process. There's a real chance that the Morgans make an example out of Johnny and change the culture around here. At least, I really hope so."

"That's a win, right?" Emily asked.

"You bet," I said and stabbed a piece of avocado. "You're going to think I'm crazy, but it kind of pains me to see Johnny taken down. He's worked incredibly hard and devoted his life to a career in pro football. I respect that. But it isn't OK how he treated me, or other women for that matter."

"Do you think the Morgans will fire him?"

"I have been asking myself the same question," I said and leaned back in my chair. "I think they'll have to. The audio is too vicious, and it's being played everywhere from local radio to ESPN. The commissioner might give them no choice but to fire him."

"Wow, I never thought I'd see the day where Johnny goes down in flames."

"So, what are the people in the office saying about all this?" I had been sequestering myself in my office to avoid the leering looks.

"Most people in sales think you're going to sue the pants off the team. A few thought you would quit by the end of the day."

"I'm definitely not quitting. In fact, I am about to do a piece for the Network. A story and a video."

Emily placed her empty lunch container on the floor underneath her chair.

"Please tell me you have a brush and some hairspray in here."

"Do I look that bad?"

"Can a professional handle this, please?"

I giggled and let her get to work.

At 2:55 p.m., I walked out of my office with my hair looking good and my head held high. After digesting my meeting with the Morgans and a long lunch with Emily, I now felt emotionally equipped to move about the stadium.

"A Diet Coke for the lady," Ryan said, greeting me outside his cube with a cold can.

"That's awfully kind of you. Just what I needed."

"I figured as much. How are you? I've barely heard from you all day."

"Today has tested my inner strength to the core, but right now I'm actually feeling good."

We walked down the stadium concourse. The commotion from the team auditorium reverberated through the cinder-block hall.

"Sounds like there's a huge crowd today. I really hope they don't bombard me with questions about Johnny," I said as anxiety fluttered in my tummy.

"They will. But don't let it rattle you."

I nodded and slowly opened the door to the auditorium. The entire room went silent and stared at me expectantly. I avoided eye contact and marched straight to my usual seat.

As expected, several beat writers and TV reporters followed.

"Blake, what's the deal? What happened with Johnny? I hear this is becoming a high-level issue."

"It's an internal matter. I can't talk about it," I said stoically.

"Come on, Blake. Aren't you going to tell us what really happened? We are your comrades, your media partners in crime."

"One day, you can read the book. Then you'll know," I said and put in my earbuds. They collectively huffed and sauntered back to their computers.

I sat up in my chair, suddenly feeling bigger, like my existence occupied more space in the crowded room of reporters. I held my own here, and with Johnny gone, there was no one who could bring me down.

Not the Bobbsey Twins. Not Garrett, who temporarily had assumed Johnny's duties.

I watched Garrett stand over the podium stage and stretch the microphone to meet his mouth.

"One, two, three. Check. Check. One, two, three," Garrett said, over-enunciating each word. Some journalists looked up at him quizzically, clearly confused as to why Johnny wasn't standing before them. Most continued to talk and ignored Garrett's presence altogether.

Garrett finally cleared his throat loudly into the microphone and the media quieted. Most still looked confused as to why this tall, skinny man wearing black glasses and a navy team fleece was addressing them.

"Good afternoon. I am Garrett, the team's digital media coordinator. I have seen many of you during press conferences here or on the road. For the next couple of weeks, I will be handling the team's media. If you have a media request, come to me. My team will be working hard to set up interviews and distribute press releases. Before I get Coach, any questions?"

"Where's Johnny and when does he come back?" a radio host blurted out. He was the cohost of the second most popular morning show in town, only bested by Hal. A former pro defensive lineman, he prided himself on pounding the team with tough questions that Hal didn't dare ask.

"Johnny is on leave. That is all I am at liberty to say," Garrett said cautiously.

"Will the team issue a release about Johnny's suspension?" a local beat reporter said, nipping on the heels of Garrett's words.

"I'm not at liberty to answer that."

"Then who is?" asked an ESPN writer intently leaning forward in her chair.

"A team-issued statement will be released at the appropriate time," Garrett said. He pushed the words out with every ounce of authority his 150-pound frame could muster, but his presence didn't carry much weight with this crowd.

I searched for the Bobbsey Twins. They were side by side, leaning against the far wall of the auditorium, arms folded tightly across their chests and lips drawn into tight frowns. They were Johnny's apprentices, having sacrificed personal lives, worked 100-hour weeks, and guarded unsavory secrets all for the promise of one day running their own team PR fiefdoms just like Johnny. Now, they answered to Garrett.

"This is bullcrap," a beat reporter said, banging his hand against the table. "Just tell us what's going on."

"What's going on is a press conference with Coach Bush," Garrett said, his voice wavering. "I will get him, and he can answer any football-related questions you have."

"Who is this kid?" the ESPN reporter grumbled.

"One of Johnny's minions," another reporter grumbled back. "We're never going to get the information we need from him. He'll tell us to go google it."

Reporters shook their heads.

"Nah, we're going to get away with murder," one said. "It's going to be a free-for-all without Johnny breathing down our necks."

Garrett had no idea what he was in for. I felt sorry for him.

As Coach Bush took the podium, Garrett scurried to the corner of the stage. Coach had aged this season. Dark rings stamped the sagging skin below his eyes and creases were etched deep in his forehead.

"I will start by telling y'all that we're here to win football games. We're here to play hard and we expect good results. We've got to turn things around and be a winner week in and week out. We're going to correct yesterday's mistakes and get it fixed by Sunday. Questions?"

"How is Andy's confidence?" Sheridan asked.

"Andy is a pro. He was testing his ankle early, but as the game went on, I didn't see a lack of confidence there. I did see some poor decision-making situations, some that he has to handle and some that we can help him handle. The problem when you play the quarterback position is that three or four glaring mistakes can be the difference in winning and losing. So, that's what we're working on right now."

After a long exchange about Andy, Garrett signaled time for one last question. A reporter asked, "How much of a disruption is the Johnny situation for the players?"

"It's not. Our focus is on Sunday. That's all."

Coach pivoted away from the media, his Nike running shoes squeaking against the wood floor as he strode toward the exit. Garrett hurried behind him.

The words "Johnny situation" reverberated in my head. I shuddered. For months, Johnny had called me out as a distraction to the team. Now, that actually might be the case. The weight of disrupting the players' routines, distracting their mindsets, and potentially contributing to a loss came crashing over me. I wanted to run after Coach Bush and apologize.

"Blake, what's wrong? You've gone pale," Sheridan said.

"All season, Johnny has told me that I was a potential distraction to the team. Now, I really am. All the players and coaches are talking about what happened. They have to deal with Garrett now instead of Johnny. It's throwing a game week into disarray."

"If the players can't handle this distraction, they don't have the mental fortitude to play in the pros. Blake, there are coaches who get fired mid-season, and players adjust and win games. Don't worry about them. Stay focused on doing your job."

"You're right. I just hate letting down Coach Bush," I said.

"Coach Bush has a lot more problems than you and Johnny," Sheridan said. "Now, remember to email me your story and video by 5:00 p.m. By the way, your hair looks great."

I patted the teased curls. Leave it to Emily to save the day.

. . .

"Heading out soon?" Emily said, poking her head in my doorway.

"Actually, yes. Can you wait a sec? I'll walk out with you."

"Sure thing, but you better get that cute little butt of yours moving. I've got places to be."

"Devonte?" I mouthed.

Emily batted her false lashes.

"I seriously don't know how you can move your eyelids with those things on them."

"These little things?" Emily winked dramatically. "I hardly notice they're there. I sleep in false lashes."

"This won't shock you, but I have never worn fake lashes. Not once in my life."

"Says the girl in front of the camera. You make it to national TV, and they'll have you in all sorts of fake stuff—lashes, hair extensions, spray tans. Just you wait."

"Sheridan Lane doesn't do all that stuff."

"She's not young and hot like you."

I rolled my eyes teasingly and pulled the suitcase out from under my desk. The thought struck me: Just yesterday, I wheeled that bag out of a hotel, thinking I was heading to my first big break with the Network. I never could've prepared myself for the saga that unfolded—sludging through a sleet storm, enduring Johnny's post-presser tirade, finding the leaked audio plastered across the internet, meeting Mr. Morgan in his office, and, the culmination of it all, submitting my video and story to the Network. While the scenes played vividly in my mind, they also felt like separate dreams, foggy around the edges, the details muted by over-stimulation and sleep deprivation.

"By the way, I rocked my story and video for the Network. Even Sheridan was impressed."

"Way to go, girl! I'm so proud of you. Pretty soon you're going to be leaving this place for bigger and better things."

"A girl can dream," I said wistfully.

"You've got that right. I'm dreaming of a big rock on my finger," Emily said.

"Whoa. I thought you had been holding off on engagement talk."

"Devonte started talking about getting engaged last week. He came back to OKC early to do his rehab here. His mom came to town too. We're really getting along. At first, I could tell she was skeptical of me. She thought I was with Devonte for the wrong reasons. Now, she sees how much I want to take care of him and how happy we make each other. She's even teaching me how to cook his favorite dinners. Watch out, because I can make one hell of a meatloaf."

"Em, that's amazing. I'm so happy for you guys."

I popped open the trunk of my car and placed my suitcase inside.

"What about your parents? How would they feel about you marrying him?"

"They may never approve, but they'll have to accept that they have no say in the matter. If they don't want to support me, they don't have to come to the wedding."

"I hope it doesn't come to that, but you have to live your truth," I said.

"Amen to that."

Thirty-One

Face Down in the Arena

My mother naturally had big, bright blue eyes. They opened wider and shone brighter than the average person's. After I recounted the previous forty-eight hours to my parents, Mom was in serious jeopardy of losing both eyeballs. They looked as if they were about to pop out of the sockets onto the kitchen counter.

"I don't know what to say, Blake. I'm speechless," she said, scrolling to the comments section of the story about Johnny and me. There were posts like "He's a pig" and "Who cares? That chick isn't hot."

"I can't read this anymore," Mom said, closing the laptop.

"After all of today's drama, I have no sense of what normal is anymore," I said. "But I do believe it all will be worth it. There are exciting opportunities ahead."

"I'm still in shock mode. Johnny has some nerve speaking to you that way. And who on earth recorded this conversation?"

"I'm dying to find out. One thing is for sure—the team is using all its resources to expose the leaker."

"They'll find him. Or her," Dad chimed in.

It was the first thing Dad had said since I arrived home. About midway through my monologue, he retreated from the kitchen to his recliner in the family room. To the casual observer, he probably appeared disinterested; however, I knew he was processing my every word in his own detached way.

Dad took a long sip of Merlot.

"I'm proud of you, Blake. You stood your ground and weathered the bullshit Johnny threw at you. Now, you're going to come out of this ordeal with a major career boost."

I couldn't help but bask in the warmth of Dad's approval.

"Thanks, Dad. I always want to make you and Mom proud."

Mom tucked a loose strand of hair behind my ear—a perfectly timed comforting stroke.

"Sweetie, it's your character that makes us proud. We raised a brave, compassionate, conscientious young woman. I'm thrilled that the Network is showing interest in you. But what we care about most is that you're happy and fulfilled."

I gave Mom a kiss on the forehead and nodded at Dad, who was swirling a near-empty wine glass.

"I probably don't say this enough, but I'm eternally grateful that you are my parents."

. . .

After eight hours of sleep and a large pumpkin spice latte, I felt like a functioning human being again. I waved at the friendly security guard and turned into the staff lot. Johnny's black Escalade was noticeably missing from its executive spot in the first row. I wondered what a day away from the team looked like for him.

I knew so little about his personal life except that he was divorced with two stepchildren. Football teams were his family. The sport defined him in every way. It was something that could happen all too easily in this business. You chased the next job, thrived off the highs of belonging to a team and the power and perks that accompanied it.

A pang of sadness hit me. I imagined Johnny sitting, bewildered, staring at undecorated walls in the multistory condo he bought a few blocks from the stadium. Deep down, he had to be feeling scared and lonely. I looked at Johnny's empty space and vowed never to let football consume me that way.

. . .

Energy pulsated through the stadium concourse, which was rare for a Tuesday. This was the players' day off, their day to lift weights, get treatment, watch extra film, move through the stadium at their own pace.

The locker room door banged open. Inside, players talked loudly over DJ Khaled's "All I Do Is Win." Two receivers emerged and slammed the door behind them.

"Hey, Boots," one said.

"Morning," I said brightly.

"Boots, we've got a spring in our step," the other receiver said cheerfully. "Because we got ourselves a new quarterback."

I stopped in my tracks.

"Wait. What are you talking about?"

"Marcus is movin' up. He's gonna start Sunday."

"Marcus is starting over Andy and Seth?" I said, shaking my head incredulously.

One receiver held up a binder.

"That's why the entire offense is at the stadium. To help Marcus watch film and get ready."

"It's our boy's turn to shine," the other receiver chimed in before they turned down the hallway toward the meeting rooms.

I skipped up the stairs, giddy to share the news with Ryan. It was hard not to root for Marcus, with his effervescent smile and kind nature. I never forgot how patiently he waited for me to interview him while I talked to Seth. Now, it was Marcus's turn to take the spotlight.

Ryan was cracking open a Dr Pepper at his cubicle as I walked up behind him.

"Thought you could use a treat this morning," I said, handing him a pastry bag with a chocolate chip muffin inside.

"Aren't you a ray of sunshine."

"Did you hear the news? Marcus got promoted to starter."

"Isn't it awesome? Having a more athletic and mobile quarterback is going to elevate this offense. I know it."

"They had nowhere to go but up after Andy's performance last week," I said softly. "I wonder what the coaches are going to do with him."

"Andy's going on IR with an ankle injury. Let's face it. He isn't 100 percent. This is the perfect way for the organization—and for Andy—to save face on getting benched."

"So, Seth is backing up a rookie," I said. "I know that's pissing him off."

"Seth had his chance. He should have played better," Ryan said.

I glanced at Ryan's computer screen. He was editing a press release about Andy moving to the injured reserve.

"Hey, how did you get all this information so early?"

He looked down at the muffin crumbs in his lap. "Garrett called me this morning around six. He'd gotten word from the GM and wanted me to start working on releases."

"I guess I should check in with Garrett. It's so quiet over here. Where are Carleton and Carson?"

"They're all meeting with HR," Ryan said and shrugged.

"I bet it's part of the investigation," I whispered.

I walked down the hall. Through the frosted glass doors of the conference room, I could see the Bobbsey Twins and Garrett sitting across from Karen's legal team and the HR director. Karen caught my eye and sent an assistant to open the door.

"Blake, please come in," she said from her seat. "We have made a swift and urgent move that you should be aware of."

The Bobbsey Twins looked paler and balder than ever. They stared into their coffee, barely acknowledging my presence. Garrett meekly waved my way.

"After some interviews and data review, we uncovered some very disturbing communications initiated by Johnny. We had no choice but to find Johnny employment elsewhere," Karen said.

"So, Johnny has another position?" I asked, confused.

"He will be joining the PR team for some minor league. We are going to get someone in here ASAP. I look forward to introducing you to candidates."

Johnny was being shipped away to minor league football. The demotion was just as bad as getting fired.

. . .

When I got to my office, I called the one person who might be able to shed light on the situation.

"Blake, dear lord, your team is a mess," Sheridan said.

"Tell me about it. Johnny is gone. Something about his 'disturbing communications.' Do you know what that's about?"

"Are you referencing the notes Johnny was sending?"

"Notes? What notes?" I asked.

"Apparently, he had Carleton and Carson give notes to young women that he signed *from JC*. Johnny wrote an intern at a radio station that her butt was wearing the hell out of her jeans. He wrote a young Iranian reporter he met at the Combine. He asked if she sold rugs, because she looked like she had a nice one."

"I'm not surprised. I got one of those JC notes myself."

"Disgusting," Sheridan said. "Well, my source with your team told me that Carson and Carleton had texts proving what Johnny had done. They didn't want to be implicated in the scandal, so they sold Johnny out."

"Sheridan, you were right. Remember at practice when you said you were waiting for the day when the ducklings bit Johnny in the ass? Well, it just happened," I said.

"I guess so," Sheridan said with a laugh. "In the end, things work out as they should."

Thirty-Two

Winning Time

My office door flew open, ushering in Emily and her signature cotton candy scent.

"Do I look any different?" she said, jumping up and down in her platform, red-bottomed heels and waving her left hand wildly. A yellow, square diamond glistened on her ring finger.

"You're engaged!"

I leaped to hug her.

"Can you believe it? I'm going to marry my true love!"

"Tell me everything."

"Last night, I made my famous spaghetti with spicy red sauce. Totally ordinary night. Devonte's mom and his brothers were having dinner with us. We said grace. Then he got on one knee. He said he couldn't wait any longer. He had something to ask me in front of the people he loved most. I screamed, 'Yes!' before he even opened the box."

"My heart melts seeing you so in love," I said, grabbing her hand. "And that rock is unbelievable."

"My man did good, didn't he?"

"Have you thought about when you'll get married?"

"Probably this summer. Devonte's knee will be totally fine by then, and the team will be off."

"Will the wedding be here?"

Emily looked away, sadness pulling at the corners of her eyes.

"That's the thing. I'm not sure where it will be. I had always dreamed of a big Louisiana wedding with my family. But I don't know if they'll come. My parents don't even know I'm engaged."

"Oh, Em. Don't you think they'll understand when they see how happy you are?"

"I'm not so sure. I'm scared to tell them because I think they'll ruin my happiness. They'll want me to call it off."

"I'm really sorry. I'm always here for you if you need to talk."

"Blake, you're such a good friend," Emily said, clasping my hand. "That's also why I wanted to ask if you'll be a bridesmaid."

"Yes!" I exclaimed. "I'd be honored."

"OK, I'd better get out of here before I really start to cry. Next stop, HR."

"Why?"

"I need to let them know. Technically, I am violating the biggest team rule here. Don't fraternize with players. I'm freaking marrying one."

"You've got a point."

With that, Emily turned on her heel.

Fifteen minutes later she texted me. *Done with this team. Packing up my cube. TTYL.*

Emily was leaving. I needed to be next.

. . .

I was headed out of my office to help Emily carry boxes when my phone rang. It was the GM. I stopped in my tracks. He never called me. In fact, he had never spoken to me.

"Hello, this is Blake."

"Hi, Blake. Can you join us in the conference room right now? Thanks."

I timidly opened the heavy glass door. The GM sat at the head of the conference table, flanked by Coach Bush and a woman with cropped, auburn hair.

"Come in. Take a seat," Coach Bush said, standing up and pulling out the chair next to him.

"Blake, we would like you to meet Stephanie Wilson. Stephanie is a candidate to be our vice president of Media Relations."

The GM motioned to a woman with a freckled, round face and big brown eyes. She wore little makeup, which gave her a youthful, no-nonsense appearance.

Stephanie stood up and straightened her fitted pinstripe jacket.

"Pleasure to meet you, Blake," she said, extending a hand.

"Nice to meet you too."

"Stephanie flew in last night for an interview and we asked her to come in today to see our day-to-day operations and meet some more people," the GM said. "We wanted to make sure she met you."

"I heard you are a rising star in the media department," Stephanie said.

"This young lady does a fine job," Coach said. "I think you two would work real well together."

I smiled gratefully at Coach Bush. He continued to be one of my biggest advocates, even despite all that had transpired with Johnny. Coach Bush had my back.

"I have always wanted to work with another woman. It often doesn't happen in a league front office—two women working together," Stephanie said.

"Have you always worked in pro football?" I asked.

"I'm a lifer. My dad coached at Michigan under Bo Schembechler. I played soccer there. After I graduated, I knew I wanted to work in sports. The sports I knew best were soccer and football. I've been learning football schemes since I learned how to walk. We talked about nickel-and-dime packages around the dinner table. After college, my dad helped me get an internship with Detroit. I've worked my way up the PR ladder ever since."

"Wow," I said, impressed by Stephanie's poise and pedigree. If the team hired her, staying on might not be so bad.

"Blake, there's another matter we would like to discuss with you," the GM said, turning to Coach and Stephanie. "Hal is still recovering. It's going to be a few weeks, maybe even a month until he returns to work. We have talked internally and with the radio station about who should fill in for him, specifically his sideline duties for the radio broadcast of the games and his pregame Network appearances. Stephanie suggested you."

My eyes widened in surprise.

"This is the perfect opportunity for the team to brand themselves on multiple platforms and integrate media," Stephanie said. "We have our digital reporter on the radio and national TV. We can direct viewers and listeners back to the team's site for additional content."

"To be transparent, I pushed back," the GM said. "You're still a rookie. This is a big load to carry. But I floated the idea to Mr. Morgan, and he endorsed it."

"I'm thrilled," I said, my leg dancing under the table in excitement.

"Sunday will be your trial run. If all goes well, you can have the gig until Hal returns."

"You'll be great, kiddo," Coach said, nodding approvingly.

"I promise not to let you down."

"There's a great deal of prep work that must be done for the game. The station will be in touch with the rundown. Tell Garrett to take you off any other projects."

"As you might surmise," the GM continued, "we want to hire Stephanie and are working on getting her released from Detroit. All of that should be worked out in the next week, but let's keep this conversation under wraps until we are ready to release an official statement."

"Of course," I said.

"That should be all," the GM said.

I stood and Stephanie and the men stood up too.

"Good luck this weekend," Stephanie said.

. . .

I buttoned my black peacoat and boarded the early bus to the stadium. Since the Network needed me on the field by 7:30 a.m. for troubleshooting, Lenny had canceled the Blake Bus. Trainers and coaches occupied about a third of the seats. I sat near the front. For some reason, I was not nervous or uneasy. It felt as if I belonged, a part of the team, a part of the media. I sat in silence, respecting the quiet focus pervading the ride.

The bus pulled into the loading dock, and I wheeled my bag down the concourse.

"I can take that, Blake," a trainer said. "I am going to store these bags in the equipment area."

"Thank you."

I stepped onto the bright turf field wearing cushioned, flat shoes and black fitted pants with pockets for my audio accessories. I came equipped.

"There she is!" Sheridan beamed. "You look fantastic."

"I hardly slept last night. Too excited. But I don't feel tired at all."

"We're going to get you miked up shortly. You have hits in the eight and nine hours up until your radio pregame show."

"Yep, that starts at ten," I said. "The radio crew is going to meet me down here."

"This is where the magic happens." Sheridan grinned.

I shoved my phone and pens into my back pocket and rummaged through my satchel for my earpiece.

"I'm sure you heard this is a trial run for me."

"I did. I also heard it was Stephanie's idea, which is a great thing. She's advocating for you."

"How did you know that?"

"I told you. I have been covering your team for several years. I have sources." Sheridan winked at me.

"Do you know her?" I asked.

"We have met and know each other professionally, but I've never worked with her. I hear great things. She's smart and professional. She's tough; she pushes her department to innovate. She's exactly the hire the team needs to make."

"I can see that just from the few minutes I met her," I said.

"You should still look for new opportunities," Sheridan told me. "In fact, the Network is creating a new multimedia position. It's fantasy football writing, blogging, and contributing to Jeremiah's fantasy show. You'd be perfect. A great way for you to cut your teeth."

"That would be amazing. When can I apply?"

"I've already put in a good word for you. Consider today's broadcast your application. If they like what they see, they'll fly you to LA for formal interviews and test runs with Jeremiah."

"Yikes, there's a lot of pressure riding on today."

Sheridan lifted my chin, her gaze kind and gentle.

"Be yourself. You have the knowledge and the heart for this job. Trust that. Trust that always."

· · ·

There were stutters and stumbles throughout the morning, but I hit my groove late in the second half. I paced myself along with the action of the team, updating the play-by-play crew on injury reports or anecdotes from the sidelines.

Marcus was a sight to behold. He scrambled out of pressure, made throws on the run, and picked up key first downs with his feet. At the end of the first half, the team led 21–7, with Marcus throwing one touchdown and running for two.

I jogged next to Coach Bush as he headed for the tunnel.

"Coach, what has impressed you most about Marcus's play in the first half?"

"Everything," he said. "This kid came prepared. He's making good decisions on the run. He's gotten us out of trouble with his feet. We've still got work to do. But a real good start for number 5."

· · ·

The locker room erupted into a dance party after Coach's postgame speech. A receiver turned up "All I Do Is Win" from his speakers and the entire receiving corps danced around Marcus.

The losing streak had ended. Marcus had resurrected the team. They had their quarterback of the future. No questions asked.

As the players sang and cheered, I took it all in. It was my first time in the locker room. On the surface, nothing special—just basic wood cubbies for each player. But this moment in time would live and breathe in my soul forever. The thump of the music. The smell of sweaty flesh. The sight of Marcus's kind, wide smile as he clapped to the beat.

No outside media was inside the locker room. They couldn't enter until Coach and Marcus spoke at the podium. For now, the team could celebrate their young quarterback in unbridled fashion.

My phone vibrated in my back pocket. It was a text from Hal.

Way to go! Call me when you finish your interviews.

After I finished the postgame show, I found a quiet corner in the cheerleaders' locker room. I hadn't eaten since dawn and my stomach growled in anger. I unwrapped a protein bar from the hospitality basket and called Hal.

"A star has been born," he said.

"You're way too kind. I made all sorts of mistakes. My tongue was slipping and sliding, too excited to properly enunciate anything."

"But you rolled along and didn't get stuck or bogged down. You got better with every minute. I'm proud of you."

"Thanks, Hal. I hope it is good enough to impress the Network."

"The Network is going to hire you. It may not happen next week. You know these things take time. But by next season, I predict you'll be back in LA."

"I hope so," I said. "How are you feeling?"

"I'm good. I'm starting to walk some. The doctor put me on some new medications that seem to be working. I should be back in the saddle after Christmas."

"That's such great news. People around here really miss you," I said and glanced up at the clock. "Hal, I'm sorry to do this but I should get off soon. The station wants me at the postproduction meeting."

"Before you hang up, there's something I want to tell you."

"What's that?"

"This stays between us. You can't utter a word to anyone."

Hal paused and breathed heavily into the phone.

"It was me."

"What do you mean?"

"The leaker. It was me," Hal said.

"How?" I asked, shaking my head in confusion. "You've been in the hospital."

"One of the guys from the station recorded the presser for me. I had asked him to email me the audio. I thought listening to it would give me something to do—keep me from getting bored. Well, the recorder was left on and it picked up Johnny's screaming. I heard the whole thing."

"Really?"

"I was so disgusted by that pig-headed fool. I had to do something. So, I sent it anonymously to that site, Under Pressure."

"I guess I should thank you, Hal. That audio has helped launch my career."

"You are launching your own career. What I did is right a wrong. I was so mad at how Johnny talked to you. He's had a fresh mouth for far too long. I'd had enough."

"Hal, it's time for things to change," I said.

I closed my eyes. Visions of games with my dad danced through my head. I had dreamed of finding my place on the sidelines for so long. The journey getting here had nearly broken me. Johnny's harassment. Seth's betrayal. My regrettable drunken tryst with Jackson. And other judgment lapses in between. I had weathered it all and grown stronger and wiser in the process.

I still had a steep uphill path to climb if I wanted to be the next Sheridan Lane. I would be competing for jobs that millions of women dreamed of and navigating entrenched sexual politics along the way. That was part of the game. But now I was better equipped. I knew my voice; my story mattered.

"Welcome to the big leagues," I told myself.

Acknowledgments

I first want to thank the readers who joined Blake as she navigated the thrilling and vicious world of professional football. I hope they enjoyed this story that is so close to my heart.

There are so many incredible people who brought this novel to life. Megan McKeever saw the raw potential in the manuscript and helped me elevate and polish it with her keen editorial eye. I am grateful for her thoughtful direction and brilliant wordsmithing.

Shaundra Taylor and Nicole Betters, who knew that an Imprint writing class would bring together a writing group that has lasted nearly a decade? Thank you for reading drafts of the novel, providing invaluable insight, and cheering me on to the finish line.

Amy Palcic, you are a trailblazer and inspiration. You are the first woman to head PR for an NFL team and the first person I wanted to read this novel. Thank you for investing yourself in this process and encouraging me along the way.

John Lopez, you have mentored me in the different stages of my career—from my days in the NFL to our time in television together and then the development of this manuscript. Thank you for reading and editing my first draft and assuring me "I had something here."

To my husband, Jeff, who graciously lent his editorial savvy many late nights when I was obsessing over sections of the book. You are my rock. My constant. My true love. I could not have written this book without you.

I am also grateful to my father, Bart Bentley, who graciously provides legal advice at a moment's notice. I am so lucky to have you as my father and my attorney.

To my entire family—my mother, Beverly; my sisters, Blair and Bette; and all the Bentleys, Olodorts, and Gunsts—I am beyond blessed to call you family. Thank you for loving me unconditionally and supporting me always. And to my grandmothers, Margaret and Marian, who are no longer with us. You are my spirit guides.

To my ride-or-die besties who have been there for me through all of life's highs and lows. Lila, thank you for reading, listening, encouraging, and being there for me in the toughest of times. Carolyn, thank you for over three decades of friendship, for letting me live on your couch one summer as I pursued my career in journalism and interned for Bill O'Reilly, and for inspiring me daily with your civic activism and pure heart. Elena, thank you for connecting me to accomplished writers, introducing me to hip-hop in sixth grade, and being an incredibly loyal friend. Katharine, you always lead with an open, giving heart—thank you for our blue-sky days and our beautiful friendship.

And to fellow writer and dear friend Emily Schaffer. You have been a guiding light in the publication process. Thank you for sharing your knowledge and insights and being a constant source of inspiration.

Bettina Siegel, your digital prowess and positivity helped launch the novel. Thank you.

The most beautiful aspect of professional sports is that it brings together people from all walks of life. I am eternally grateful for the people I have worked with and learned from during my career in sports journalism.

Finally, I want to acknowledge women everywhere who courageously stand up for themselves in the workplace. It's scary. It's hard. But it's so important. Your voice matters.

Bentley Author Q&A

It's obvious from the start that gender plays an important role in this book. What inspired you to write such a pointed story? Why now?

I started writing this novel at the most inconvenient time in my personal life. I had recently returned to my job in sports journalism after giving birth to my first child. I was navigating my first football season as a mother with little sleep, uneven hormones, and a layer of baby weight (which people are quick to point out when you work on camera). This novel had been percolating in my subconscious for years, but I had been too immersed in the sports media world to write it. The time away during my maternity leave and the challenges I was facing as a new mom with a demanding work schedule gave me a new perspective. I found most of my alone time came while I was pumping breast milk at work, so I would use those quiet moments to mentally draft the characters. Over the next few years, I wrote the manuscript intermittently while also having a second child. Then, I shelved it. I was busy "mommying" and working. It wasn't until news broke about disturbing harassment allegations in professional football that I decided to revisit the novel with a new lens. I started with a blank page and renewed determination to detail the sexual politics women face in sports journalism. Be pretty but not too sexy. Know your sport but don't outsmart the men. Be a great mother but don't take off time from work. It can feel like an impossible tightrope. That's what I set out to capture.

How has your own experience with gender and discrimination informed the contents of Sideline Confidential? *Was it painful to relive these experiences?*

I've had the pleasure of working with some wonderful people throughout my career. But there have been men who have said and done things from a position of power that were degrading and hurtful to me. As a young reporter, I struggled to stand up for myself or I would play along and act flirtatious or coy. I wanted so badly to succeed that I didn't push back. I also lost my way a bit during that time. I witnessed behavior—affairs, lewd comments, drunken escapades—that skewed my moral compass. My forty-year-old self cringes at the mistakes I made when I started my career, but I am wiser for it.

....

You've spent years crafting stories that appear in the media. How does the experience of writing a book compare to the experience of reporting? How does it feel to be telling your own story now?

My reporting career unfolded on television, often on the sidelines of a football game. I gave quick, informative reports and felt infused by rushes of adrenaline. The process of writing a manuscript couldn't be more different. It's slow, methodical, solitary, and necessitates caffeine breaks. A writer also makes herself much more vulnerable through writing a novel, especially when she is drawing from her own life. It has been scary putting myself out there in the world in this way. These words will live and breathe—they'll be critiqued and questioned—in a way my TV reporting never was. That being said, writing *Sideline Confidential* has felt like the greatest accomplishment of my career.

You're a seasoned sports journalist, so your connection to Blake's character is clear. What other aspects of her character do you identify with?

When I started working in professional football, I was young and naive just like Blake. I also traversed a similar path in that I faced frustrating double standards and a few "BB rules" of my own. As I mentioned, like Blake, I also misaligned my moral compass and got caught up in the prestige of working in such a powerful league. It took some soul searching, but I realized that I needed to forge a new path for myself and really focus on crafting my journalistic skills. I ended up moving to Beaumont, a small town east of Houston, where I became the first woman sports anchor on the evening news.

Are there any aspects of Blake's character from which you feel you differ?

In the end, I didn't get that big network job. I eventually moved back to Houston and worked in sports journalism for a decade before I decided to change careers so that I could spend more time with my family. I'm not sure that Blake would make that decision. In my eyes, she's determined to see her career through to the national stage and prepared to make the necessary sacrifices.

Who was your support system in your time as a media personality? Did you have someone like Sheridan to look up to as a mentor figure? Or people like Hal and Emily who had your back?

Although I worked with and alongside some wonderful people who certainly had my back, Emily, Sheridan, and Hal are fictional characters. Emily is the coworker women dream of having. She's daring, brave, loyal, and a whole lot of fun. When creating Sheridan, I drew from experiences I had with successful women in the industry. There's a conversation that Sheridan has with Blake toward the end of the novel where she talks about missing treasured moments with family and friends and even sacrificing relationships for her job. I remember having that exact conversation with a national reporter in a hotel bar in Indianapolis. She told me that the constant travel and the nature of her work (interviewing superstar athletes) made many boyfriends uncomfortable. She struggled to stay in a long-term, committed relationship. That stuck with me. Hal is a combination of the talented, good-hearted people I worked with in radio. I am forever grateful to them for making me a regular on their shows, sharing their inside knowledge with me, and helping me craft my media skills. One of those radio hosts, John Lopez, worked with me in radio and television and even provided feedback on this novel.

How do you think it would have affected Blake to not have that support system?

I don't think that Blake could have picked up the pieces and forged her own path without Emily, Sheridan, and Hal. Emily gave Blake the emotional support she needed as she dealt with Johnny's blows and the shame she felt after her tryst with Jackson Ways. Sheridan not only provided real-world context about the industry but also encouraged Blake to follow her professional dream and gave Blake her big break with the Network. It's women lifting other women up. I love that. I also love Hal coming in at the end to expose Johnny's harassment. It shows that this book isn't about women versus men. It's about people confronting toxic work cultures and courageously standing up for what's right.

In Chapter 29, Blake makes it her goal to empower other women in professional sports using the platform she's been given. How does this relate to your personal mission?

That is the "why" for this novel. It's my platform to empower women who work not only in sports but in any male-dominated workplace that is laced with sexual politics. There are Johnnys everywhere. In the film industry, banking, politics—the list is long. It is incredibly hard and scary for young women in entry positions to find their voice and stand up for themselves. I want this book to tell them that they aren't alone. Many of us have been there and we can support each other by listening, speaking up, telling our stories, and giving each other a voice.

....

What would you like readers to know about you?

I love sports. I played college volleyball and I consider my happy place to be golfing and hiking with my husband. Sports has taught me countless valuable lessons in life. How to focus, push myself beyond limits, recover and rest, breathe deeply. I could go on forever. But I think what makes sports so special is that they bring together people from all walks of life—be it cheering in the stands, competing on the field, or coaching on the sidelines—and it exposes what is raw and beautiful about the human condition.

....

Is there anything you didn't get to say in Sideline Confidential *that you wish you could say now?*

I am incredibly grateful to the women who broke gender barriers in sports journalism and opened doors for all those who followed. From *New York Times* hockey reporter Robin Herman, who was the first female journalist to interview players inside a men's professional sports locker room, to Lesley Visser, who was the first woman to be a TV analyst for an NFL game, to Robin Roberts, who went from being a sports anchor in Hattiesburg, Mississippi, to a cohost of *Good Morning America*. To all the fearless and relentless trailblazers out there, thank you!

Bentley Reading Group Guide

1. In Chapter 1, Johnny lays down initial ground rules for Blake: she has to ride her own bus, and she is not allowed in the locker room—all because Johnny does not trust Blake around the players. Later, Emily adds these rules also exist because Blake is a liability to him. Johnny obviously does not have a healthy attitude toward women, but do you think his caution is fair? What would you do if you were in his position?

2. What are the characteristics of Johnny's "old-school boys' club mentality" that Bentley mentions? How pervasive is this mentality in the workforce and is this mentality more acute in the sports world?

3. Blake falls for a couple of men who play the field with women. How did Seth and Jackson win Blake over and then cause her heartache? Using specific examples from the book, how would you characterize their mentality?

4. Compare and contrast Johnny's behavior in question 2 with the playboy behavior in question 3. Why did Blake fall for one but not the other? Is there anything that they have in common?

5. In Chapter 8, Blake receives acclaim for going to a strip club. What do you think the author is trying to say about the male perception of women here? Why is it important?

6. Identify key moments for each of these figures and how those moments shaped their characters. What were your first impressions? What do you think of them now?

   a. Johnny

   b. Garrett

   c. Seth

   d. Ryan

   e. Emily

   f. Hal

7. Silence plays an important role in this book. What are some occasions where Blake's coworkers' silence has a negative impact on her when they could have spoken up instead?

8. What are some examples of the "double standard" that Johnny had for Blake? How is it different from the way that her other coworkers treat her?

9. Discuss some of your own experiences with workplace discrimination—as someone who has been on the receiving end of it, as someone who has observed it, or as someone who has been responsible for it before.

10. How do you think you would have handled the situation at work if you were Blake? Why did she choose to stick it out so long?

11. Do you think Blake should have sent that recording? What would have happened if Hal hadn't sent it either? What do you think the outcome would have been if she did send it?

12. In Chapter 29, Sheridan tells Blake that she has prioritized her job over everything else in life—investing in relationships, spending time with her family, having children. Do you think that women can have it all in cutthroat industries like sports journalism? Can they have a fulfilling relationship, children, and a thriving career?

13. Blake's observation about Johnny's devotion to football in Chapter 30 seems very significant. And again, in Chapter 31, she realizes it's his whole life. We get a sense of Johnny's humanity in these moments. Why is this important? What do you think this says about Blake's character?

About the Author

BROOKE BENTLEY GUNST is a former television anchor and award-winning sports reporter. After graduating with a master's in journalism from the University of Southern California, she spent two years working for the Houston Texans as a media personality and over a decade working in sports journalism. Brooke now devotes her time to championing local nonprofits, including Homemade Hope, where she served as the development director. She and her husband live in Houston and are raising two young boys. You can connect with her at www.brookebentley.com.